AN URGENT KISS

Captivating Kisses
Book 6

Alexa Aston

ARE YOU SIGNED UP FOR DRAGONBLADE'S BLOG?

You'll get the latest news and information on exclusive giveaways, exclusive excerpts, coming releases, sales, free books, cover reveals and more.

Check out our complete list of authors, too!

No spam, no junk. That's a promise!

Sign Up Here

www.dragonbladepublishing.com

Dearest Reader;

Thank you for your support of a small press. At Dragonblade Publishing, we strive to bring you the highest quality Historical Romance from some of the best authors in the business. Without your support, there is no 'us', so we sincerely hope you adore these stories and find some new favorite authors along the way.

Happy Reading!

CEO, Dragonblade Publishing

Additional Dragonblade books by Author Alexa Aston

Captivating Kisses Series
An Unexpected Kiss (Book 1)
An Impulsive Kiss (Book 2)
An Innocent Kiss (Book 3)
An Unforeseen Kiss (Book 4)
An Enchanting Kiss (Book 5)
An Urgent Kiss (Book 6)

The Strongs of Shadowcrest Series
The Duke's Unexpected Love (Book 1)
The Perks of Loving a Viscount (Book 2)
Falling for the Marquess (Book 3)
The Captain and the Duchess (Book 4)
Courtship at Shadowcrest (Book 5)
The Marquess' Quest for Love (Book 6)
The Duke's Guide to Winning a Lady (Book 7)

Suddenly a Duke Series
Portrait of the Duke (Book 1)
Music for the Duke (Book 2)
Polishing the Duke (Book 3)
Designs on the Duke (Book 4)
Fashioning the Duke (Book 5)
Love Blooms with the Duke (Book 6)
Training the Duke (Book 7)
Investigating the Duke (Book 8)

Second Sons of London Series
Educated By The Earl (Book 1)
Debating With The Duke (Book 2)
Empowered By The Earl (Book 3)

Made for the Marquess (Book 4)
Dubious about the Duke (Book 5)
Valued by the Viscount (Book 6)
Meant for the Marquess (Book 7)

Dukes Done Wrong Series
Discouraging the Duke (Book 1)
Deflecting the Duke (Book 2)
Disrupting the Duke (Book 3)
Delighting the Duke (Book 4)
Destiny with a Duke (Book 5)

Dukes of Distinction Series
Duke of Renown (Book 1)
Duke of Charm (Book 2)
Duke of Disrepute (Book 3)
Duke of Arrogance (Book 4)
Duke of Honor (Book 5)
The Duke That I Want (Book 6)

The St. Clairs Series
Devoted to the Duke (Book 1)
Midnight with the Marquess (Book 2)
Embracing the Earl (Book 3)
Defending the Duke (Book 4)
Suddenly a St. Clair (Book 5)
Starlight Night (Novella)
The Twelve Days of Love (Novella)

Soldiers & Soulmates Series
To Heal an Earl (Book 1)
To Tame a Rogue (Book 2)
To Trust a Duke (Book 3)
To Save a Love (Book 4)
To Win a Widow (Book 5)
Yuletide at Gillingham (Novella)

King's Cousins Series
The Pawn (Book 1)

The Heir (Book 2)
The Bastard (Book 3)

Medieval Runaway Wives
Song of the Heart (Book 1)
A Promise of Tomorrow (Book 2)
Destined for Love (Book 3)

Knights of Honor Series
Word of Honor (Book 1)
Marked by Honor (Book 2)
Code of Honor (Book 3)
Journey to Honor (Book 4)
Heart of Honor (Book 5)
Bold in Honor (Book 6)
Love and Honor (Book 7)
Gift of Honor (Book 8)
Path to Honor (Book 9)
Return to Honor (Book 10)

The Lyon's Den Series
The Lyon's Lady Love

Pirates of Britannia Series
God of the Seas

De Wolfe Pack: The Series
Rise of de Wolfe

The de Wolfes of Esterley Castle
Diana
Derek
Thea

Also from Alexa Aston
The Bridge to Love (Novella)
One Magic Night

PROLOGUE

Merrifield, Norfolk—1793

A S THE CARRIAGE carried Hugo Drake closer to home, he felt his belly knotting. He was returning from his first year away at school, which he felt he'd been fortunate to survive. While he had enjoyed the academics offered and thrived, especially in maths and geography, the rest of his experience had been abominable. His contact with his fellow students had been even worse than he had imagined, their ridicule and taunting leaving him an emotional wreck.

He knew he was different from others. The stammer marked him thus. He had stammered for as long as he could remember. He would know what he wished to say, and yet it simply would not come out of his mouth, leaving him mute. Or he would become stuck on a word, repeating the beginning of it over and over and over until others laughed—or shamed him. Though he had longed to do so, he had made no friends at school. Now, he dreaded coming home because he would be berated by his father.

Other boys had their fathers—and sometimes even their mothers—come and retrieve them from school at the end of each term. Hugo's escort home had been a surly footman. Even his father's servants looked down upon him, despite the fact he was the heir apparent to the Earl of Merriman. His life stretched out endlessly before him, and all he could see was the misery to come.

The carriage arrived a little after half-past seven that evening. It was still light outside, and Hugo wondered if he would be called into his father's study. A part of him wished the meeting would be over and done, but the other half hoped it would be delayed until tomorrow morning, allowing him a brief respite. At one point, his parents had gone away to town for the Season each year, but his father remained at his country seat most of the year now.

When the vehicle came to a halt, dread rippled through Hugo. The door opened. He hesitantly went down the steps which had been placed by the footman, making his way to the front door, where Storey regarded him with disdain. The butler was a close confidant to Hugo's father. Since the earl despised his son, so did the butler. He promised himself when he became the earl, he would rid the house of this man and any other servant who had disparaged him in words or deeds.

"Lord Merriman will see you tomorrow morning," Storey said brusquely.

Not a word of greeting, which was exactly what he had expected. Hugo was hungry, but he knew Storey would never think to feed him, and Hugo was too proud to ask for anything.

"Be in his lordship's study at nine o'clock," the butler added, walking away.

He wondered where Mama was. At one time, she had tried to champion him to his father, but she had long ago been beaten into submission. She no longer had the strength or will to defend herself, much less a stuttering son. Still, he loved her and headed to her rooms, hoping to find her awake. Oftentimes, she escaped into sleep. Hugo could not blame her.

Knocking softly, he opened the door and entered, closing the door behind him. She had a small sitting room which came before her bedchamber. He moved through it, then eased the door open, finding her seated in a chair by the window.

She turned, her face softening as she caught sight of him, a rare smile appearing on her lips. "Hugo. My darling boy."

He crossed the room to stand before her, savoring her embrace and the faint smell of lilacs, which always reminded him of her.

Pulling away, she clasped him by the shoulders and asked, "How was school? I am so sorry your father did not let you come home for any of the holidays."

That had hurt the most, seeing the other boys leave to go home to loving families, while he remained with the tutors at school. Fortunately, they had left him on his own for the most part, so he had read late into the night, slept in, and then explored the school and the areas outside it to his heart's content.

Knowing he could not lie to her now, though, even though he saw the sadness in her eyes, he replied, "Wh-wh-what d-do you th-think?"

Tears welled in her gray eyes, so like his, as she enveloped him in her arms again.

"My heart is heavy, waiting to hear your reply, my boy. You are such a kind, intelligent person. Was it simply awful?"

Feeling safe within these four walls, he was able to answer her with one clear, clean word. "Yes."

She led him to her bed, and they both climbed upon it together. Her arm went about him as they talked over the school year. Hugo had learned when he felt safe, he could get more words out. They didn't seem so muddled. He told Mama about the subjects he enjoyed. Books he had read and languages he had begun to study.

"My, it sounds as if you have grown not only taller, but also intellectually," she said, kissing the top of his head. "But you must get some rest, my darling. So must I. We have to be at our best tomorrow."

He knew the hidden meaning behind her words. They both needed to be well rested in order to have their wits about them when they were in the presence of the earl.

"I will s-see you tomorrow, Mama," he said, crawling from the bed and heading upstairs to his own bedchamber.

His trunk awaited him, though no servant had unpacked its contents. He believed other households ran differently. That servants weren't meant to be so rebellious or openly disrespectful. For a moment, he wondered if his father had issued an edict for servants *not* to wait on him. It did not matter. He had learned from an early age to be self-sufficient, and so he opened and unpacked the trunk, putting his belongings away.

Suddenly, his belly growled, rumbling in protest of not having eaten for many hours, but he pushed the thought aside as he undressed and slipped into his nightshirt. He climbed into bed and lay in the dark a long time, sleep evading him. The nights at school had been the worst of times, anxiety keeping him awake because he had never known when the other boys might come for him. Sometimes, they merely laughed at him or made fun of him, imitating his stammer and laughing riotously as they did so. Other times, though, they dragged him from his bed, beating him for the pure fun of it. They knew not to touch his face, however, and so he would go to classes the next morning, his body battered and tender from numerous blows. Hugo knew of the code of silence and never told on those who bullied him. He'd had no friends and doubted he would make even one during the school years ahead. Other boys would be afraid to be associated with him.

At least he was back at Merrifield. For the most part, his father would ignore him. He could go days—even weeks—without laying eyes on the earl.

Suddenly, he heard his door push open and knew it had to be Dilly.

Sure enough, his three-year-old sister appeared next to his bed. She reached out with chubby fingers and touched his cheek.

"Thank you for coming to see me, Dilly. Would you like to get into bed with me?"

She nodded. Hugo helped her up, and she snuggled against him, her warmth a comfort to him.

Dilly was actually Delilah. When she was born, Hugo had trouble saying her name. All he could get out was Dilly, and so that is what he called her—and what she called herself. Dilly was the one bright spot in his life, and he loved her completely, more than anything or anyone on this earth. She was also the only person he never stammered around. If only the world were full of Dillys, he might actually be normal.

With his sister by his side, Hugo finally fell asleep into a deep, relaxed sleep.

When he awoke, Dilly was no longer in bed with him. He supposed she had returned to her own bed so that she would not be scolded by her nursemaid. Kittrell had also served as his nursemaid, and Hugo could not recall one kind word ever spoken to him by her. Still, she was usually pleasant with Dilly.

At least water had been delivered to him the previous evening, and he used it now to wash before he dressed. He combed his hair carefully, wanting to look presentable when he met with his father.

Going down the hall to the schoolroom, he saw Dilly and Kittrell already there. He entered, mustering a smile, and said, "G-g-good m-morning."

The nursemaid barely glanced in his direction, and he took a seat at the table next to his sister. A maid came in, bringing breakfast for the three of them. As usual, he ate in silence.

Dilly, however, talked quite a bit. His sister's vocabulary and use of language had exploded since the last time he had been home. Thank goodness, she had not been cursed with the stammer which plagued him.

When they finished eating, Kittrell whisked Dilly away, leaving Hugo on his own. He wandered about the schoolroom, opening and examining a few books he had used in this very room when he'd had a tutor before he left to go away to school. He wondered if Dilly would also leave for school someday and hoped if she did, her experience would be better than his.

When the appointed time came, he ventured downstairs and stood in front of his father's study, steeling himself before he knocked upon the door.

"Come."

Just the sound of his father's voice sent chills up Hugo's spine.

Opening the door, he stepped inside, closing it behind him. He went and stood in front of the desk, his father's eyes on the newspaper he read. Hugo stood a good quarter-hour, watching his father methodically turn the pages. His gut told him that the earl wasn't reading the newspaper at all. That he was merely toying with his son, making him wait.

Finally, his father put the newspaper down and acknowledged his son's presence.

"The headmaster wrote me a most interesting letter," the earl began.

Panic shot through him. He had not known of this. He supposed the letter had been given to the footman who had escorted him home. Knowing not to speak, he simply waited for his father to tell him what he wished him to know.

The earl reached for the letter, which sat on his desk, and held it up. "He writes that you actually have a brain inside that head of yours. That your command of writing Latin and Greek is strong. He also praises your ability regarding mathematics."

He couldn't help but feel a bit pleased that his father had received good news about him, especially since everything else Hugo did seemed to disappoint the earl.

Frowning, his father continued. "However, he tells me that you made absolutely no friends and that your physical abilities and skills on the playing field are abysmal."

When teams had been chosen, the captains aways argued over who would take Hugo, who was always the last boy left. He never understood why they spent time doing so because he never got in to play in a single game. He knew he was smaller than most other boys his age, but his stutter did not affect him physically. Apparently, though, all the other boys believed that it did.

"The headmaster also writes that your oratory skills are non-existent." His father snorted. "I would have expected as much." Tossing the letter aside, his father's gaze met his. "Do you understand how great an embarrassment you are to me? Why, I will never be able to show my face at my club in town because all my peers will have heard from their own boys what a waste of humanity you are."

When Hugo stood mutely, the earl slammed a fist upon the desk. "Answer me, damn you!"

"Y-y-y-yes, Fa-fa-father. I kn-kn-kn-know th-that I embar . . . embar . . . embarrass you."

Rage filled the earl's face, turning it bright red, and he stood quickly, knocking over the chair he'd sat in.

"It is humiliating having a son such as you. Humiliating! My peers judge *me* because of *your* deficiencies. Your faults."

Hugo knew what was coming. He had known all along, but there was no way he could ever prepare himself for what took place next.

"This is the second time I have had to live through this," his father muttered, glowering at him.

Confusion filled him. "Wh-wh-what?"

"I spent my entire life being humiliated by my younger brother. He, too, sounded exactly like you did. Couldn't get a word out without mucking it up. I was a laughingstock. I did everything I could to separate myself from him, even begging my own father to send us to different schools to spare me the shame. Thankfully, Papa did so."

Hugo knew his father never would have defended his own flesh and blood. He was glad this unknown uncle had escaped being near the man before him, one who was cruel and heartless and had no love for his only son.

"And I have heard gossip that says his son is exactly as worthless as you are. An embarrassment to the Drake family name."

It was interesting to learn that he had both an uncle and a cousin and that they both suffered from the curse of stammering. He had not known that it ran in families. It made him never want to have children of his own, simply because he would hate for them to go through the pain he already had—and would continue to endure.

"My father tried to beat the flaws out of my brother, and he proved to be unsuccessful." An evil gleam lit the earl's eyes. "I intend to meet with success, however."

The next minutes were ones Hugo endured. The curses that came with each blow. The sting and then pain of the cane, which tore into his flesh. He did equations in his head, trying to escape from the reality as his father beat him bloody.

Finally, he collapsed on the floor, falling to his hands and knees, doubting he could stand on his own two feet without help. He imagined crawling from the study, through the house, and up several flights of stairs, thinking it beyond him, wishing he could die, here and now, and end his suffering.

He heard the cane being dropped into the stand where his father kept it. He knew a servant would need to be summoned to take him back to his room and wondered if his father would ring for one or let him lie on the carpet. He struggled to retain consciousness and then felt himself drifting away.

Eventually, the door opened. By then, Hugo was aware of his surroundings. He looked up to see his father motion to him on the floor.

"Get him out of my sight." It amazed him that the earl's tone was so cavalier, as if he were asking teacups to be cleared.

The footman lifted him at the neck, dragging him across the carpeted room. Once they were on the other side of the door and it was closed, however, strong arms scooped him up.

Tears blinded him as the footman carried him all the way to his bedchamber, the first time that had ever happened. Surprisingly, he was gently placed upon the bed.

Looking up at the servant, he saw it was not someone he recognized. And what surprised him most was that he saw sympathy in the man's eyes.

"I will be back soon, my lord. Do not try to undress without my help. I will bring ointment and bandages and see to your wounds."

He lay on the bed, crying because of the kindness in the

stranger's voice. Deliberately, he caused his mind to go blank, something he had much practice at doing. He did not think of the ordeal he had just undergone. Instead, he drifted, thinking of summer days walking through the woods at Merrifield. Wading in the stream, the breeze ruffling his hair.

When the footman returned, he began ministering to Hugo in a gentle manner. No servant had ever shown him such compassion. Only Dilly had ever been this gentle with him. Even his own mother had been too afraid of her domineering, rage-filled husband to behave in such a fashion.

"Wh-wh-what is y-y-your name?" he asked.

"Alfie," the footman replied.

"Alfie," he repeated, glad of the softness of the name. He had difficulty with hard consonants at the beginning of words, such as Bs and Ps, but Alfie seemed to roll from his tongue.

"W-w-w-will you g-g-get in tr-trouble? He-he-helping m-me?"

"If I do and am dismissed, so be it," Alfie declared. He paused, studying Hugo for a moment. "I have heard the servants mention you, my lord. They said such terrible things. No one should be spoken of as they do you, especially those who should be serving you. They should be grateful to hold the position they do. I am here to let you know that I am not only your faithful servant. I also hope to be your friend."

Hugo didn't know it at the time, but Alfie would be his only friend for many years to come. What he did know was when he became the Earl of Merriman, he would make Alfie his butler. He knew this servant would help him be respected in his own household.

As the footman peeled away the bloody clothes and washed and dressed the raw, ferocious wounds, he thanked Alfie from the bottom of his heart, even as he vowed to someday conquer both his tormentors and the speech impediment which haunted him.

CHAPTER ONE

Cambridge—1803

HUGO WALKED THROUGH the rooms which had been rented for him by Mr. Becker, a clerk to his father's solicitor. He had arrived in London with instructions to see the family solicitor before making his way to Cambridge, only learning once he arrived that the man was too busy to see him. The solicitor had assigned one of his clerks to look after Hugo, and it had been Mr. Becker who had traveled with him to Cambridge, helping him to rent these rooms he would live in during his time at university.

Turning to face the clerk, he now put into practice things he had been working on his entire life. He took a breath and thought of what he wished to say, hearing the words in his mind.

"Thank you for helping me become settled, Mr. B-B-Becker."

Hard constants at the beginning of words still gave him trouble, but after years of practice, he could speak more clearly and with less stammering than he had as a child.

"I was more than happy to accompany you to Cambridge, my lord," Becker replied. "And if you have need of anything, please write to me. I know that I will be able to handle whatever matter you need addressed on your behalf."

While at the solicitor's office, Hugo had learned that he would receive a quarterly allowance, which would help pay for these rooms and his meals, as well as other incidentals. He had no intention of going back to Merrifield at the end of each term, as other university students would do. He intended to remain in Cambridge year-round until he took his degree.

It had been hard to say his goodbyes to Mama and Dilly, but he knew it was best to stay away from Merrifield and his father. The earl had not physically assaulted him in several years, not since Hugo had sprung to his full height, three inches over six feet. On the rare occasions he was called in to meet with his father, he hovered above the older man, knowing his size intimated the earl.

Once more, very methodically, he asked, "Do you have any p-plans to be a solicitor yourself?"

Becker smiled broadly. "I do indeed, my lord. I am most eager to become a solicitor myself, but I come from a most humble background. I learn daily, however, and hope to one day be able to practice on my own. Even if it is out of a very small office."

Boldly, Hugo said, "When that d-day comes and I am the Earl of Merriman, I . . ." He paused, slowing down. "I will hire you myself."

"You would?" Becker asked, incredulous. "I might serve as *your* solicitor?"

He nodded, collecting his thoughts. "When I b-b-become . . . when I take the title, I will make changes. M-m-many changes."

In awe, the clerk said, "You have given me a worthy goal to strive for, my lord. Thank you ever so much."

He smiled. "You have shown me kindness, Mr. B-Becker. You have l-l-looked me in the eye. Made me feel . . . comfortable." Hugo was especially proud that he got out the word comfortable since it was so long. "Keep this b-between us."

"Of course. I cannot thank you enough. Well, I should be off now so that you might settle in. I need to book a room for this evening and arrange to take the mail coach back to London tomorrow morning."

Hugo thought on whether or not he should ask Becker to stay with him, and then decided it might be too much. "Have a safe j-journey."

"Enjoy your studies, my lord. I hope you will have a wonderful time in Cambridge. Goodbye."

After the clerk left, he spent time unpacking his trunk. It would be wonderful to be living on his own, without anyone underfoot. He hoped he would learn to relax more, and he certainly would practice speaking. That had been difficult to do while he was at school and others were constantly around him. Once his task was completed, he decided to go to the inn over the road for his evening meal. If he liked the food served there, he would frequent the place since it was so close.

He used the key Becker had given him and locked the door behind him, crossing the street and entering The King's Arms. It was still a bit early for dinner, and the inn's public room was only about a third full. Much more to his liking. Too many people and loud conversations disrupted his train of thought, and he found it difficult to communicate in those circumstances. He dreaded the day he would have to attend the Season and be thrust into a ballroom full of strangers, having to try to make conversation and dance, much less look for a bride. Thankfully, that was far down the road.

He sat at an empty table and ordered an ale from the barmaid who had appeared, and then he asked, "What is g-good here? To eat?"

She smiled. "Just about everything, my lord. We get many compliments on our beef and mutton dishes. The stews and soups also are reliable dishes to choose from. Are you a student new to Cambridge?"

He merely nodded.

"Well, you've come to the right place. Many of your fellow students dine here. What shall I bring you besides ale?"

"Choose f-f-for me," he told her, and she gave him a saucy smile. Thankfully, she did not ask him about his stutter. Too many others boldly did, and he was often left without words trying to explain something which he himself did not fully understand.

She returned with the ale moments later, and he sipped it

slowly, wondering what these next years would bring.

Then he heard his name called and tried not to react. If the caller thought he had been mistaken, he might leave Hugo alone. But he heard it a second time.

"Drake? I thought that might be you."

Glancing up, he recognized the man who had come to stand near his table. Rising, Hugo offered the Duke of Reddington his hand.

Thinking hard, he said, "It is . . . nice to see you, Your G-Grace."

"And excellent to see you as well, Drake. Mind if I sit with you?"

This would have been the only person welcomed at Hugo's table. Reddington had been two years ahead of him in school, a duke since he was twelve years of age. Reddington had come across a group of boys practicing their usual cruelties upon Hugo, and the young duke had immediately put a stop to their bullying. He still could hear Reddington's words ringing in his ears.

Do not touch him again—else you will have me to deal with.

Though the taunting had subtly continued, the physical abuse had stopped after the duke's intervention. Hugo had been four and ten at the time. By the time Reddington graduated and moved on a few years later, the other boys left Hugo alone. Even the jeers had died down, most likely due to his new, tall frame. No one bullied him physically or verbally. It was as if they simply forgot all about him, and Hugo moved through his remaining years of school as a wraith, acknowledged by no one except his tutors.

"Have a seat, Your G-G-Grace."

The duke did so and said, "Your speech is much clearer, Drake. My congratulations to you for mastering your stammer."

He paused a long moment, trying to put the words together, and then said, "You helped me with that. Even though I still struggle. You m-m-made them leave me alone. I f-f-find when I relax and have no worries, I can speak without m-much of a stammer."

"What will you study at Cambridge?" the duke asked. "Since I have not seen you before, I assume you have just arrived and are beginning your university days."

"Mathematics."

Reddington nodded. "I recall you were quite good at maths. Took several prizes, I believe, if I recall correctly. Well, good for you, Drake."

The duke glanced up and waved. Hugo glanced over his shoulder and saw a man headed toward them. Immediately, he tensed. It was one thing to sit and try to have a conversation with Reddington. It was altogether something different with a stranger at the table. He tried to think of a quick excuse to leave, but the barmaid set his meal before him at that precise moment.

"Here you go, my lord." Her eyes flicked to the duke. "What might I bring you, Your Grace?"

By then, the other man had reached them, and the duke ordered for the both of them. Hugo knew there was no way to escape now, and so he rose, as did the duke, ready to meet someone new.

"I believe the two of you might somehow be related," His Grace said. "Hugo Drake, this is Anthony Drake."

He looked at the newcomer and recognized a resemblance between them. They both had dark hair and similar facial features. Offering his hand, he said, "Nice to m-meet you."

The other man smiled widely. "It is so good to meet you, Mr. Drake. I feel that we do have some relatives in common. Please forgive me if I seem too familiar. Might you be the Earl of Merriman's son?"

Immediately, Hugo knew Anthony Drake must be the cousin his father had mentioned all those many years ago.

But what of his stammer?

"Have a seat, Drakes," the duke said cheerfully, and they all seated themselves at the table. "Go ahead and eat, Hugo. I am going to have to call you Hugo and this one Anthony to keep the two of you separate. That means you should call me Matthew."

"I c-c-ca . . . I . . . no. That will not d-do."

"It will if I say it does," Reddington said, a twinkle in his eyes. "It is not just anyone that I give leave to call me Matthew, but my wish is that you would do so, Hugo."

He nodded mutely, shocked by this offer of familiarity with a man of such high rank. Then his cousin claimed his attention, and so he faced him.

"I am the earl's son," he said slowly. "I l-learned about you . . . years ago. You do not . . . stammer."

"I do when I am tired," Anthony revealed. "It has taken me years to conquer my stutter. I can help you do the same if you would like me to work with you."

"How?" he asked, feeling helpless. "I have . . . found a f-few things to d-d-do over the years. I speak slowly. I think b-before about what I w-w-want to say."

"Those are good things to do," his cousin agreed. "I practice both. I have learned to slow down and not get too excited, else the stammer appears quickly. I also am mindful of what I say, sometimes choosing one word over the other because it is easier to pronounce."

"Yes!" he said excitedly, his morale soaring, being in the presence of another kindred spirit for the first time.

The barmaid set down the others' food and drink, and Anthony took a big swig of his ale.

"I am sincere in my offer. If you wish, I can work with you. I have taught myself things to do. Matthew helps me with some of them."

When Hugo looked at him questioningly, his cousin said, "One thing is to read aloud daily. Just to yourself. The more you do so, the more comfortable you become with hearing yourself saying words correctly aloud. Then, for a quarter-hour each day, Matthew and I read aloud in unison together. I am comfortable in his presence, which is a key to squashing the tendency to stammer. Reading in unison with another has made a vast difference."

"I would l-like to try that," he said, hope building within him. His cousin had yet to stutter or stumble over any words, which thoroughly impressed Hugo.

Grinning, the duke said, "We also sing. Quite a bit."

"S-s-sing?" he asked, puzzled as to what that had to do with stammering.

Anthony shrugged. "I am not certain why it helps. It simply does. I think because singing involves a lot of stops. You sing one phrase and wait a few beats before picking up with another phrase. I have learned to speak in small chunks of words. If you listen to me carefully, you can hear that I do pause after every few words. It may be something you might wish to practice yourself." He paused. "Matthew and I sing every day. He has a pianoforte in our rooms."

It did not surprise him that a duke would be so indulgent as to have a pianoforte while at university.

Enthusiastically, Reddington said, "I have always enjoyed playing a great deal. It soothes me. It is also an enjoyable way to pass my free time. Anthony is correct. When he sings, you never hear one stutter come from him."

Hugo watched as the pair exchanged a glance, and Anthony nodded subtly.

Turning to him, the duke said, "We have a large set of rooms nearby. One bedchamber is empty now. A friend of mine completed his studies last term. We had not decided whether or not to replace him with a fellow student, but I believe that you would be a good fit for us, Hugo. What do you say?"

Disappointment filled him. "I j-j-just r-r-rented rooms today."

"That is easy to remedy," Reddington said nonchalantly. "There are always students looking for rooms to let in Cambridge. If your landlord cannot find someone to replace you—which I doubt—he still already has what he has been paid for the quarter, does he not?"

"I have . . . paid for three m-months." He shook his head sadly. "I have n-no additional f-funds to pay you."

"You do not need to pay me a farthing," the duke said breezily. "My rooms are already paid for. In fact, Anthony pays me nothing toward the rent."

"It is true, Cousin. I am at Cambridge on scholarship. I met Matthew in a seminar, and we became fast friends. He allows me to share his rooms at no cost to myself."

"I . . . don't . . ."

"You do not need to worry about a thing, Hugo," Reddington assured him. "We shall finish our dinner and then go to your rooms. Between the three of us, we can have everything moved by tonight."

They finished their meal, and the duke said, "Come down the way so you can see what you think. We are very close to The King's Arms, and so we dine here often. Lizzy, the barmaid who waited upon us tonight, often serves us. She will even hold back special treats for us."

They took him to a set of rooms on the same side of the street as the inn. It was just as they said. The duke's rented rooms were large and airy. A pianoforte sat in a common room. Anthony insisted they sing at least one song to demonstrate to Hugo how therapeutic music might be to one who stammered. He had never sung before in his life, although he was familiar with the song which Reddington began to play for them.

He joined in singing, timidly at first, and then realized he wasn't stumbling over his words. Beaming at them, he began to sing loudly in a rich bass.

When the song ended, the other two applauded his efforts, and Matthew said, "Bravo, Hugo! How do you feel?"

He grinned shamelessly. "Like a n-new man," he declared.

"Success will not happen overnight," Anthony shared. "It is going to take hours of practice on your part. Know that I, too, still have to think about what I say and not let words spill from me too quickly." His cousin smiled. "But in time, I think you will be speaking most eloquently, Hugo."

They returned to his rooms, and he quickly packed while

Reddington went to visit with the landlord downstairs.

When the duke returned, he said, "Things are settled, Hugo. Your landlord had someone else with him when I went to see him just now. The young man was looking for a few rooms to let, and I informed him that these were now available. Your landlord returned your rental fees to me."

Reddington handed the pound notes over. "It is yours to do with as you wish."

"Won't you k-keep this?" he pleaded.

"Absolutely not. I am the Duke of Reddington. I am made of money." He paused. "What I am more in need of is a friend. I will be frank, Hugo. Having become a duke at such a tender age, every boy and man I met from that moment on was either afraid of me or fawned over me. I was rather lonely growing up because of that. I have made a good friend in Anthony. I believe you, too, will become my lifelong friend."

When Hugo fell asleep that night, he was filled with hope.

For the first time ever.

CHAPTER TWO

London—April 1808

LADY TIA WORTHINGTON was happier than she had been in many months. At this point last year, she and her twin sister were about to make their come-outs into Polite Society, something they had both looked forward to for their entire lives. Unfortunately, her father had collapsed and died suddenly on the eve of the Season. Mama had whisked them away from town so that they might do their mourning in the country at Millvale.

She had not spent a single moment mourning the loss of the duke. Her father had been a cold, distant man, ignoring his four children for the most part. Especially his daughters. The only one who had gained even a modicum of attention was her brother Val, who had succeeded his father as Duke of Millbrooke. Val had recently become a father for the first time at the beginning of March. He would bring his wife Eden and little William to town next week so they might attend the Season. Tia adored her new sister-in-law, a former governess, and William was fast stealing her heart.

She was eager to go this afternoon to take tea with her older sister Ariadne, who had wed Julian, Marquess of Aldridge, during her first Season. They had a daughter called Penelope, and Tia could not wait to see her young niece, who had recently begun to walk.

More importantly, she would finally get to see Lia today. Her twin had always been her closest friend, almost an extension of Tia herself. Lia had met Viscount Cressley while they had been visiting their aunt Agnes at Traywick Manor in the Lake District last autumn. Lia had fallen in love with Viscount Cressley, a neighbor, but they had left Traywick Manor and returned to Kent without anything resolved between the couple. Lo and behold, Rupert had shown up at Millvale with a special license and drafts of marriage settlements, along with his heartfelt declaration of love. He and Lia had wed in the village church at the beginning of December. They had stayed through Christmastime and then returned to Cumberland.

Tia had exchanged a few letters with Lia, but it was not the same as talking in person. That was why she was so ready to see her twin this afternoon when they met for tea at Ariadne's. Her older sister had come up with what most of the *ton* would consider a most peculiar notion—bringing your children to town for the Season. Ariadne had talked to several of the ten cousins in their extended family, while Tia and Lia had spoken to the others. All ten had agreed with Ariadne and would bring their own children to town each year. That way, not only could parents spend more time with their offspring, but the new set of cousins would also be able to grow up in one another's company and form strong bonds of friendship.

The only cousins who currently had children were Ariadne, Val, and Lucy. Lucy had given birth to her daughter Elizabeth a month ago. She and Judson, the Marquess of Huntsberry, had written and said they would come to the Season next year. For now, they wanted to have more time at home with their newborn. Tia suspected Val would have done the same if it had not been for her making her come-out. Her brother was very protective of all his sisters, and he had told Tia he wanted to be present this Season for her.

Dru, Lucy's sister and the Countess of Martindale, was increasing. She and her husband Perry had decided to skip this Season altogether. Dru had written of how large she had grown and how travel was difficult for her. She promised her cousins she would come to next Season, though, and show off her new babe, which would arrive this coming July.

Two of the remaining cousins, Verina and Justina, were too young to make their come-outs, so they would not be in town with Aunt Agnes. Tray, their older brother, was finishing up at university, and he had shared that he would not come to town until next spring. The last of the cousins, Con, would be at tea today. Tia was very fond of Con and looked upon him as another brother.

Tia breakfasted in her bedchamber, since it was also her mother's habit to do so. Once Val and Eden arrived in town, however, she would take the meal downstairs with them. She went and practiced the pianoforte for an hour after she ate, something Lia excelled at. Tia could play adequately. She might have even been better at the instrument if she weren't so lackadaisical when it came to practicing. She liked hearing music when others played, but she had to concentrate too much on her fingering patterns when she played herself, which took the joy out of music for her. Mama had encouraged her to practice, though, simply because she would be expected to entertain when they had guests. She didn't want to embarrass herself in front of others, so she had practiced the same three selections multiple times over the past month and would feel comfortable playing any of these compositions for guests.

She returned to her bedchamber, which seemed so empty without Lia sharing with her these days, and retrieved her bonnet and reticule. Tying the bonnet beneath her chin, she went downstairs and found Mama already waiting for her in the foyer. They had an appointment with Madame Laurent this morning. Even though Tia had an entire wardrobe made up for her last Season, gowns which she had yet to wear, Mama thought she needed at least a few new ballgowns for *this* Season.

It didn't take long to reach the modiste's dress shop, and they entered, finding only one other client seated. Tia thought the older woman striking in appearance. She had abundant black hair, which was graying at the temples, as well as very unusual gray eyes.

One of Madame's assistants appeared and greeted them. "Good morning, Your Grace, Lady Tia. If you would like to come to the back, my lady, I will help you in your fitting today. Madame is already there with Lady Merriman's daughter."

She followed the assistant and caught sight of the other young lady being fitted for gowns. It was obvious she was the daughter of the woman seated in the shop because they favored one another so much. The girl had the same raven hair and gray eyes. Where the mother had an air of sadness about her, though, this girl looked extremely lively.

"I am Lady Delilah Drake," the young lady said. "Please tell me that you, too, are making your come-out this Season. Are you as terrified as I am?"

Tia couldn't help but laugh, already liking this young lady. "I am Lady Tia Worthington, and I, too, will be making my debut into Polite Society. It is so very nice to meet you, Lady Delilah."

"I have tried to be friendly to a few other girls I have come across during my dress fittings," Lady Delilah confided. "They did not wish to be friends at all." Leaning closer, she confided, "In fact, one of them boldly told me that she would not be making friends with anyone making her come-out because she considered all those girls to be her competitors. She told me that she planned to land a duke, and nothing would stand in her way in doing so."

Tia had not considered others in her come-out class as a threat and said, "Well, I am not looking for a husband this Season. What I am looking for is to make friends—and enjoy the many social affairs."

Lady Deliliah's eyes widened in surprise. "You are not looking to be wed?" Then she smiled. "Why, I find that quite refreshing."

As the assistant helped Tia from her gown, she said, "Eventually, I do wish to wed. I have three siblings, and all of them are very happily married. Surprisingly, they all made love matches."

The other girl gasped. "I have never considered love as a factor in taking a husband. Why, I did not know those in the *ton* ever considered wedding for love." She shook her head. "My own parents certainly were not in love."

They continued gossiping as they tried on various gowns, and Tia found herself taken with Lady Delilah's outspokenness.

"Do you have any siblings?" she asked.

Her new friend's face softened. "I have an older brother. He has always taken such good care of me. He is the Earl of Merriman. My father passed two years ago. He was bedridden the two years before that. He suffered a horrible attack of apoplexy and never left his bed after it."

Tia nodded sympathetically. "My own father, the Duke of Millbrooke, also was struck by apoplexy last spring. We lost him that same day. It is why my come-out was delayed a year, due to being in mourning."

"Do you think we can become friends, Lady Tia?" Lady Delilah asked earnestly. "Having never had a sister, I have been looking forward to my debut for years now. Yes, I do hope to find a husband, but I also wish to form some lasting friendships."

"I do not look upon you as competition in the least bit," she declared. "I am most happy to be your friend, my lady."

The other girl smiled sweetly. "Then you simply must call me Dilly. Mama demands that I introduce myself to others as Delilah, but my brother has always called me Dilly. He could not say Delilah when I was born. He began calling me Dilly and still does to this day. I actually prefer it. Dilly sounds much more friendly and fun than Delilah, in my opinion. To me, Delilah sounds haughty and judgmental. I promise you that I am neither."

"Then Lady Dilly it shall be," Tia declared.

"Oh, we are going to have such fun together this Season," her new friend said.

She hoped that would be the case. Tia had anticipated sharing everything with Lia. With her sister now a matron, things would be different. It would be lovely to have Dilly as a friend and confidante.

After another half-hour, both girls had completed their fittings. They returned to their mothers, who seemed to be getting along well, and Mama introduced Tia to Lady Merriman, who introduced Delilah to Mama.

Lady Dilly said, "Mama, I think Lady Tia and I are going to be close friends. Might she and Her Grace come to tea tomorrow?"

Tia looked to Mama, who said, "We would be happy to accept your invitation to tea, Lady Merriman."

The countess smiled. "Then we are happy to host you and your lovely daughter, Your Grace. How fortunate we were that our paths crossed today. Why, we might have gone through half the Season before being introduced."

Madame Laurent hovered nearby, and Mama asked, "Are you finished with Thermantia's wardrobe now, Madame?"

"Yes, Your Grace. I will have everything delivered to His Grace's townhouse by the end of the day."

"I will return for my own fitting in two days, then," Mama told the modiste.

"We look forward to serving you, Your Grace," Madame Laurent said. "Have a lovely day."

They said their goodbyes to Lady Dilly and her mother, and Tia and Mama returned to their waiting carriage.

"Did you practice your pianoforte this morning?"

"I did, Mama. I have mastered three pieces. Why, you will think you are listening to Lia instead of me when you hear me playing them," she bragged.

Her mother nodded, satisfied, and then asked, "What did you think of Lady Delilah?"

"I find her quite nice. She is the first friend I have made this Season." Tia frowned. "However, she told me she has met other young ladies during the fittings for her gowns. Not one of them wished to be friends with her."

Mama nodded sagely. "That is because you are all on the Marriage Mart, Thermantia. You are rivals, trying to win the favor of the eligible bachelors in attendance. While it is good to make the acquaintance of many young ladies, you must always keep in mind that you must place yourself first. *You* must be the one who walks away with the best available gentleman."

Her mother's attitude irked Tia. "Mama, I want—"

"I do not wish to hear anything about love matches, Thermantia. Yes, your three siblings have made them, and I am actually happy they did so. You, however, have never been one who was overly sentimental. I expect you to make a brilliant match because of your looks and family's standing. As the daughter of a duke and the sister to another, there is no limit as to the match you will make. I am advising you to aim no lower than a marquess. A duke would be preferable. I believe there are a couple of eligible dukes who will be in attendance this Season. Valentinian, of course, will assist you in narrowing your marriage choices, as will I. He did so for Ariadne, and he will do the same for you."

Tia did not remind her mother that Val had little to do with Ariadne's marriage. She and Julian had met and fallen in love quickly. Yes, Val had liked Julian, making a friend in him, and Val did approve of their union, but he had told Tia he would not interfere with her choice, unless the man she chose was horribly unsuitable.

Her brother knew that Tia was not ready to settle into marriage yet. While Lia had always dreamed of being a wife and bearing children, Tia was the more outgoing of the twins. She wanted to simply enjoy the many social events of the Season without worrying about finding a husband. Not every girl wed at the end of her first Season. Some came back and did another—or another. Of course, there were some girls who, after four or five Seasons, simply gave up hope and were placed upon the shelf by others. Those were the wallflowers, and Tia did not expect to be in that category. She was outgoing and friendly. While she was not vain in regard to her looks, she knew others found her to be quite attractive. She planned to enjoy as many activities as possible. When the time came to take a husband, she hoped, liked her siblings, that she would know in her heart which gentleman was the one for her. If it were a love match, that would be all the better, but she did not wish to hold out for one.

After they returned home, Tia started a letter to Verina and Justina. Her cousins had come with their mother to Millbrooke and stayed several months after her father's death, and she, Lia, and Mama had accompanied Aunt Agnes and the girls back to Cumberland for another two months. In those months, she had grown close to both these cousins. She would finish the letter after she had seen the others at tea, so that Verina and Justina would have the most current news regarding the extended family.

She made her way downstairs and met Mama in the foyer so they could go to tea. They were admitted to Julian's townhouse after their arrival, and the butler led them to the drawing room. She was eager to visit with her older sister, knowing Ariadne would be able to tell her more about what to expect during the Season, and she was also looking forward to seeing Penelope.

Most of all, though, Tia was ready to be reunited with her twin because she had missed Lia more than she ever could have imagined.

CHAPTER THREE

TIA LISTENED AS they were announced and allowed into the drawing room. Her eyes swept the room, finding Ariadne and Julian present. She and Mama went to greet them, and Tia teared up as her sister embraced her.

"I have missed you, sweet Tia," Ariadne said. "My, you have a maturity about you since we last saw you."

"I am not on the shelf yet," she teased, going to Julian for another, warm embrace.

"It has been too long, Tia," he said.

She adored her brother-in-law, a former London dock worker who wound up becoming a marquess. Julian was large and muscular, his eyes light, with two, dark slashes of expressive brows. He was protective of his wife and daughter, and that protection extended to her, as well.

"Come and sit," Ariadne said. "The others should be here soon."

She studied her sister for a moment. Ariadne had always been the beauty in the family, with her copper hair and sky-blue eyes. She also was incredibly kind and thoughtful. Together, Ariadne and Julian had purchased an orphanage and spent two days a week with the children who resided there. Tia and Lia had visited Oakbrooke Orphanage, and they had been moved by how the children adored Ariadne and Julian.

"Where is Penelope?" she asked.

"Her nap is almost over," Julian said. "You will not believe how much she has grown. And she is starting to speak." He grinned. "Mama was her first word. We are working on Papa."

The butler announced the next visitor, and her cousin Con breezed into the room.

"It is wonderful to see you all," he said. "Aunt Alice, you never seem to age."

Mama harumphed as he kissed her cheek. "And you are as glib as ever, Constantine."

"I am practicing my compliments for the upcoming Season," Con said. "If every young lady making her come-out is as pretty as Cousin Tia here, why, I will need to write an entire book of compliments in order to shower my many dance partners."

"Are you truly thinking about marriage?" she asked her cousin.

Laughing, he said, "Not a whit," causing them all to chuckle. "Val and I said we would wait until we had titles of our own. As Duke of Millbrooke now, it was time for him to wed, and he has already produced an heir. How is William?"

"More handsome than his father," she told him. "But completely bald."

That made Con laugh harder. "I suppose Val and Eden have yet to arrive in town, or they would be present at tea today."

"They intend to come to town next week," Mama informed him. "Eden is still recovering from childbirth. Valentinian wants to show off his new duchess, though, to Polite Society, so they will be here in time for the opening ball. Have your parents arrived in town yet?"

"They will also come sometime next week," Con shared. "Mama wrote to me and said that Aunt Agnes is not coming for the Season, though."

"I had a letter from Agnes only yesterday," Mama said. "She decided to remain at home this spring. Tray will be finishing university, and she wanted to be there and help him settle in permanently at Traywick Manor."

"I will miss having Aunt Agnes here," Tia said. "She is a favorite to all of us."

The door flew open, and Lia rushed in, headed straight for Tia. They clung to one another tightly.

"I have missed you so much," both said in unison, causing each to tear up.

"You would think they have not seen one another in years," Rupert said, biting back a smile as he greeted everyone.

Two teacarts were rolled in, and Ariadne asked Tia to pour out along with her. She almost protested, knowing the honor should go to Mama because of her rank, but she realized her sister was giving her practice at one of the necessary social skills. She was grateful for the opportunity.

Plates were filled, along with teacups, and then Lia said, "We have news to share."

Immediately, she knew what her twin would say, anticipating the announcement.

"We will have a child come November," her sister said, her gaze meeting Tia's.

Congratulations were issued, and Julian told Rupert, "There is nothing like having a child. You think of them before anything else. All you want is for them to be healthy and happy. I guarantee you that you will fall in love every day with your babe, just as you do your lovely wife."

"I am hoping for twins," Rupert revealed. "And if they have Lia's red hair, that will be a bonus."

"Red hair is not fashionable," Mama protested. "All four of my children got their father's red hair in varying shades. It is much to overcome."

Julian took Ariadne's hand. "Well, I adore my copper-headed beauties, Your Grace. Both of them."

Rupert kissed Lia's cheek. "And my auburn-haired wife is the most beautiful woman on earth, so I hope that at least our daughters will have her rich shade of hair."

Hearing her brothers-in-law admiring red hair made Tia feel

slightly better. She was the only strawberry blond in the family, and she had never met another with hair her particular shade.

"I think Tia's hair will help her stand out in her come-out class," Con said, giving her a smile. "Gentlemen will be certain to remember you before other ladies, Cousin."

Mama snorted. "I only hope Thermantia's hair color will not ruin her chances of making a suitable match."

She shook her head, and her gaze met her twin's. Mama always seemed to choose pessimism over optimism. It was something they were used to by now.

"How are you feeling?" Ariadne asked. "For a time, I was violently ill with Penelope."

Julian chuckled. "The servants placed chamber pots every few steps around the house. Even on the landings of the stairs. My poor darling could barely walk three paces without retching."

Tia hadn't realized that her sister had been so sick while increasing. She did not know if that was always a part of what carrying a babe entailed, and worried because she absolutely hated being ill.

"It did not last the entire time," Ariadne said, obviously seeing Tia's worried expression. "How are you faring, Lia?"

"Well, we did keep a chamber pot in the carriage as we came to town. Sometimes, the motion of the wheels comforted me. Other times, it made me dizzy and sick. It was a bit unpredictable."

"Do you think it will keep you from attending events?" she asked, worried that her sister would not come to balls.

"Rupert and I have decided we will attend some events, but we are taking our cues from Ariadne and Julian. We will not try to go to everything, just the affairs which interest us."

"Well, you better come to the opening ball," Tia said. "I must have you there with me."

"Oh, we would never miss that," her twin assured her. "I cannot wait to see you make your come-out, Tia."

She wondered if her sister might have regrets in having wed

before making her debut into the *ton*, but watching her with her husband, who had taken Lia's hand and laced their fingers together as they talked, let Tia know that her twin had everything she had ever wanted, especially now that she was with child.

The door opened, and a nursemaid brought in Penelope. She wriggled in the servant's arms, so the woman set her down. Immediately, Penelope toddled toward them, grinning at her parents.

Julian stood and swept his daughter up, tossing her into the air and catching her several times before taking a seat again, Penelope in his lap. Once more, her gaze met that of her twin's, and they shook their heads, knowing their own father had never held them, much less played with them. Julian was an exceptional, loving father, and Tia was so happy Ariadne had made a true love match.

"She has grown," Mama said. "I am surprised she walks quite steadily for one so young."

"Penelope loves to walk outside," Ariadne said. "We spend a great deal of time with her in the gardens or out on the lawn. Julian is thinking of getting her a dog."

"A dog?" Mama asked, looking as if she'd bitten into a sour grape. "Whatever for?"

"As a companion, Your Grace," Julian said easily, giving his daughter a bite of bread with jam slathered on it. "I know most dogs are used in hunting, but they can also make for good pets. Several breeds are loyal and faithful. I think it would be nice if Penelope had a dog who helped watch over her."

"You watch over her enough as it is, Aldridge," Mama said. "Between you and her nursemaid, Penelope needs no one else."

"Well, I think it a fine idea," Con said. "Perhaps I, too, will get a dog when I have children. In ten or twenty years," he added, and they all laughed merrily.

Tia and Lia wound up on the floor after tea, Penelope moving between their laps as they played with the little girl. Tia saw the wistful look in her sister's eyes.

"You are going to be a wonderful mother," she said. "And Rupert—who is mad for you—will be *almost* as doting a father as Julian."

Lia kissed the top of Penelope's head. "I truly look forward to motherhood." She reached for Tia's hand, squeezing her fingers. "Oh, I am so incredibly happy, Tia. I never knew I could find such joy in every day. I want the same for you. The only part of living at Crestbrook which I do not enjoy is missing you. We simply must find you a husband who lives within five miles of us so that I can see you more often."

"What if I come and visit you after the Season?" she suggested. "Once you return to Cumberland, I could accompany you. I could even stay until the birth of your child if you would like."

Her twin frowned. "As lovely as that sounds, you will most likely be making plans for your wedding."

Tia shook her head. "No, not me. I do not plan on wedding for at least a year or two."

Lia studied her. "But what if you fall in love this Season?"

"I have no plans of doing so," she said blithely. "I am going to go to balls and dance until dawn. Stroll the gardens at garden parties and inhale all the lovely blooms. Be clever and win at cards at routs. I am ready to enjoy life, Lia. Enjoy being free."

Lia squeezed Tia's fingers again. "I hope you have a wonderful time during the Season, but I would like you to be open to the idea of love. Who knows the kind of gentlemen you will meet? One might be in town, right now, thinking the very same things as you. Then he will see you across a ballroom and fall madly in love with you—and you with him."

"I doubt it."

Her sister shook her head. "You have no control over love, Tia. I know what I speak of. I fell in love with Rupert and was miserable because I did not think he loved me. I was worried about attending this Season because I did not think I could see him dancing with and courting other women."

"You would have stayed home just to avoid him?" she asked,

shocked.

"I cannot say for certain. Everything changed once Rupert showed up at our door and swept me off my feet. Love can be so very odd, Tia. And yet it is the most wonderful feeling in the world. My love for Rupert grows stronger each day."

She raised their joined hands and kissed Lia's. "That is because you found the love of your life. Every day will be better than the one before. Honestly, Lia, I simply want to enjoy this time in my life. If love comes, I will not ignore it. If it never does, I will accept that, too."

"Rupert and I will help you find a husband," Lia said fervently.

She chuckled. "The two of you have never even been to a Season. I think I would trust Val and Con helping me more than the two of you. At least they will be acquainted with many of the gentlemen present and help guide me toward more suitable ones."

Lia brought Tia's hand to her cheek. "I just want you to experience all the happiness I have found. It is hard not being with you every day, Tia."

"We have this Season together," she said, determination filling her. "We will always have the Season. Ariadne is right. This time is about more than attending social events. It is for our growing families to come together and enjoy being with one another. Just think—this time next spring, you will be a mother, bringing your own babe to the Season. Lucy and Dru will come with their children. Verina will be making her come-out. We will be able to spend time with Ariadne. I have a feeling that the Season will become my favorite time of year."

Penelope walked back to her parents, and Tia shared, "I made a friend today. At Madame Laurent's."

"That is wonderful. Tell me about her."

"Her name is Lady Delilah Drake, but she prefers to be called Dilly."

"Dilly. That is an unusual nickname."

"Her mother insists that she introduce herself to others as Delilah. Her brother could not say her name when she was born, and he christened her Dilly. He is the only one who calls her that, but she asked if I would do so, as well."

Tia recounted her conversation with Dilly, and Lia was surprised to hear how other young ladies had refused to be Dilly's friend.

"I never realized how competitive the Season was," Tia said. "Of course, Mama has already lectured me about how I should only consider the suit of gentlemen who are either a marquess or duke. She will press me in the next few months to find a husband."

"Val will stand up to Mama," Lia assured her. He will protect you from her wrath."

"I hope so. When I do wed, I do not care what my husband's rank might be. I simply want someone I feel comfortable with. Someone I can enjoy building a life with. I want a man who will value me and yet allow me a bit of independence." She paused. "And he must be a family man. None of this straying from our marriage vows. I want my husband to be faithful to me and pay attention to our children."

"It would help if he could also be friends with Rupert and the other men in our family," Lia suggested.

Tia nodded. "I think that will be the barometer for me to measure a man's worth. If Val and the others like him, then I will consider a future with him."

Lia leaned over and hugged her. "I hope this Season will be everything you have dreamed of, Tia."

"I hope so, too."

She was eager for the Season to begin. She had her family to support her, and had made a new friend in Lady Dilly Drake. Tia believed the next few months would become the best of her life.

CHAPTER FOUR

HUGO REMAINED SILENT as Alfie dressed him for the day. His valet had already shaved him and trimmed Hugo's hair this morning, all in an attempt to make him presentable for his trip to White's. He had never set foot inside the club, but he held a membership to it as the Earl of Merriman. Going today and being amongst his fellow peers would be a test, one which he very well knew he might fail. He couldn't allow that to happen, though.

Because of Dilly.

If he never had to come to London again, Hugo would have been perfectly happy. He'd only been to the great city twice. The first time had been his initial meeting with Mr. Becker. The clerk had not been the least judgmental as Hugo had stammered his way through his conversation with the man. In fact, he had taken so to the clerk that he had promised Becker he would make him the Drake family solicitor once his father passed and Hugo took his title as Earl of Merriman.

The earl's death had occurred two years ago, just before Hugo had completed his studies at Cambridge. His father had been struck with a fit of apoplexy, which had left him paralyzed along the right side of his body, leaving him bedridden. The earl had lost the ability to speak, as well. He still held his title, however, and so Hugo had no say regarding the estate.

Fortunately, Merrifield had a wonderful steward. Mr. Rains had remained in close contact with Hugo, sending weekly reports of how things fared. It was through this correspondence that he began to learn what was involved in managing a large estate. He studied each letter Rains sent, learning everything he could.

In addition, he asked Matthew to help him understand what was unclear. His friend had already returned to Redfield by then, his studies completed. Ironically, the duke's country estate was a mere ten miles from Merrifield, although Redfield was located west of Brandon in Suffolk, while Merrifield, which was near Thetford, was in Norfolk. Merrifield did lie right on the border of Norfolk and Suffolk, though, and Hugo knew he would see a good deal of Matthew once he returned to reside at Merrifield.

In a wonderful gesture of friendship, Matthew had returned to Cambridge a few months after Hugo had first written to him regarding his father's ill health, and his friend had stayed a week. Together, they had read every report Rains had sent, and Matthew guided Hugo through what occurred on a country estate. He explained the responsibilities that would fall to Hugo once he became the earl, things his own father had never broached with him. Then again, Merriman had little to do with his son, especially as Hugo had gotten older.

Once Matthew left, Hugo's thirst for knowledge regarding estate management continued. He poured over books in various libraries, drinking in knowledge. When the day came and he was named the Earl of Merriman, he wanted to be completely prepared.

During his father's lingering illness, he never returned home, however. Remaining at Cambridge became very important to him, as did the lessons he partook in with his cousin. Anthony had been a godsend. He taught Hugo how to focus more intensely and worked with him on his breathing. They read aloud together daily, and he also read aloud for an hour or more on his own, getting used to forming words and speaking them. He, Anthony, and Matthew had sung every day while Matthew had been with them. The duke had even left the pianoforte behind when he returned to Redfield. Anthony had challenged Hugo, and he had taken up the instrument, finding a music tutor. Nowadays, Hugo played at least an hour a day for the sheer joy of it. Half the time, he chose classical compositions, while the rest of the time he played country tunes so that he might sing along with them.

The stammer always lingered under the surface. He understood, thanks to Anthony, that he would never completely conquer it, but with concentration, proper breathing, and daily practice speaking and singing aloud, Hugo had a good control of his greatest defect. He tried to remain as worry-free as possible. Working alongside Rains, he managed Merrifield and its tenants well.

He also looked to Mr. Becker for advice. When Hugo received word of his father's death on the eve of setting out for home, he had stopped to call in London in order to see Becker. He had stayed in contact with the clerk, who now had gone out on his own and was working as a solicitor. Hugo had told him he wished to become his client. Becker had accompanied Hugo back to Merrifield for the funeral services, and they had spent a good week discussing the estate and investments, both those currently held and recommendations Becker had for the future.

Even Matthew had come to visit Hugo that first week he was home and had found Becker to be wise beyond his years. Matthew promised Becker when his own solicitor retired, he would direct all his business to the former clerk. That had occurred six months ago, and now Becker was well thought of by his peers, having earned the trust of a duke and an earl so early into his career.

Becker had also set up Hugo with a financial adviser at a bank, not a man his father had used. Hugo wanted a fresh start and divorced himself from any holdings his father had. Based upon advice and suggestions from his new banking adviser and Becker, he had diversified his wealth. Already, two years into his earldom, he was seeing a tidy profit beyond what Merrifield brought in.

But today was the day Hugo had dreaded for years. He adored Dilly and would do anything for his sister. That meant accompanying her and Mama to town in order for Dilly to make her come-out this Season. While he had no intention of searching for a bride, he did need to be at the various social affairs in order to see the kind of gentlemen who were paying attention to Dilly. He would need to get to know these men—and that meant starting before the Season began. His visit to White's today was the start of Hugo entering Polite Society himself, and he couldn't help but worry about how that would go.

Would he see those who had bullied him in the past? Would they recognize him? Or even remember him? He hadn't a clue. He only knew he must become actively involved in Polite Society for his sister's sake. Dilly was a lively girl, full of fun and mischief. She could be a bit rash and leaped often before she looked. He would need to be present to temper her, as well as help her look deeply into the gentlemen who became her suitors.

Fear of rejection haunted him. He had never had friends before Matthew and Anthony, unless he counted Alfie. The footman now served as Hugo's valet. He had wanted to replace Storey with Alfie, but his friend had no interest in being the butler of a country household. Alfie had asked instead if he could be Hugo's valet and travel with him wherever he went, be it the country or town. He had a suspicion that this was Alfie's way of looking after him, but he did not press him. Instead, he allowed the footman to be elevated to valet—and removed both Storeys from Merrifield. Actually, he had done almost a clean sweep, ridding the country household of most of its servants. Alfie had been able to tell Hugo who would be loyal to him and which servants had belittled him over the years, due to their allegiance to the former earl or because they had disparaged him for his stammering.

Mama had helped in the hiring of new servants. Frankly, she had become a new woman after her husband's death. She had moved as silently about the house as her son had, not wishing to draw her husband's notice, and had rarely left her rooms. Since the earl's death, she was still a bit quiet, but she was more present in his life and that of Dilly's. She also volunteered at the village church and seemed happier than he had ever seen her.

"There. That ought to do it, my lord." Alfie stepped back and studied his handiwork. "I do believe I have mastered the art of tying cravats. And now that your wardrobe has been updated, you will be a man dressed in the height of fashion. Look out, men at White's—Lord Merriman is entering your fold."

He couldn't help but chuckle at his friend's teasing. "You know how to keep me in good spirits, Alfie," he praised.

The valet turned serious. "I know how frightening it must be to contemplate going to White's, my lord. You do not know who will be there. How you will be accepted." Alfie smiled encouragingly. "But I have faith in you. You have conquered your stammer. You will do the same with Polite Society."

"It will help that Reddington will be present," he said, knowing he might not have gone at all without his friend promising to meet him at White's.

"His Grace will take good care of you," Alfie assured him. "He always has. As does Mr. Drake."

The moment Hugo had assumed his title, he looked for a way to bring his cousin to Merrifield. He had been fortunate when Anthony completed his studies at Cambridge and had taken a position as a sexton at a church just outside the university town. Anthony had cared for the church's property, as well as run the bell for services. He had even dug graves for those parishioners lost. With his employment being so close, they had continued to live together.

Once Hugo returned to Merrifield as the earl, he met with the vicar who held the living in Merrivale, the nearest village. The vicar had been old when Hugo was young, and he was in his late sixties. The clergyman had conducted the services for Hugo's father, and then they had met the following day. When the vicar learned that Hugo's cousin had graduated from Cambridge and was eager to assume the living at Merrivale, he had graciously retired. Immediately, Hugo had sent word to Anthony, and he had put in his notice at his current church, arriving at Merrivale three weeks later. He now lived at the vicarage and was but three miles from Merrifield. It had comforted Hugo to have his cousin and mentor so close by.

"Yes, my cousin does keep his eye on me," he agreed. Standing, he said, "I suppose I am off to White's."

"Give my best to His Grace," Alfie requested.

"I most certainly will."

He took a final swig of his coffee. Hugo never went down to breakfast, finding he was not hungry in the mornings. Alfie did, however, always bring him a cup of coffee. The hot beverage brightened his mood, making him feel somehow sharper. He had Coggins have the carriage brought around and told the butler once his coachman dropped him at White's, he would have him return, knowing Mama and Dilly might have another appointment scheduled and be in need of transportation.

It had surprised him all it took for his sister to be made ready for her come-out. Mama had commissioned an entire new wardrobe for Dilly. While Hugo did not begrudge his sister having new gowns to wear, it had shocked him when Mama explained that Dilly would not be able to don again any of the gowns to the balls held that Season, and she would also not repeat wearing any gowns worn to a *ton* affair. He thought it a waste, just another example of how out of touch Polite Society was with the rest of the world. Still, he would do everything in his power to see that Dilly gained a husband this Season, one who was worthy of her.

Mama had also hired a dance master to perfect Dilly's steps. Both a music and art tutor had been engaged for a short while, and now Dilly's playing of the pianoforte was quite good. Her sketching and painting left much to be desired, though, and he doubted she would consider pursuing art.

Hugo entered his carriage, working on slowing his breathing

as they traveled through the bustling streets of London. Already, after a few weeks in town, he sorely missed the countryside. He did not like noise or large crowds, and London was full of both. Dread filled him, thinking of the opening ball to be held in about ten days' time. He had passed along all the invitations he had received to his mother, allowing her to respond to the events she deemed suitable for Dilly to attend. He would escort the pair to these—and not attend a single extra event he did not have to go to.

The coach arrived at White's and he exited it, instructing his driver to head home and be at Lady Merriman's disposal for the rest of the day.

"Yes, my lord," the coachman said, tipping his cap to Hugo.

After two years, it still amazed him how his servants proved deferential and professional. Then again, he had rooted out all the bad ones, and Mama had done an excellent job of replacing the old guard with the new.

He moved to the door, telling himself he was as good as any man who passed through these doors. That he was an earl, a quite wealthy one, and he had a friend waiting for him.

Once he was admitted, a genial-looking man stepped forward. "I am Pollard, my lord, head of White's."

Pausing a moment, he then replied, "I am Lord Merriman."

The man's eyes lit up. "Ah, His Grace told me to be expecting you, my lord. Welcome to White's. I am here to make certain your every need is met. Might I show you about in order to familiarize you with our establishment?"

"Of course."

Hugo followed Pollard, seeing everything from the dining, card, and billiards rooms to the coffee and two morning rooms. Pollard was friendly, which made him comfortable. He tried not to look at the other gentlemen in the rooms they passed, not wanting his confidence to waver. His gut told him he would eventually run into former classmates. Some of those would be the very men who had bullied him unmercifully, but he was an adult now, not a small, cowed boy.

A servant stepped up, and Pollard said, "This is Tommy, my lord, one of the best servers at White's. Tommy, this is the Earl of Merriman, a good friend to the Duke of Reddington."

The server nodded in acknowledgement and said, "His Grace has just arrived, Mr. Pollard. He is seated in one of the morning rooms and asked that Lord Merriman join him as soon as possible."

"I can do so now," Hugo said.

"Before you leave, my lord, please let Tommy know all your preferences regarding food and drink. Your taste in newspapers, as well. Anytime you visit us at White's, we want it to be an enjoyable experience."

"I prefer coffee with cream. No sugar. If it is tea, then it is the opposite. Sugar and no cream. The only food I will not eat is liver, and I read newspapers voraciously, all the ones printed in town."

"Very good, my lord," Pollard said. "Tommy will remember your preferences, and I will let our other staff members know of them, as well."

"If you follow me, my lord, I will take you to His Grace," Tommy said.

He did so, once more passing others who sat, drinking hot beverages, reading newspapers, and talking with fellow peers. Hugo didn't realize he was holding his breath until they entered a room and he spied Matthew, who broke out in a huge smile.

"I will bring your coffee now, my lord," Tommy said, discreetly exiting.

"Merriman!" called Matthew, rising to greet him. "We are finally in town together."

Instead of a sedate handshake, the duke threw his arms about Hugo, slapping him on the back. He knew others were carefully observing Matthew's behavior and would take note of the closeness between them.

As they sat, he leaned toward his friend. "Was that merely a show of friendship, or are you letting the members of White's know that I have the ducal stamp of approval?"

Matthew laughed heartily. "You are never one to mince words, Hugo." He paused. "I *am* glad to see you, but I did not think a rousing show of support by me toward you would go unnoticed. After all, I have had others observing my every move for over a dozen years now. And what the Duke of Reddington is seen doing is soon imitated by others. Whoever the Duke of Reddington offers his friendship to will be seen as a gentleman others will wish to meet. Who knows? You soon may prove more popular than I have ever been."

Hugo shook his head. "You are as outrageous as usual." He smiled. "And as kind as you were from the moment you took notice of me."

His friend brushed aside the compliment. "How is Anthony? He is not the best writer of letters."

"My cousin is kept busy by the parishioners of Merrivale. And even though he can write eloquently, you know he prefers conversations in person."

"Do the two of you still practice speaking together?" the duke inquired.

"When I go and visit him, we will retreat to his study and do so. For the most part, we each practice on our own, though. I know it is something I can never grow lax about. I spent too many years dreading opening my mouth. Now that I can speak clearly and concisely, I never wish to lose that skill."

"How is your sister's preparation for the Season coming along?"

"She is as busy as ever. She had a dress fitting yesterday, and then she practiced her dancing and pianoforte playing before Mama took her to tea with some friends. They actually went to the theater last night. I have not even seen either of them since yesterday morning."

"Oh, you will see plenty of them beginning next week. You will escort them to so many events, they will begin to blur."

He studied his friend. "Do you enjoy going to these social affairs?"

Matthew shrugged. "Sometimes. I will admit that oftentimes I am bored. Every mama with an unmarried daughter chases me about. I find their daughters uninteresting and usually hide in the card room at balls." He sighed. "Perhaps now that you are in town, we both might look for a bride."

Hugo shook his head. "Not me. Not this year. My only intention is to see Dilly wed. I will look to you, though, for help in seeing which candidates have the most potential. As a duke, I am certain you know everyone in Polite Society."

"I do know most, if only by reputation. I must say, keeping your pretty sister away from the rakes and rogues will be a difficult task."

"You think Dilly pretty?" he asked.

"Your sister is very pretty," Matthew assured him. "And every gentleman—be he good or bad—will be sniffing about her."

Worry filled him. And worry was not good for him. It bothered his thinking. It caused him to lose focus.

"Might I have a seat here?" a voice asked. "White's is filling up this morning. I have never seen it so crowded before a Season began."

He glanced up at the tall, lean man, noticing his unique amethyst eyes and aquiline nose.

Matthew said, "Of course, Dyer. This is my good friend, Lord Merriman. Viscount Dyer."

"A pleasure," the viscount said, offering Hugo his hand.

"Likewise," he said.

"Please, do not let me interrupt your conversation. I simply want something to drink and the latest newspaper. Ah, wait. Here is Tommy, ready with what I need."

"Lord Dyer," the servant greeted. "Your beverage and newspapers."

"You are a gem, Tommy," Dyer said. "If I were not poor, I would steal you away from White's and make you my valet."

"I am quite happy to serve the members of White's, my lord," Tommy said.

Hugo wondered at the remark the viscount made, wondering if he teased about being poor. It did not seem something which should be shared.

"Are you truly poor?" he asked boldly, something quite out of character for him.

Dyer laughed. "I tease about it. I do have a quarterly allowance provided to me, courtesy of my father, Lord Marley. For now, I watch the money I do have carefully. When I eventually come into my title—and I hope it will be many years before Papa passes on—I believe I will still be scrupulous with my funds." He smiled. "Until then, I am on my own. I pursue my interests and do my best to avoid wooing any young ladies during the Season. While I am always a ready dance partner, I let them know I have no interest in wedding until I am settled with my title."

"That is very frank," he said, liking the open honesty of this man.

"Please, do not let me interrupt your conversation," Dyer told them. "I have plenty to keep me entertained."

He opened a newspaper and began reading, allowing Hugo and Matthew to pick up where they left off.

"As I was saying, you must be vigilant in watching over your sister," Matthew said. "I can help you as you narrow down the list of candidates for her hand."

"Beg pardon," Lord Dyer said. "My cousin is making her own come-out this Season. She is the youngest sister of the Duke of Millbrooke, and I will be assisting him in helping her find a husband. Perhaps we might pool our knowledge of the eligible gentlemen that take an interest in our relatives. If any of us discover something unsavory which would discourage a match between the young ladies in our care and an unscrupulous suitor, it could benefit us all."

Liking the idea, Hugo said, "I would appreciate any information which comes to you, Lord Dyer. I cherish my sister, and I would not see her with some cad."

"Perhaps you might join my cousin and me at Tattersall's this afternoon at two o'clock then," suggested the viscount. "Millbrooke just arrived in town this morning, and he asked me to look at a new horse with him. I would be happy to introduce you to him, Lord Merriman." He turned to Matthew. "Of course, I believe you know my cousin, Your Grace."

"Not well," Matthew admitted. "What I do know of Millbrooke, I like." He looked to Hugo. "What do you say, my friend? Shall we join the Duke of Millbrooke and Lord Dyer at Tattersall's this afternoon?"

Knowing it would be helpful to have another duke among the circle of his acquaintances, especially with Dilly making her come-out, Hugo said, "We would be delighted to spend some time looking at horseflesh with you, my lord."

CHAPTER FIVE

W HEN IT CAME time for them to leave White's for Tattersall's, Matthew explained to Viscount Dyer that he had a quick errand to run, and he and Hugo would meet Dyer and the duke there. They went outside to the Reddington ducal carriage, where Hugo climbed in, seating himself and closing his eyes. For two, full minutes, he breathed in and out slowly, trying to establish his equilibrium once more.

When he opened his eyes, Matthew was seated across from him, and the carriage was in motion.

"I thought you could use a respite from all the conversation," his friend said, always mindful of how being around others for too long could grow to be too much for Hugo. Anthony, as well.

"I am grateful for your awareness of my situation, Matthew. I did like Lord Dyer, though. Quite a bit."

"I had not really ever held a conversation with him," the duke explained. "I simply knew who he was, and we have nodded pleasantly at one another a few times over the years. I have heard that he is extremely close to his cousin. Millbrooke gained his title a year ago. The duke has also wed. It is good Millbrooke is looking after his younger sister during her come-out. I think it an excellent idea for you and the duke to get to know one another and exchange information regarding suitors."

"I agree."

"I asked my driver to simply drive the streets for a bit before he heads to Tattersall's and our engagement there. Let us recite poetry together, my friend. It will soothe you."

He had begun reading poetry aloud when he lived with Matthew and Anthony. The three had often read the same poems over and over, and Hugo had many of them memorized by this point. Matthew began reciting *I Wandered Lonely as a Cloud* from Wordsworth, a favorite of theirs. As the carriage traveled through the streets of London, they also repeated the verses of Wordsworth's *Tintern Abbey* from memory.

Finally, he asked if they could sing one song before reaching Tattersall's, and Matthew readily complied. Music continued to be a great liberator for Hugo, and he sang with gusto now, his deep bass harmonizing with Matthew's tenor.

When they finished the song, he nodded, satisfied. "I am at peace again."

"I know your time at White's was a bit overwhelming today. You did a fine job, Hugo. You spoke when addressed and even asked a few questions of Lord Dyer."

"He proved to be a popular fellow. I lost count of the number of gentlemen who stopped by to greet him—and us, of course."

Hugo had been proud that he had not stumbled over any of his words, especially when being introduced to others. Some of them had included the very bullies from his past. Most, however, seemed as if they were meeting him for the first time, leading him to believe he had not made any lasting impression upon any of his tormentors. Of course, he had not been referred to as Hugo Drake in introductions today but rather Lord Merriman, and others would not associate the small, scrawny, stammering boy with the large man he had become. He had worried about confronting those who had done him harm. Now, he realized he was most likely the only person who even held memories of those terrible times. At least it would give him a fresh start in society.

"He is well known throughout Polite Society," Matthew agreed. "I knew, though, that being with Lord Dyer and conversing as much as you did would leave you strained."

"Being with you and reciting poetry and singing was exactly the remedy I needed to refresh myself. I cannot thank you enough."

"How does Anthony do it?" Matthew mused. "He gives a sermon each Sunday, speaking at length, and then he must greet the parishioners as they leave the weekly service. I would think that overwhelmingly hard."

"My cousin has had more practice than I have at being around others," Hugo explained. "And once Sunday services are over, Anthony seeks solitude for the remainder of the day."

"Do you enjoy having him nearby?"

"Without a doubt, having Anthony close has made a world of difference. I am also grateful that you and I are not too far from one another." He hesitated a moment and then asked, "Were you serious when you mentioned that we should look for brides this year?"

Matthew shrugged. "It is an idea I am growing accustomed to. I know I am but five and twenty and that many men in my position wait another five, ten—even twenty years—before wedding, but I would like to have a family, Hugo. It has been just Mama and me for so very long."

"Are you surprised that your mother never wed again?"

"No, not a bit."

Curious, he asked, "Did they love one another?"

Matthew considered his question, and for the first time in their acquaintance, Hugo saw his friend hesitating.

"Let me say this. I have never asked Mama if that is so. From what I witnessed, there was no love on his part for her. She might have, early on in the marriage, thought that she loved him, but she quickly saw love had no role in their relationship."

"My parents had no relationship at all," he told Matthew. "Sometimes, I thought my father did not want to even be the same room with my mother. She was so incredibly timid around him, afraid of setting him off and having to endure another beating. Mama is still a quiet woman, but she is no longer tense in the company of others. She is eager for Dilly to wed, however, and I assume she wants the same for me. I will have to peruse the Marriage Mart at some point in order to gain a wife and subsequent heir. For now, I plan to focus on Dilly's suitors this Season and see her settled before thinking of marriage for myself."

The vehicle had stopped, and Matthew consulted his pocket watch. "We are right on time."

They exited the carriage just as another grand one pulled up nearby. It was as fine as Matthew's, and Hugo noted the emblem on the door, realizing the Duke of Millbrooke had arrived. Sure enough, Viscount Dyer bounded from the vehicle, and he was followed by a man of similar age, one who was tall and whose chestnut hair gleamed in the sunlight.

Introductions were exchanged between the four men and then Millbrooke said, "My cousin tells me that you have a younger sister who will make her come-out this spring, Lord Merriman."

"Yes, Dilly is terribly excited about entering Polite Society and making new friends."

"My sister Tia is the same. I have three sisters," the duke shared. "Two are already wed to the Marquess of Aldridge and Viscount Cressley." He grinned. "I also have wed, and my duchess recently presented me with William, our firstborn."

"That must be difficult, having to leave him in the country to come to town for the Season," Matthew said.

Millbrooke shook his head. "Not at all, Your Grace. My sister has started a new tradition within our family. We come from ten cousins, spread across three families, and all ten of us have decided we will bring our children to town with us each year."

Hugo looked at the duke blankly. "Seriously?"

Millbrooke laughed. "It is a wild idea my sister Ariadne had, but I believe she is right in such radical thinking. She said parents should not be separated for months at a time from their children. Ariadne also wishes for all our children to get to know one another, and what better time for the next generation of cousins to do so than when we are all in town for the Season?"

He thought the idea unique. It was the custom of members of the *ton* to leave children in the hands of their nursemaids and governesses while the parents journeyed to town for the social Season each spring. He assumed that would be what he would do, but this outlandish idea of not abandoning the children yearly intrigued him.

"Come," Millbrooke said. "Let us go inside. I only arrived in town this morning and do not want to spend too much time away from my duchess and son."

They entered and were greeted by Mr. Tattersall himself, who showed the duke three different horses available for purchase. Although Hugo was an accomplished rider, he knew very little about how to select good horseflesh and said so.

Immediately, Lord Dyer and Millbrooke dominated the conversation, both of them experts at obtaining horseflesh. He listened carefully, knowing this information would be valuable to possess. Both he and Matthew interjected a question or comment every now and then, but for the most part, Hugo did not have to speak much. Still, listening kept him on his toes, not knowing when someone might ask a question of him.

He also found himself relaxing more in the company of these two newcomers, a feeling he had not experienced since he had first met Anthony and Matthew five years ago. He hoped he might see more of the pair as the Season progressed. He knew not every titled gentleman he encountered would be as interesting or kind as these two cousins, but he believed he would enjoy time spent in their company, discussing suitors for their two sisters or any other topics.

The duke purchased the second of the horses he had been shown, and the four men left Tattersall's, returning to their two carriages.

Millbrooke offered his hand to Matthew and then Hugo. "It was nice to meet you both and spend a bit of time with you. As I mentioned earlier, I do like the idea of getting together and talking about the various gentlemen who become interested in our two sisters. Might I ask if either of you are wed?"

"Neither of us," Matthew replied for the both of them. "While I have begun to think I might test the waters and consider looking for a duchess this year, my friend here wishes to wait until his sister is settled in marriage before he peruses the Marriage Mart himself."

"Hopefully, we will see you soon at White's again," Lord Dyer said. "My parents will be in town early next week. Perhaps you might like to come and take tea with us."

Hugo replied this time. "Yes, that would be lovely, my lord."

"I only wish Lucy and Dru, my two sisters, could be in town this Season," the viscount continued. "Lucy recently gave birth to a babe and is recovering from childbirth, while Dru is far along in her increasing and too uncomfortable to come to town this spring."

"You will also need to come to tea—or even dinner—and meet my duchess," Millbrooke volunteered. "I wish to give her a few days to rest before I plan any social engagements for us, however. William is but five weeks old, and I am mindful that it will take time for Eden to recover from his birth. If Tia were not making her come-out this Season, we might have stayed home ourselves. We are here, however, and as older brothers, I know we will do right by our younger sisters, won't we, Merriman?"

"Of course, Your Grace."

They parted ways, going to their separate carriages, and Matthew told Hugo that he would drop him at home.

When they arrived, he said, "I would ask you in for tea, but I am all talked out. I plan to retreat to my study and enjoy a cup of tea in solitude."

"I will see you soon then," his friend said. "And Hugo, you did very well today. Take pride in yourself. Today was just the start. I know this Season will be difficult for you, but you have the drive and determination to make it a success, both for yourself and Lady Delilah."

He entered his townhouse, greeting Coggins, and headed up the stairs. He reached the landing and ran across Dilly. She was wearing one of her new day gowns and looked quite lovely in it.

Before he could compliment her on it, she said, "Oh, Hugo. You are finally home! Do you realize I have not seen you all yesterday or today? I have wonderful news to share with you. I made a friend at the modiste's yesterday. A friend!" she repeated, beaming at him.

He was glad to hear this because she had come to his study a week earlier in tears. Apparently, none of the girls she had met so far had wished to become friends with her. Dilly had looked forward to the Season, not so much to find a husband, but to form lasting friendships. His heart had been heavy, knowing her overture of friendship had been rejected by others.

"It is good to hear this."

"She is coming for tea now," Dilly continued, her excitement apparent. "Oh, I cannot wait for you to meet her. Her mother was a bit frightening to me. I tried not to be intimidated by her."

"No one should ever intimidate you, little sister," he said fondly. "But you and Mama must entertain your friend at tea this afternoon without me. I simply cannot be around a guest now."

He hoped she would pick up on what he said without having to explain it to her. Then again, he had worked incredibly hard over the last five years and rarely stuttered around anyone, especially Dilly. He doubted she realized how exhausting it was for him to be around others. Already, his head was pounding, and he needed the solace of being alone to recuperate from this long day.

"No, Hugo," Dilly said, stamping her foot for emphasis. "I want you to meet her. I want her to like me. And you."

This was a petulant side to Dilly which he had never witnessed before. She had never been unreasonable or disrespectful to him. The only thing he could think of to have made her act this way was the new friend she had made. Still, he tried to give this friend the benefit of the doubt now and shook his head.

His tone firm, he told her, "You do not need my presence for someone to like you. If she accepted an invitation from you to come to tea, then she already is your friend. You can speak of your come-outs. All the things you will be doing this Season."

"Hugo, I need you at tea," she pleaded.

Normally, he did everything he could to make his sister happy, but suddenly he was so weary after the long day of being around others he wished to impress. Any focus he had had fled, and he worried he would not be able to even string two words together. This was a not time to regress and return to stammering. Not on the eve of the Season. Dilly needed him at his absolute best. More importantly, he did not want to slip up and embarrass Dilly in front of her new friend. For all he knew, the girl might be a terrible gossip. If she began spreading the news of his stammer, it could seriously affect his sister's chances at making a suitable match.

Frowning at her, Hugo sternly said. "No. I am going . . . to my study. For tea . . . by myself. I do not wish to be . . . disturbed. I am in no . . . mood to entertain a silly . . . girl."

His sharp tone caused Dilly to wince, and he saw tears form in her eyes. Feeling awful, he added, "I cannot be around . . . anyone else today. I would only . . . be a hindrance to you. Talk about all matters feminine. I will meet this friend. Another . . . time."

Her jaw dropped, and then her mouth set stubbornly as she stormed off, heading up the staircase.

If Dilly had not been so put out with him, she would have picked up on the subtle clues as he begin halting as he spoke. When he was overtired, he knew to break phrases down and speak in them, not in full sentences. Knowing he would apologize to her later once she had calmed, Hugo went down the stairs, only to see that Coggins had admitted a young lady, who now stood in the foyer, looking at him with frank disapproval.

"I suppose . . . you are . . . my sister's new friend," he began, aware his concentration was faltering fast, as he spaced out his words, afraid he would begin stammering and completely embarrass Dilly—and himself. "And that you heard ... every word we ... exchanged."

With a disdainful look, the young lady said, "You, my lord, are apparently not the man you sister brags about. She adores you. When we met yesterday morning, all she could do is praise you to the rafters. It seems the least you could do to please her would be to sit at tea with her and the first friend she has made in town. Obviously, you are not interested in making her happy—or getting to know me. Do us both a favor, Lord Merriman, and avoid my company when we meet at the Season. Life is too short for me to waste it on a two-faced soul such as yourself."

He could not believe she had spoken so brazenly, dressing him down as a governess would a misbehaving charge. Upset that this young lady had overheard his argument with Dilly, Hugo thought he should apologize to her, but it was too late. She alrcady had motioned to Coggins.

"If you would, Coggins, please take me to the drawing room now. I am eagerly looking forward to tea with Lady Dilly. I believe we will become fast friends."

Hugo watched her sashay up the stairs, the swing of her hips causing his mouth to go dry. When she reached the landing and turned, their gazes met. She glanced at him dismissively and continued up the staircase.

Taken aback, he retreated to his study, thinking this young woman a hoyden. No properly raised girl of the *ton* would ever address an earl in such an impertinent manner. Hugo determined that she would not be a good influence upon Dilly. Why, she was already using his sister's nickname, which no one did but him. He would need to nip this friendship in the bud and encourage Dilly to be friendly with more demure, unassuming young ladies. While he admired candor when used in small doses, this young lady had taken things too far. She was not for Dilly.

Ringing for tea, he sipped a cup, his eyes closed, recovering from the long, trying day.

CHAPTER SIX

T IA MARCHED UP the stairs, anger sizzling through her. Lord Merriman had ruined her good mood, which had begun after she had finished practicing the pianoforte this morning. She'd left the music room and found Val and Eden had come to town much earlier than expected. Naturally, William accompanied them, and Tia had gone directly to the nursery to see her nephew. Eden was there and handed William over, allowing Tia to rock the babe to sleep.

They had gone to the drawing room, where Val and Mama sat talking. Eden explained how she was feeling more and more like her old self, and Val had suggested they come to town now instead of waiting until next week. He urged his wife to see if Madame Laurent could squeeze her in for a dress fitting because he wanted Eden wearing something splendid for the opening ball of the Season. Her former wardrobe as a governess was nowhere near adequate, and Val wanted his duchess to shine. Fortunately, their local dressmaker in Willowshire had made up several day gowns for Eden, but she would need more than a few ballgowns since the Season went through spring and summer.

Mama had insisted the three of them leave at once to go to the modiste's shop, saying that no matter which clients were present, Madame Laurent would make time to see a duchess. Val had said he would have Con go with him to look at a horse he was interested in purchasing since the ladies would be busy.

Madame Laurent was swamped, but just as Mama had predicted, when a duchess came calling, everyone else was momentarily cast aside. Discreetly, of course, but Eden went to the front of the line, all the same. Once her measurements had been taken, Madame had said to trust her in both the design and materials which would be used to make up several ballgowns for Eden. The modiste even told them she had hired another seamstress, and all of the Duchess of Millbrooke's gowns would go to her—and be completed before anyone else's gowns were even begun.

They had returned home after that, and Eden had come to Tia's bedchamber, eager to see the gowns her sister-in-law would be wearing to the Season. Tia proudly showed off the first night's creation, one which flattered her figure and coloring. Eden was tired after journeying to town and then being fitted, so she had gone to nap, while Mama and Tia had made plans to go to Lady Merriman's for tea. Unfortunately, Mama's gown had caught on something as she descended the stairs from their carriage, creating a large tear in it.

Refusing to go inside the townhouse because of the rip, Mama had encouraged Tia to attend tea, saying she would send the carriage back for her once the coachman had dropped her at home. If her lady's maid could not repair the gown, then Mama said she would give it away.

Tia was only glad Mama had not been the one to be present in the foyer just now. If she had heard how Lord Merriman had refused to come to tea, she would have turned around and left. No one insulted a duchess in that manner. She supposed she, too, should have left, only the carriage no longer waited for her. Besides, she would not abandon Dilly. Here the poor girl thought her brother hung the moon, but he seemed like a typical, self-centered man of the *ton* to Tia. Her own papa had been grumpy regarding social events, be it tea or a ball, and Tia thought Dilly should not have to suffer her friend's absence because her brother was a clod.

The butler paused before the drawing room doors. "My apologies, my lady. His lordship is usually . . . most kind."

Despite what this servant said, Tia believed what she had overheard was the real Lord Merriman, not the façade he put on for others in Polite Society to view. And perhaps he was kind to his sister most of the time, but she had already decided after seeing him interact with Lady Dilly that she would not care to make his acquaintance.

She looked pointedly at the butler, her lips pressed together, and he realized she was not going to comment. Instead, he opened the door and announced her arrival.

"Thank you," she said as she swept past him and into the drawing room, spying Lady Dilly and her mother rising from their seats. As she made her way toward them, she calmed herself, placing a gracious smile upon her face.

"Lady Merriman, Lady Dilly, it is so nice to see you again. I must apologize for Mama's absence."

Briefly, she told them about the torn gown and how Mama had returned home.

"I do not blame her, Lady Thermantia," the countess said. "I would have felt awkward myself with my gown in such disrepair. I only hope it can be saved, especially if it is one Her Grace favors."

She had no idea whether Mama liked the gown or not. That was not the kind of relationship they had. She and Mama did not talk about much of anything. Mama usually gave Tia orders and expected them to be followed. That was one of the reasons she did not wish to wed this Season—because Mama expected her to. Tia had always had a bit of a rebellious streak, where Lia was much more compliant and unassuming.

"Have a seat, Lady Tia," her friend urged.

She noticed Lady Merriman had called her by her given name, which is how Mama had introduced them at the dress shop. That was a sticking point. While Ariadne had not minded the name given to her at birth, the other Worthington siblings had rebelled, creating diminutives out of their given names. She determined she would be called Lady Tia this Season, and decided Lady Merriman would be the first place to start.

"My lady, I hope you would address me as Lady Tia, as your daughter does," she said sweetly. "Papa and Mama gave me and my siblings very long names. We usually opt for a shorter version of them. My twin, Cornelia, goes by Lia."

"Oh, Lia and Tia!" exclaimed Lady Dilly. "I quite like that."

Lady Merriman frowned slightly. "While nicknames are all well and good for intimate occasions with only family members present, I believe your mama is right in insisting that you be addressed as Lady Thermantia, my dear. After all, my own darling daughter is Delilah, a simply beautiful name."

"I like Dilly better, Mama. You know that."

The countess frowned. "Dilly sounds like a silly creature," she said sternly. "Simply because your brother could not pronounce your name when you were born does not mean you should continue to use it."

"I like Dilly," her friend said stubbornly. "I wish you would call me Dilly, Mama. As Hugo does."

So Hugo was the brother's Christian name. Tia had never met a Hugo. She thought the name brooding and arrogant, like the man himself.

"You will be Delilah entering Polite Society," Lady Merriman insisted. "It is a lovely name and will win you far more respect from others than Dilly ever would."

Not wishing to see the pair continue to argue, Tia said, "I do like the name Delilah. It is very polished. Even romantic."

The countess frowned. "Romance has no place in a young lady's life, especially not as the Season begins. You would do well to rid yourself of any romantic notions, Lady Thermantia, and simply allow your mama to help guide you in your search for a husband."

The woman was grating on her nerves now. Smiling sweetly, she said, "While Mama will certainly play a small role, it is my brother, the Duke of Millbrooke, who will determine which gentleman is suitable for me." She did not have to share with this woman that Val would allow Tia to take her time in taking a husband, much less that Val wanted her to select her mate.

"Tell us about your brother," the countess said.

Being careful to use his title and not speak informally, she said, "Millbrooke became the duke after we lost our father last year. His death occurred just before the Season began, and so we retreated to Kent to do our mourning in private. Millbrooke is wed and the father of a son."

Lady Merriman looked pleased hearing that. "Then it sounds as if His Grace's steady hand will help you immensely."

Tia wasn't about to tell this woman that Val had wed a governess. True, Eden was the daughter of a viscount, but she thought some within Polite Society might judge Eden harshly because of her former occupation. Val would make certain that the *ton* gave his wife the respect due a duchess. Of that, Tia was certain.

The rest of tea passed pleasantly. Lady Merriman only added to the conversation occasionally, allowing Dilly and Tia to get to know one another better. She thoroughly enjoyed Dilly's company. Her new friend was quick-witted and seemed to be high-spirited.

When tea concluded, Tia rose. Taking Lady Merriman's hand, she passed along her mother's invitation.

"Since Mama was upset that she could not have tea with you today, she asked if I would invite you to dine with us tomorrow evening."

It had actually surprised her when Mama mentioned dinner rather than tea, but she wanted to issue the invitation as intended. Then she recalled that Mama had said to include Lady Dilly's brother.

Frowning, she added, "Naturally, Lord Merriman is also invited to accompany you."

It seemed the countess had been hesitating, but now she

brightened. "Yes. We would be delighted to join Their Graces for dinner tomorrow, my lady."

"Mama said to come at seven. We will have a drink before dinner. Hopefully, you can stay a bit after dinner." Looking to Dilly, she asked, "Do you play an instrument or sing?"

"I sing rather well. My brother is the one who plays the pianoforte beautifully, however. You must ask him to do so. Why, I will speak with him and see if he will accompany me while I sing."

So, the grumpy lord played the pianoforte. Tia would be happy to let him have at the instrument. It would save her from having to play in front of company.

"Their Graces would enjoy it if the two of you would entertain us tomorrow evening," she said graciously. "I must leave now."

"Should our coachman escort you home?" Lady Merriman asked.

"No, that will not be necessary. Mama said she would send the carriage back. It should be waiting for me now. Thank you again for a lovely time, my lady." To Lady Dilly, she said, "I look forward to seeing you tomorrow evening."

"I will walk out with you," Lady Dilly said.

As they left the drawing room and headed down the corridor, Tia said, "I overheard you and your brother discussing him coming to tea this afternoon."

Lady Dilly stopped in her tracks. "I am mortified that you did so. I apologize."

"*You* have nothing to apologize for. It was your brother who was behaving so rudely."

"Hugo is never like that," Lady Dilly said. "Frankly, I do not know what came over him. Usually, he is calm and never ruffled."

She didn't care. "You seem to put him on a pedestal. You must remember that he is an ordinary mortal, just as the rest of us are. Frankly, I thought it wrong of him to speak to you in such a manner."

Lady Dilly took Tia's hands in hers. "Please, do not judge Hugo harshly. He is a good man. He simply has . . . difficulties. I do not wish to speak of them."

Tia didn't care what difficulties the man had. He was no gentleman and did not deserve his sister's devotion. A good brother like Val did, but not the earl.

"Pass along my mother's dinner invitation to him. If he does not wish to accept it, please know that we are eager for you and your mother to come, even without his escort."

"I will make certain he does come," Lady Dilly said resolutely. "I want you to see the side of him that I see every day."

She did not need to see the side which was obsequious when in polite company. She had already viewed the impatient man—and found him lacking.

They continued downstairs, and Lady Dilly embraced her in the foyer. "Thank you for coming to tea today, Lady Tia. And for calling me Deliliah after Mama made her preferences known. I suppose Mama is right. I should reserve my nickname for those who are closest to me. That would be you and Hugo. If I find a man I am particularly interested in, I will allow him to address me as Lady Dilly."

"Well, I expect everyone to call me Lady Tia," she revealed. "I simply will not answer to Thermantia. My goodness, I think Thermantia sounds as old as Methuselah and twice as disagreeable."

They both laughed, and Tia took her leave. The carriage awaited her outside, and she nodded to the coachman before allowing a footman to hand her up.

All the way home, she thought of her new friend and the fun they would have during this Season. As for Lady Dilly's brother, she would merely avoid him. As she had told the disagreeable earl, she had no intention of wasting time in the presence of those who were negative and unpleasant. Tia would enjoy every moment of the months ahead—and bring Lady Dilly along with her.

CHAPTER SEVEN

TIA FACED A dilemma. She had informed Mama that Lady Merriman had agreed to come to dinner, along with her two children. Tia wanted to tell her mother that she did not want Lord Merriman at their dinner table, but that would involve explaining the conversation she had overheard. If she did so, Mama might rescind the dinner invitation, as well as keep her from even seeing Lady Dilly. Her mother always harped upon how special their family's status was in Polite Society. If she heard how boorish Lord Merriman had been, refusing to host Tia at tea, she might believe something was lacking with Lady Dilly and her mother. Tia could not chance that.

She decided not to reveal the conversation between the siblings and simply would avoid speaking to Lord Merriman tonight, other than issuing a polite greeting when he arrived. She longed to discuss this, though, with Lia and decided to go see her twin after she practiced her pianoforte this morning. It was time to begin working on a new piece because it had occurred to her that she might not only be called upon to play in her home but other places where she was a guest, as well. If she only had three numbers in her repertoire, it would become apparent to others, especially the spiteful young ladies whom Lady Dilly had mentioned.

She applied herself now and began perfecting the finger patterns in a work by Beethoven. When she had devoted an hour to her practice, Tia went to the nursery to spend a couple of minutes with William. Eden was there with her son, and she asked her sister-in-law how she was feeling.

"Much better these days," Eden replied. "Val worries too much about me. Yes, I was a bit tired in the beginning. Giving birth is not easy to do. But I am more like myself in the past week or so. I was a bit tired coming from Kent to town, but thank goodness we live closer than Cumberland and can reach London in such a short time."

Eden had been the governess to Verina and Justina in Cumberland, far in England's northwest. After Tia had traveled that great distance last year to visit her cousins, she readily agreed with Eden. Perhaps when the time came for her to wed, she would ask the gentlemen who courted her where their country estates might lie. She was not overly fond of journeys that lasted for days and days. She stifled a giggle, thinking what she required in a husband might be far different from what others might be looking for.

"I am going to call on Lia now," she told Eden.

"I know how the two of you must miss one another. You shared not only a womb but a bedchamber and a strong friendship all these years. Please give her my best."

"Mama said that we are to have dinner with Lia and Rupert tomorrow night. You will be able to see her then. It will be Lia's first time to entertain in town. I know she is looking forward to it."

Tia kissed the top of William's head and asked Parsons if a footman might be freed up to escort her to Lady Cressley's residence.

"I will not require the carriage," she informed the butler, thinking it silly that people in town would wait a quarter-hour for horses to be harnessed to a carriage, only to drive them two blocks to their destination. Tia was a country girl at heart and used to walking long distances, something she enjoyed.

The footman escorted her to her twin's new London residence, and she hoped that Lia would be amenable to walking in Hyde Park since it was such a lovely day. Now that her sister was a matron, she no longer required an escort to places. It was just one of the odd rules of the *ton*, and Tia was glad Lia could now serve as her sister's chaperone, even though they were the same age.

She was admitted and taken to Lia's sitting room, where her sister was working on a beautiful piece of embroidery. Lia was skilled in all kinds of needlework, while Tia did not have the patience to sit with a needle and thread for more than a few minutes.

"Tia!" her sister cried, her welcoming smile drawing Tia in.

She embraced her twin and then asked, "If you are feeling up to it, might we walk in the park now?"

"I am hale and hardy this morning. That is, after I was ill in my chamber pot when I awoke this morning. I long for the day that will end."

"Oh, I was supposed to give you a message from Eden. She thought of it after we'd had tea, and you mentioned being queasy. You should keep a slice of bread at your beside and eat a few bites of it before you rise in the morning. She said it helped settle her belly when she was carrying William."

Lia chuckled. "I am ready to try anything." She patted her belly. "As much as I have always longed for a child, he or she is certainly making me work hard in carrying them."

"Do you feel the babe within you yet?" she asked, knowing nothing about how a woman became with child, much less what one felt like growing inside a person.

"No. I met with the local midwife just before we came to town. She called it quickening and said that I should feel the babe stir at around five months or so. That will be sometime in July."

"Will you and Rupert stay for the entire Season?"

Lia took Tia's hand. "That depends upon you. If there is a wedding, naturally, we will want to attend."

Laughing, she shook her head. "You know my philosophy has

been to come to the Season and simply enjoy all the various events. Perhaps I will consider taking a husband next year. For now, I intend to have as much fun as I can."

Her sister pursed her lips in thought, and Tia cut off what she knew Lia would say next.

"You think I will fall in love. Well, I am determined not to do so. At least not this Season. I know you are blissfully happy with Rupert, and I am thrilled to see your happiness. I know myself, however. I will wed when the time is right for me. That means do not wait about town for me. When you and Rupert are tired of the social swirl, retreat to Crestbrook. And remember, I can always come and visit you."

Lia grinned mischievously. "Even if the carriage ride is obscenely long?"

"Well, there is that," she said, laughing. She squeezed Lia's fingers. "But I would walk to the ends of the earth to spend time with you."

"Let me claim my bonnet, and we shall go have a nice stroll and chat in the park."

Ten minutes later, they were at the entrance to Hyde Park and strolled arm-in-arm through its beauty.

"It is quite inconvenient for you not to be in bed next to me. I have something to talk over with you," Tia confided.

"Go on," her sister encouraged.

"I met a wonderful girl at Madame Laurent's shop during a fitting, and I believe we are destined to be good friends. I cannot wait for you to meet Lady Dilly."

"Dilly? Why, it seems she goes by a nickname as you do."

"She is Delilah—but prefers Dilly. Her mother is just like ours and wants her to be known as Delilah, however. But that is not what I want to talk over with you."

"I am intrigued."

"Mama and I were to have tea with Lady Dilly and her mother. Mama's gown caught on something as she climbed from the carriage, ripping a large hole in her it. She refused to go in, but she encouraged me to do so because she knows how fond I already am of Lady Dilly. Unfortunately, I overheard a conversation which upset me a great deal."

Her twin indicated a bench nearby, and they sat upon it.

"What happened?"

"Lady Dilly had told me how wonderful her older brother is. She seems to worship him. When I was admitted by their butler, however, I heard him tell her that he did not want to play host at tea to her guest, calling me a silly girl—when he had yet to even meet me! He claimed to be too tired and refused his hosting duties. Lia, he spoke to her in such a clipped, harsh tone. It made me feel sorry for her. And then, he came downstairs, where I was in the foyer."

"Oh, dear. I know you all too well, Tia. You confronted him, didn't you?"

"Well, I had to defend my friend, didn't I? I called him out on his rude behavior and then told him I had no interest in making his acquaintance. That if we came across one another at events, I would choose to ignore him and not waste any time with him."

"Oh, this is not going to go well," Lia fretted. "Especially if you wish to remain friends with Lady Dilly. You cannot ask her to choose you over a beloved brother."

"Even worse, Mama told me to pass along an invitation to Lady Merriman. I asked the countess to come to dinner this evening. She is to bring her two children with her."

"We have always known not every gentlemen of the *ton* behaves in a gentlemanly manner," her sister reminded her. "Mama has warned us of this. Val and Con, too. I say be politely distant to this brother whenever you encounter him during the Season. It is not as if he will be a suitor to you."

"True," she said, mulling over Lia's advice. "From what I gather, he is not wed, but it seems men wed later than women do. I will see how Val reacts to him tonight. Of course, with Val being a duke, I am certain Lord Merriman will be on his best, most charming behavior at dinner. It is just so disappointing to have made my first friend and dislike her brother so much."

"Perhaps you caught him when he was having a bad day," Lia suggested.

"That might be true, but he could have at least apologized to me when we spoke. Or gallantly changed his mind and come to tea. Instead, he merely seemed a bit embarrassed that I had overheard how dismissively he treated his sister." She sighed. "Let us talk of other things now. I do not wish to spend another minute discussing Lord Merriman's deficiencies. Are you ready for the opening ball?"

Lia smiled. "Rupert and I have yet to dance with one another. I am most eager to partner with my handsome husband."

They spent a pleasant hour discussing the first events of the Season, comparing which ones they would be attending. Lia shared that she was only ill from the babe in the early mornings, unlike Ariadne, who had been sick throughout the day for months.

"I believe I will do quite well at the events we attend." Lia placed her hands upon her belly. "It is hard for me to believe a babe grows inside me now. I only have a small bump so far."

"That will not last for long," Tia said, laughing. "You were not present at Millvale to see it, but Eden's belly seemed to pop overnight, swelling to three times its size by the time she gave birth to William. If you have any questions, Lia, go to Eden or Ariadne with them. You know Mama never wishes to talk about such intimate matters."

"When the time comes and you find yourself interested in a certain gentleman, we should talk again. There are things I must share with you."

"About kissing?" Tia asked, curious what her twin referred to.

"Yes. Kissing and . . . other things," Lia said vaguely. "I want you to be prepared for your wedding night. All I can tell you, Tia, is that lovemaking is the height of living." Her sister's face grew rapturous. "You will find yourself soaring to the heavens and beyond."

"I am so happy to see you this way, Lia. You are a wonderful wife, and you will make for the very best of mothers. Will you do as Ariadne has asked and bring your babe to town with you next spring?"

"I already love this babe fiercely," her sister revealed. "I would never desert my child for months at a time, simply to go to social affairs. Ariadne is wise in knowing this. I think it will be wonderful for all the cousins to bring their children to town each Season. Just think how much fun we would have had if we and our cousins had all come to town and we had gotten to know one another from the time we were children? Yes, Rupert and I have discussed it, and we are in agreement. We will always keep our children with us."

"You are fortunate you wed a man such as Rupert."

"You will find a good man yourself, Tia. I feel it in my heart. You are so strong in your convictions. You will be a woman who demands to be an equal partner to her husband, and I know the man you wed will value family as much as you do."

"Well, it certainly will not be someone such as Lord Merriman."

They both broke out into laughter.

"I am growing hungry," her twin said. "Come home with me. You can stay and eat something with me. I am selfish, Tia. While I have enjoyed every moment of marriage, I have missed you something awful. I want us to make the most of our time together in town."

Tia stood and pulled her sister to her feet. "Come along. After all, you are eating for two now. We must make certain your babe is well fed."

They left Hyde Park and returned to Rupert's townhouse, stopping by his study so that Tia might see him for a few minutes.

"I shall go and tell Cook to make up a small tray for us. Perhaps some cheeses and fruits," Lia said.

She left the study, and Tia looked at her brother-in-law. "Mys sister is incredibly happy with you, Rupert."

His face softened. "I never thought to make a love match. I know now that Lia is my soulmate. No one who walks this earth could make me feel the way my Lia does."

"I would not have allowed her to wed just any man," Tia teased. "I still think it quite romantic that you chased her halfway across England and presented her with a special license."

His gaze met hers. "When Lia left Cumberland, it was as if a part of me had been cut off, Tia. I knew I had made a terrible mistake in not declaring my feelings for her. I would have sailed the Seven Seas in search of her. I will be grateful until my dying day that she forgave me for being so beef-witted and not telling her that I loved her."

"You are together now, Rupert. That is all that matters. And soon, you will have a physical manifestation of your love when she delivers your babe. The child will be made up of the best parts of both of you."

"I still marvel at the fact that we are to become parents soon. We have discussed it for many hours, Tia, and we want to be nothing like our own parents. Of course, I never knew my mother since she died giving birth to me, but my father was so distant. Lia says your father was the same. I believe your mother tries to be a little different now that she is a widow."

"Mama is a woman brought up in her time. Thanks to Ariadne, our generation will behave differently as far as our children go. We will be loving parents, spending vast amounts of time with the children we produce. We—and they—will all be better for it."

"Well said." He grinned. "Especially for a woman who has yet to find love."

Tia wanted to stop all this talk of love. Yes, her siblings had been fortunate enough to make love matches, but she was quite independent. She could not see herself loving someone to the point to where she relied upon them so much. As long as the man she wed was kind and respectful to her—and affectionate to their children—she would be happy. The one thing she would demand is his active involvement in raising their children. That would be hard to find, especially with the attitude of most men of the *ton*.

Lia returned and said, "Come out to the terrace. The day is so pleasant, I thought we might eat outdoors."

Rupert smiled at his wife. "The two of you go and talk. I know you still have much to say to one another since you have been apart for months." He then looked at Tia. "Remember, you are welcome at Crestbrook at any time. Though I may not be a blood relative to you, I feel you are the sister of my heart."

"I feel the same about you, Rupert," she shared. "I am fortunate that all my siblings have wed such amiable people."

They left Rupert laughing and went to the terrace. Tia spent another couple of hours with her twin, reluctant to leave. She finally said her goodbyes and returned home in time for tea, which Mama would expect. Once the Season began, she would not be able to see Lia as much. Mama had already told her they would entertain callers each afternoon, which would limit her time with her sister. Still, she would make the most of her time with Lia, even as she enjoyed the fruits of the Season.

CHAPTER EIGHT

HUGO AVOIDED HIS sister and mother all the next day. Actually, he had skipped dining with them the previous evening, not ready to be around people, especially after he had disappointed Dilly. He had spent much of today away from the house. Not ready to brave White's again, he had walked Hyde Park for several hours. When the British Museum opened, he made his way to Montagu House in Great Russell Street and spent the rest of the day amongst Sir Hans Sloane's treasures. The physician had collected over seventy thousand items by the time of his death, bequeathing his collection to the British government, and it had become the foundation of the museum. Hugo enjoyed losing himself amongst the antiquities from far-flung places such as the Far East to the Sudan, and especially appreciated the items from ancient Greece and Rome.

He could not hide forever, however, and finally made his way home. Once he arrived, he realized how late it was. He had even missed tea. Alfie marched him to his rooms, telling him to strip off what he wore.

"Whatever for?" he asked.

The valet's stern look matched any aggravated headmaster's. "You are accompanying your mother and sister to a duke's house for dinner. Lady Merriman is displeased with you, to say the very least. She has berated me simply because I knew not where you had taken off to. I walked the streets for hours, trying to find you."

"I was visiting the British Museum," he said, feeling chastised. "I am an earl, you know. I do not have to report my every move to my mother."

Alfie sighed. "I know that, my lord, but you left me in an awkward position. I cannot defend you *and* be courteous to your mother. Next time, simply tell me where you are going and do not vanish."

"All right," he quietly agreed. "Do we know what duke? Is it Reddington?"

"No, it is not His Grace," said Alfie, who was familiar with Matthew because of Hugo's close friendship with the duke. "Another duke. I didn't catch his name, but Lady Merriman is happy to be invited to his home."

He wondered if it was a friend of Mama's. Or might an invitation have come from the Duke of Millbrooke? Hugo had enjoyed the man's company yesterday and found him most knowledgeable about horses. Yes, it must be Millbrooke. If that was the case, no wonder Mama had been so upset with him being gone all day.

"There. You are presentable," Alfie declared. "And not a moment too soon. Get downstairs, my lord. Do not keep your mother waiting."

Hugo hurried to the foyer, where he found Mama and Dilly. His sister looked anxious. Mama looked put out.

"It is about time, Merriman," Mama said. "We were about to leave without you. Alfie assured me he would have you here. You are fortunate to have such a loyal valet."

"I know I am, Mama. Shall we?"

He escorted them to the carriage and handed both of them up. Hugo was still getting used to the idea of being invited to dinner. He worked on his breathing, slowly inhaling through his nose in deep breaths, and then exhaling quietly through his mouth.

"I know you are head of this household, Merriman, but you simply must tell someone where you are going. What if you had not turned up and we had to go to His Grace's without you?"

"I apologize, Mama." He glanced to Dilly. "And to you, as well, Dilly."

Mama sighed. "Try not to call your sister that childish pet name, Merriman."

His gaze met Dilly's. "I am sorry. For everything."

Her nod let him know she knew he was apologizing for his behavior regarding tea yesterday. He still wanted to speak to Dilly about her new friend, however. He did not think it wise for his sister to be on close terms with such an outspoken young woman. What he worried about now was pronouncing Dilly's given name. For some reason, the *l's* in Delilah gave him fits. Even after all these years of practicing, trying to tame his stammer, Delilah was the one word he had the most trouble saying.

"I hope you will become good friends with His Grace," Mama continued. "Millbrooke may be new to his dukedom, but he is quite influential."

So, they were headed to Millbrooke's to dine. At least he knew what table he would be sitting at tonight.

"If you can cozy up to Millbrooke—as well as maintaining your friendship with Reddington—it will benefit Delilah."

"How, Mama?" Dilly asked. "Why would Hugo being friends with two dukes help me?"

Mama snorted. "It is all about what people see, Delilah. If they spot your brother in the company of two dukes, they will take notice. They will think more of Merriman, and their favor will extend to you."

Dilly shook her head. "I am not certain I truly like Polite Society, Mama. I would rather be judged for my own good character and not men seen with my brother."

"Keep those kinds of opinions to yourself, Delilah Drake," Mama warned. 'In fact, you should express no opinions at all when you are speaking to others this Season. You do not want to chase off a gentleman because of something you say."

Exasperated, Dilly asked, "Then what am I supposed to talk about?"

"The weather is always a safe topic," Mama replied. "Answer questions you are asked, but please keep your replies short. Men do not like a lady who prattles on and on."

His sister blew out a breath. She visibly bit back the retort on her lips, causing Hugo to smile at her.

"My sister will do just fine this Season, Mama. She is very pleasant to be around. I think others will find her quite amiable."

The carriage turned onto a square, and he knew they would disembark soon. Hugo gathered his courage. The door opened, and he stepped from the vehicle, handing down Mama and then Dilly.

"Enjoy yourself this evening," he whispered to his sister. "It is not every day one is asked to dine with a duke and his family."

They were admitted by the butler, who led them upstairs to the drawing room. He heard them being announced, and they entered the room. Immediately, he spotted Millbrooke, who stood with three ladies. He assumed one would be the wife he had mentioned, along with the sister who was making her come-out and his mother.

Millbrooke smiled. "Ah, Lord Merriman. Come and join us."

As Hugo escorted his mother and sister across the room, the others turned to face them. He quickly scanned their faces.

And stopped in his tracks.

The impertinent miss from yesterday was among them.

It struck him that *she* was the sister the duke had referred to. The one who was to make her come-out. How was he to separate Dilly from this young woman without offending one of the most powerful men in Polite Society?

"Merriman," Mama whispered, tugging on him.

Hugo realized he had stopped and started up again, bracing himself as they reached the group. He had a suspicion that Millbrooke had not sent the invitation because they had met yesterday. Something told him that it had come from the dowager duchess since her gaze was focused on his mother.

"I am so glad that you have forgiven me for missing tea with you yesterday, Lady Merriman."

"These accidents happen," his mother said. "Thank goodness it was not the opening night of the Season when your disaster occurred."

The two women chuckled, and the duke said, "I know Mama and Lady Merriman have met. Might I introduce you to my duchess?"

He turned his attention to the attractive woman with a very pleasant smile. "I am grateful you could join us this evening, Lady Merriman."

"Allow me to present my children, Your Graces," Mama said, pride evident in her voice. "This is my son, the Earl of Merriman, and Lady Delilah Drake."

They exchanged greetings, and then the duke said, "I know my sister met you two ladies at the modiste's, but I would like to introduce Lord Merriman to her. This is Lady Tia Worthington, my lord. I spoke of my sister yesterday when we at Tattersall's."

"You went to Tattersall's with him?" Lady Tia said, obviously surprised. "Lord Merriman?"

"Yes. Con and I met Lord Merriman and the Duke of Reddington there. They assisted me in selecting a new horse."

Lady Tia looked at him skeptically. "So, you spent yesterday with my brother, my lord. I hope visiting Tattersall's did not tire you. Looking at so many horses can be overwhelming."

He heard the dig in her voice and chose to ignore her brazen rudeness. "His Grace knows his horseflesh. He chose a . . . very good horse."

He had wanted to say a magnificent horse, but he feared tripping over a word of so many syllables. He was afraid if he stumbled—or stuttered—Lady Tia would pounce upon it. Whether Dilly realized it or not, she was not someone to befriend.

The butler brought a tray around with drinks, and he accepted one. He would only take a sip or two. The same would be true during dinner. He found if he drank spirits, his guard came down. Tonight was not a night to allow that to occur.

Trying to make himself a part of the conversation by asking a question he knew would allow others to talk, Hugo said, "I hear you are a new mother, Your Grace. Congratulations."

As he suspected, the duchess began talking about her infant son. Her husband chimed in, as did the dowager duchess and even Lady Tia, all bragging about the babe. His mother and Dilly asked questions about William, leaving Hugo to listen to the conversation. He studied Lady Tia as she spoke about her nephew. She seemed genuinely fond of the child. In fact, other than her caustic remark to him when they first arrived, she seemed very charming. He could see how Dilly had been taken with her.

She had a unique shade of hair. It was a soft red with blond streaming through it, a color he had never seen on another living soul. Her blue eyes were as clear as a summer sky. She possessed a willowy frame, not the current fashionable curves of so many other young ladies her age. If he had not had his previous encounter with her, he would have said she was quite pretty in the face. Having heard her acidic tongue, though, he knew better than to be fooled by her exterior beauty.

The butler called them in to dinner. The duke led his wife and mother in, with Lady Tia and the dowager duchess following them, while Hugo offered an arm to Mama and Dilly. When they reached the dining room, he saw Lady Tia visibly upset, and soon he realized why.

They had been seated next to one another.

He went to his seat and quietly said to her, "Neither of us is happy with this arrangement, my lady. I suggest we make the best of it and not make our family members aware of the enmity between us."

She flashed him a smile. "Certainly, my lord."

A footman helped her to sit, and Hugo took his place to her left. He now dreaded the meal, knowing it might go on for a couple of hours.

The soup course was served, and he politely turned to her, hoping to salvage the situation. "The soup is quite good."

She frowned. "Is that all the conversation you have for me? If so, save your breath, my lord. I promise to concentrate on my food. You can talk with my brother and the others instead."

Lifting her wine goblet, she sipped from it, then turned back to her soup.

He had never met a more unpleasant female. Not that he had met many in his lifetime. For the most part, he had avoided women. He became tongue-tied around them. Matthew had noticed it during Hugo's second year at university and asked him if he were a virgin. After he had gotten over being asked such an impertinent question, his friend had insisted that he learn about intimacy. Matthew had found a willing widow who would teach Hugo about lovemaking, and he had visited her once or twice a week during his time at Cambridge. She had been quite the tutor, and he was pleased in the skills he had developed, confident he knew how to please a woman in bed.

Since then, however, he had been with no woman. He barely saw any women other than Mama and Dilly, save for a few servants. He knew it would be important to woo and wed so that he might get an heir. That would be for after he saw Dilly settled. Once he had her settled, he could think about himself.

In the meantime, he asked a few more questions. He had found others enjoyed talking about themselves, so if he inquired about them, they usually spoke and he listened.

The meal was very good, and he was proud he hadn't had to engage Lady Tia further.

Then Millbrooke said, "Since it is only the two of us, Merriman, what say we dispense with port and cigars and accompany the ladies to the drawing room? Perhaps you might even play for us, Tia," the duke suggested.

She smiled brilliantly. "I would be happy to do so."

They adjourned, returning to the drawing room. The butler offered Hugo a drink, but he waved it away. He was curious to hear Lady Tia play.

She did so without music, having memorized the piece. Her playing was adequate but lacked any depth. It seemed as superficial as she herself was.

When she finished, they applauded her efforts, and she went to a settee where Dilly sat.

"You should play for us, Merriman," Dilly suggested.

"You play?" His Grace asked.

Hugo nodded.

"Go and play something for us, Merriman," the dowager duchess urged.

Knowing he could not graciously refuse his hostess, he moved to the piano and sat, cracking his knuckles.

"He insists upon doing that before he plays each time," Mama said to the others. "A terrible habit, but he does play beautifully."

He took a deep breath and struck the first keys. Within seconds, he was lost in the music, only coming out from its spell when he struck the final chord. Quickly, he rose and returned to his seat, the others applauding enthusiastically.

"My, you play incredibly well, my lord," the duchess said. "I have never heard another play with such feeling."

"Thank you, Your Grace."

The others began talking, and he felt eyes upon him. Turning, he saw Lady Tia gazing at him thoughtfully. Let her look all she wanted. He neither wanted nor need the chit's approval.

When the evening came to an end, he heard Dilly making plans with Lady Tia and decided he would need to speak to his sister and have her break them. This was not someone he wanted Dilly to be around. It did not matter that she was the sister of a duke. Lady Tia was not good enough for his Dilly.

The duke and his family walked them downstairs. As he descended the staircase, Lady Tia fell in beside him.

"You are an accomplished pianist, my lord. I envy how you become so absorbed in the music. I have never been that way. I spend too much time thinking of which finger belongs on what key."

"Music must be felt in your soul, my lady. Apparently, you have none."

She looked taken aback at his cruel words, and Hugo immediately wanted to apologize. He was not this kind of man. Just because he thought ill of her, he never should have voiced his opinion, especially so harshly. He would apologize.

But the words stuck in his throat. His tongue grew thick. Fear filled him that he would start stammering, and all he could think of how this woman would cackle with glee at his predicament. Then he caught sight of her eyes misting with tears, and he hated himself for making such a heartless remark to her.

"You are as callous as I first believed you to be, my lord. I had thought to offer you an olive branch, simply for Lady Dilly's sake." She paused. "I will never make that mistake again."

Quickly, she hurried down the stairs, catching up with Dilly. Hugo stood watching her, appalled at his own behavior. He had known cruelty in his youth and had vowed never to be as vicious as those who had hurt him.

Why had he spoken as he had to her? Why did it seem as if his very blood boiled when he looked at or spoke to Lady Tia?

He left the house, handing up Mama and then Dilly. Turning back to his hosts, who had followed them outside, he manage to get out, "Thank you for a lovely evening, Your Graces."

"I am glad we could do this," Millbrooke said. "Will I see you at White's tomorrow?"

"Yes, Your Grace. I shall be there tomorrow morning."

Hugo climbed into the carriage. The door was closed, and the coachman set the vehicle into motion. He remained silent as

Mama and Dilly chattered on about dining with a duke and two duchesses. Dread filled him, knowing what he must say to his sister.

When they arrived home, Mama went immediately upstairs. That gave him the opportunity to ask Dilly to join him in the library. He accompanied her there, seeing her high spirits and flushed face.

"Dilly, please sit," he said once they entered the room.

"What? Is something the matter, Hugo?"

"Yes."

Concern filled her face as she took a seat next to him. "What can I do?"

"I do not want to encourage a friendship between you and Lady Tia," he said flatly.

Dilly shot to her feet. "What?"

"Please, sit."

"No," she said, defiance in her eyes. "I will stand. Why do you not want me to see her, Hugo?"

"I think she will be a bad influence upon you."

"But . . . why?"

Delicately, he said, "I will only say that when we have spoken, I have not found her to be pleasant in the slightest."

Confusion filled his sister's face. "I do not understand. Lady Tia is very nice, Hugo. Yes, she is quite lively, but that is what I like about her."

"You are not to continue the friendship," he said flatly.

Her mouth set stubbornly. "Are you going to continue to be friends with her brother?" Dilly demanded.

"Yes. The duke is—"

"Then *I* will continue to be friends with Lady Tia."

With that, Dilly stormed from the library. Hugo watched her go, knowing he had made a mess of things.

And he hadn't a clue what to do next.

CHAPTER NINE

As Hugo sat in the chair and allowed Alfie to shave him for the second time that day, the valet chastised him.

"Stop brooding, my lord."

"I have every right to brood," he snapped. "I have lost control of my household."

It was true—and it frightened him. Control is what helped him get through each day. He knew he was tightly wound, always having to watch every syllable which left his lips. Control had meant that he had conquered his stammer. Well, perhaps not conquered it, but he had it well in hand. And now, at a critical point in his life, he was on the brink of spiraling downward.

All because of Lady Tia Worthington.

Dilly had ignored his request to stop seeing the chit. Actually, he did not view it as a request. He had issued an order and expected his younger sister to obey him. As the Earl of Merriman, he was head of his family and responsible for them. He expected obedience. Yet not only had his sister disobeyed him, his mother had undermined his authority, as well.

Mama had come to him the day after their dinner at the Duke of Millbrooke's, grumbling because Dilly had come complaining to her. Mama had told him that he knew absolutely nothing of the Season. That he might view himself as an expert on many things, but he would need to bow to *her* wishes and recommendations as far as whom Dilly might associate with.

When Hugo had explained that he did not believe Lady Tia was suitable company for his sister, Mama had laughed it off, telling him that Dilly's friendship with a duke's sister would elevate her into the upper echelons of Polite Society. Mama let him know in no uncertain terms that she would also foster a friendship between the two girls, and she expected him to do the same.

Hugo had lost that battle decisively, and so he had kept to himself much of the past week. He had continued his long, solitary walks through Hyde Park, as well as spent hours in the music room at his pianoforte. Those two activities brought him comfort.

He had forced himself to go to White's upon three different occasions. He had found Matthew there on two of them and sat with his friend but had also spoken to other members present. He did not share his current dilemma with Matthew, not wanting it to be revealed that he could not control the two women in his household. While at White's, he had spent time in the company of Lord Dyer and the Duke of Millbrooke. Both men had been quite friendly, and Hugo could not understand why the duke's sister was so venomous. Then again, he had not been at his best when they had spoken to one another.

Would he wish to be judged by others on the basis of a few lines of conversation?

He had been judged his entire life for his stammer. Perhaps he had done Lady Tia a disservice. She had overheard him speaking rather harshly to Dilly and merely defended her friend. Then she had actually made an overture to him, but he had cut her to the quick with an ugly remark.

Hugo decided he must be a better man. He would seek out Lady Tia this evening and offer a profuse apology to her. He had been in the wrong and needed to admit it. Things were strained between them, so he did not know if she would even listen to him, much less accept his apology. Still, he owed it to himself—and Dilly—to make the attempt.

Alfie finished shaving him and then helped Hugo dress in his evening black. He would be wearing these fancy dress clothes on many occasions, beginning with tonight's opening ball of the Season. He knew Dilly was excited about it, but she had barely spoken to him during the past week. When he had come across her in a room, she made an excuse to leave it. At tea and meals, she never engaged him in conversation. He hated the growing rift between them and would do anything to heal it, especially because Dilly might soon be leaving his household and going to one of her own.

From the very beginning, they had always been close, despite the five years' difference in their ages. It was hard to imagine not having easy access to his sister. That led him to think of Lady Tia again. He had learned at dinner the other night that she was a twin, and that sister was Viscountess Cressley. Hugo wondered what it would be like to be a twin and suddenly no longer have accessibility to the person you had always been closest to. His sympathy grew for Lady Tia.

He only hoped she might forgive him. It would prove crucial in repairing his relationship with Dilly.

Alfie finished fussing over his cravat, and the valet left the bedchamber. Hugo had asked for Alfie to come early so that he might do what he considered his prelude to being around others. Just as when he practiced the pianoforte and played scales before launching into a composition, speaking was the same to him. He sang two different songs, feeling the tension melt away, then he practiced several difficult phrases with consonants which gave him trouble.

After that, he repeated the word Delilah one hundred times, getting ninety-seven of them correct. When amongst the *ton*, he knew to address his sister as Delilah. He would also be mentioning her to others, and he prayed he would say her name correctly this evening.

So far, no one at White's seemed to associate him with Hugo Drake, the undersized, stuttering boy who was picked upon.

Even Matthew had begun referring to him as Merriman in front of others, and Hugo hoped no one would connect his past with his present.

He left his rooms, surprised to find Alfie coming toward him.

"Lady Merriman wishes to see you in her bedchamber, my lord," the valet informed him.

"Very well."

Hugo made his way along the corridor and tapped upon Mama's door. She answered his knock herself and motioned for him to come inside.

"I know things are strained between you and your sister," Mama began. "Perhaps this will make everything better."

She handed him a small box, and he opened it, finding a pair of diamond earrings inside.

"These are not a part of the Drake family gems. They have been in my family for many years, handed down from mother to eldest daughter. My own mother made a present of them to me on the opening night of the Season when I made my debut. I wish you to give these to Delilah tonight before we leave."

"No, Mama. I cannot. That would take away a moment reserved for you and her."

"In due time, I will let her know she is to pass them down to her eldest daughter. For now, however, you must repair the hurt between the two of you. This would be a good way to do so, Merriman."

She was right, but he hated taking away a special moment between mother and daughter because he had mucked up things with his sister. Still, the goal was to help Dilly find a suitable husband. Hugo would need to be on speaking terms with his sister for that to occur.

"Very well, I will see you downstairs," he said, heading toward his sister's bedchamber.

He did not even need to knock because her lady's maid opened the door to leave just as he arrived. He entered and found Dilly sitting at her dressing stable, staring at her image in the glass. She saw him in the mirror and turned to face him.

"Why are you here?" she asked, her tone sharp and unforgiving.

He swallowed. "To tell you something—and give you something."

Dilly rose and came to stand before him. "Are you going to apologize to me? To Lady Tia?" she asked angrily.

Solemnly, Hugo said, "Yes. I am sorry for the pain I have caused you, Dilly."

She threw her arms about him, holding on tightly. "I have hated being estranged, Hugo." Dilly released him. "You have been so unlike yourself."

"I love you, Dilly Drake. I only want the best for you. If I have misjudged Lady Tia, I am man enough to admit it."

Taking his hand, she kissed it. "Thank you. Thank you." She kissed it again. "Lady Tia is truly wonderful, Hugo. We have spent so much time together this past week, and it is as if I have a sister of my own now in my new friend. I appreciate you apologizing to me, but better yet, go through with what you have told me and apologize to her. She has done nothing wrong."

"What has she told you? About me?"

Dilly frowned. "Nothing. It is odd that she does not wish to mention you to me at all. Believe me when I tell you that I have asked her why there seems to be such enmity between the two of you."

It was a promising sign that Lady Tia had taken the high road and not revealed either of their conversations to Dilly. His sister might not be so forgiving if she had known how ungentlemanly he had behaved toward Lady Tia.

"I promise you that I will seek out Lady Tia this evening and offer her a sincere apology."

She embraced him again, and Hugo believed all was well again between them.

"I told you I have something for you." He held the box up, offering it to her. "Mama should be the one giving this to you, but she graciously allowed me to do so in her stead."

Dilly looked to the box and back to him. "What is it?"

"Mama said it is something from her family. Passed down from each mother to her oldest daughter. She thought if I gave it to you, it might help restore goodwill between the two of us."

Opening the box, Dilly gasped. "Diamond earrings! They are beautiful, Hugo."

"Be sure you tell that to Mama and thank her properly. I feel I stole a precious moment between the two of you, being the one to present them to you."

"To be honest, it means more coming from you than from her," his sister admitted. "Oh, Hugo, I am so glad things are right between us again."

"So am I, little sister. Put them on now."

Dilly returned to her dressing table and sat, fastening the earrings to her earlobes. She admired herself in the mirror and then turned to face him.

"No gentleman will be able to resist you this evening," he declared.

She grew serious, taking his hands in hers. "I know I embark upon a new chapter in my life tonight. While it excites me, I cannot help but feel a bit sad, Hugo. I will most likely leave this house at the end of the Season."

"We will always be brother and sister," he assured her. "And we will forever be friends. While I expect you to depend upon your new husband, know that you can always come to me if you need to talk over something."

"When will you wed?" she asked.

"It is my duty to see you settled, Dilly. Only then will I con-sider taking a bride."

"Oh, wouldn't it be wonderful if we both found someone this Season? Why, we could marry our betrotheds in a double ceremony."

Laughing, he squeezed her hands before releasing them. "I do not picture that happening, little sister. Let us focus on you and your happiness in the weeks to come. We should not keep Mama waiting."

He offered her his arm and escorted her downstairs. When they reached the foyer, Mama looked at him questioningly. Hugo nodded, letting her know all was well between him and Dilly.

His sister smiled. "Thank you for such a lovely gift, Mama. I absolutely love my new earrings. I shall wear them to every event I attend this Season. They will give me confidence."

"I am happy to find that you like them, Delilah."

They went out to the carriage, and Mama began peppering Dilly with last-minute reminders. His sister nodded, taking everything in. Hugo thought most of these unwritten rules of the *ton* completely nonsense. He listened as Dilly was told to dance with a gentleman only once on this first evening.

"But at subsequent balls, you may dance with a partner a second time if you wish to encourage him," Mama said. "A gentleman who asks a lady to dance twice is showing his interest in that particular girl. But never, ever dance with a man thrice. It will simply bring out the gossips in full force, and they will crucify you."

Dilly was reminded not to overeat at the midnight buffet so that she would remain light on her feet as she danced. She was told never to go to any room and be alone with a gentleman, else she would be compromised. An exception would be to go out onto the terrace with a partner and stroll its length if a gentleman asked, simply because there would be other couples outside doing the same, so they would act as chaperones for each other.

Taking Mama's hand, Dilly said, "I understand everything, Mama. Please do not worry about me. I am going to do my best tonight—and every night of the Season. Hugo will be looking after me, learning about each of the gentleman who shows an interest in me. He and the Duke of Millbrooke will share any knowledge they acquire about gentlemen, be it good or bad."

Mama looked pleased. "Is that so, Merriman?"

"Yes, Mama. When Millbrooke and I met, it was suggested

that since we both had sisters making their come-outs, we might pass along anything of note to one another. If a man is a rake, we will certainly keep him away from Dilly. And Lady Tia," he added.

The carriage came to a halt, and Hugo glanced out the window, seeing the road clogged with carriages which had nowhere to go.

"Oh, this happens every opening night of the Season," Mama lamented. "We shall have to walk the rest of the way."

They disembarked from the carriage, Hugo escorting them another two blocks. They entered the home of Lord and Lady Parker and joined the receiving line. He skimmed the line, which snaked up the staircase. His eyes stopped when he found Lady Tia. Their gazes met, and his heart began beating faster.

"Excuse me," he said. "I see someone I must speak to."

"No, Merriman," Mama said sharply. "You are not to leave the receiving line. Once we have been greeted by our hosts and enter the ballroom, you will stay with the two of us. You must meet every gentleman who will sign Delilah's programme. Only then will it be acceptable for you to move about the ballroom."

For Dilly's sake, it was his responsibility to make a good impression on others. If etiquette prevented him from leaving the receiving line, he must accept this.

"Very well," he said brusquely, allowing his gaze to meet Lady Tia's again.

Hugo bowed his head in respect, and she tilted hers slightly in acknowledgement. That would have to do.

For now.

CHAPTER TEN

TIA AVERTED HER gaze, her heart thumping loudly in her chest. She had thought Lord Merriman was about to cut the line and come to speak with her before his mother seemed to caution him against doing so.

But why?

She had nothing to say to the man, despite how handsome he appeared in his evening clothes tonight. His hair, black as night, caused her fingers to now itch, and she wished she could run them through his thick locks. Why would she think something such as that? Yes, he was very attractive with those unusual gray eyes. He looked even taller and broader in the severe black evening wear. She stole another glace at him and saw he was now talking with his sister. Tia felt a bit sorry for her friend, having only her mother and one brother in support of her debut this evening.

Looking around, she saw she was surrounded by a portion of her large, loving family. Of course, Mama was by her side this evening for the opening night's ball. Val and Eden were also here and had escorted them to this ball. Ariadne and Julian were nearby, talking with Con and his parents. Though her aunt Charlotte could be rather opinionated, her uncle Arthur was sweet and kind. And naturally, she had Lia and Rupert with her tonight. Ten in all to support her on what would be the biggest night of her life. She was on the cusp of meeting so many new people, and excitement flowed through her.

Yet why did her thoughts now turn back to Lord Merriman, a man who did not even like her? Tia was used to everyone she met liking her. She could not think of one disagreeable person. A thought came to her, and she wondered if everyone had always been amiable to her simply because she was the daughter of a duke. Would the eligible bachelors who asked her to dance tonight only do so because of her social connection to Val? Or would they be nice to her because a duke's sister would come with a hefty dowry? Things she had never fretted about started to cause worry now, along with her problem regarding Lord Merriman.

They had only spoken for a short time during their two encounters, and the last time he had cut her to the quick with a biting remark that hurt her feelings terribly. She was determined not to let him prevent her from her friendship with Lady Dilly. Where the earl was acerbic and brusque, his sister was as outgoing and lively as Tia herself. The only difference between them was that her friend fully intended to wed by Season's end, while Tia had thought to keep her options open and hoped to delay marriage for a year or two. Yes, she had come into the Season with the idea that she would not rush to take a husband, but little William's presence in the family nursery was having a strong effect on her.

Perhaps it was also the fact that Lia was increasing that might change Tia's mind about postponing marriage. She and her twin had always done everything together, and Tia wanted her children to be close—and close in age—to Lia's. They would mean making a match sooner than she had thought to do so. A thought occurred to her that because they were twins, one or both of them might actually give birth to a set of twins themselves. How special that would be!

Lia touched her arm. "You seem deep in thought. Are you nervous about this evening? If so, you should not be."

"I will admit that I am a bit anxious. Look at all these wonderful ballgowns and the pretty girls wearing them."

Her twin clucked her tongue. "You are the most beautiful girl making her come-out, Tia Worthington. Why, your dance card will fill up before you blink three times."

"I hope so. You know how much I enjoy dancing."

"Just remember that Mama has said you will not have much of a chance to speak with the gentlemen you dance with this evening. The dances are too lively for any kind of extended conversation." Lia gave her a knowing smile. "But I am certain that Val's drawing room will be filled to the brim tomorrow with flower arrangements sent to you."

Mama had told them both last year when they were schedule to make their come-outs that gentlemen would send bouquets to ladies they were interested in. They would also come calling the following afternoon after an event.

"Do you see your friend here?" Lia asked. "I would enjoy meeting her."

Tia pretended to scan the crowd and then said, "Yes, I see her."

She described the color of Lady Dilly's gown and the girl herself since pointing was absolutely forbidden, and her twin nodded, having spied Lady Dilly.

"She is very pretty. Is that her brother standing with her? They make a striking pair, both with that wonderful dark hair and brows. I suppose that is Lady Merriman, their mother, with them. I can see she once was a great beauty herself."

Nodding, Tia said, "Yes, it is obvious they got their good looks from their mother. She is still very attractive for her age."

The receiving line began moving, and they soon found themselves in front of Lord and Lady Parker, their hosts for the evening. Val presented her to the couple, and Tia made her curtsey to them.

"I hear you are making your come-out this Season, Lady Tia," the countess said. "I wish you much success." The woman smiled at her. "There are quite a few eligible bachelors here in attendance this evening. I hope you will find more than one to your liking."

They moved into the ballroom, and Mama had them stop on the left side of the room.

"We will stand here," Mama declared, seeming like an invading force who planted its flag.

"I thought we were supposed to move about the room and meet others," Tia said, confused.

Val chuckled. "Mama is playing the ducal card, Tia. While others may go about the room, greeting old friends and being introduced to new ones, it is expected for dukes to make their stand. Others come to them, not the other way around."

"Oh, I see."

Mama stared at Val. "You introduced Thermantia to our hosts as Tia, Millbrooke."

Before Mama could continue, Val firmly said, "I did so intentionally, Mama. That is her name. While Thermantia is a beautiful name, it is also a mouthful. Besides, Tia is fonder of the diminutive form of her name. We will respect her wishes and introduce her as thus tonight."

She gave her brother a grateful smile. He was using his authority with Mama, and she saw her mother nod, acquiescing to her son's wishes. Tia had never liked her full given name, and as many of her cousins had done, she had always gone by a shortened version of it. She felt sorry for Lady Dilly, who would constantly be introduced as Delilah.

Others entered the ballroom, stopping at their party of ten. Tia's dance programme began filling up. She had worried that she would have huge gaps upon it and have to sit or stand on the sidelines, watching others dance the night away. Thank goodness, it seemed that would not be the case.

Then she heard Val say, "Reddington. Merriman. It is good to see you this evening. Let me introduce you to my family."

She looked up and saw Lord Merriman with Lady Dilly and their mother. Another gentleman was with them. He was quite handsome, with cornflower blue eyes and a dimple in his chin. He was about six feet in height and lean as a whippet.

Val made the introductions for their group, saving her for last. The Duke of Reddington gave her a ready smile.

"Your brother has told me you are making your come-out this Season, Lady Tia. Might you do me the honor of dancing with me this evening?"

"I would be happy to do so, Your Grace," she told him, handing over her programme.

Her brother looked to Lady Dilly. "While I may be an old married man, I am still a duke, Lady Delilah. It might bring a bit of notice to you if I partner with you for a dance. I plan to dance the first dance with my duchess, but would you be available for the set after that?"

Her friend agreed to dance with Val. Tia thought it kind of her brother to do so.

The Duke of Reddington said, "Well, I am a duke myself. We must let everyone see how highly dukes think of you, Lady Delilah. Might I also claim a dance from you?"

As the duke signed the programme, Tia felt eyes upon her. She turned and saw Lord Merriman looking at her intently. She feared he was about to ask her for a dance.

And she was afraid that he wouldn't.

Why would she wish to dance with him? He had displayed nothing but boorish behavior to her, but she felt her mouth growing dry as their gazes met.

"Might you . . . accept a dance with me, Lady Tia?" he asked in his deep, rumbling voice. For some reason, hearing it caused a tingle to ripple along her spine.

She had no glib remark and knew it would be awkward if she turned him down in front of so many. Her eyes cut to Val, and he nodded encouragingly. She knew he had become friendly with Lord Merriman this past week. She did not know what she was missing or why this earl did not like her, but for propriety's sake, she passed her dance programme to him.

He returned it after signing it, saying, "Thank you." Then looking to the group, he said, "If you will excuse us. I must make certain that my sister meets others present this evening. Since this is my first time at the Season, Reddington has promised to take us about the room and introduce . . . D-Delilah around."

As the others said goodbye, Tia noted the earl had almost called his sister Dilly and then corrected himself. She had not known he, too, was a novice to the Season and was as new at this as she herself was.

Her attention was drawn by more people stopping to visit with them, and soon, her entire programme was filled.

Lia gave her a triumphant smile. "See? I told you that you would prove to be popular."

"With all this dancing, I am going to be quite weary by the time the ball ends."

"May Rupert and I call on you tomorrow afternoon? I want to see the many bouquets you receive and look upon the gentlemen who make a point of calling upon you."

Tia laughed. "You are more than welcome to visit. Only know that Mama, Val and Eden, and even Con will be present to look over any suitors."

Lia squeezed Tia's hand. "My, the drawing room will be full even before your suitors arrive." Then she grew serious. "Have ever so much fun tonight, my sweet twin. This is the moment you have been waiting for. Enjoy it to the fullest."

The musicians began tuning their instruments for play, and she eagerly awaited her first partner. She glanced at the name on her programme and recalled him being an earl of medium height with kind eyes.

"Forsythe," she repeated softly to herself as he approached, wanting to learn the names of those she would be dancing with each time.

He reached her and bowed. "It is Lord Forsythe, my lady, come to sweep you away."

"That is wise of you to introduce yourself, my lord, especially since I have already met so many new people tonight. My head is swimming with all the names and faces."

He gave her a winning smile. "I knew from the moment I saw you that your dance card would fill quickly. You will meet a plethora of people tonight, Lady Tia. I hope as your first partner of the evening that I will make a lasting impression upon you."

She liked his forthrightness and told him so, causing his brows to rise.

"I see you are a woman who speaks her mind. That is most refreshing. Shall we?"

Lord Forsythe led her to the dance floor, and soon Tia was caught up in the lively country dance. The earl was light on his feet and made for a wonderful first dance partner. This ball would certainly live up to its potential.

Several dances later, her latest partner returned her to Val, who stood with Con. Her brother had insisted that Eden go and sit with Mama because he did not want her to overexert herself.

"Has anyone made an impression upon you so far?" Con asked.

"A few," she told the pair.

Glancing down at the dance card now attached to her wrist, Tia saw the next dance had been reserved by Lord Merriman. Her heart sped up, and she told herself not to be so ridiculous. Moments later, the earl joined them, and both Val and Con greeted him as an old friend.

"I am glad you are one of the men dancing with my sister this evening," Val said. "You are someone whom I can trust and not need to watch like a hawk. I think I will go and claim my duchess for another dance."

"Thank you for dancing with Dilly," Lord Merriman said before Val departed. "Delilah. I must remember to refer to her as Mama wishes."

"What of your sister's feelings?" questions Con. "Shouldn't she be known by the name she wishes to go by?"

"She has always been . . . . Delilah . . . to all others. I am the only one who addresses her as Dilly."

Tia spoke up. "So do I. Lady Dilly asked me to call her by that name."

His gray eyes darkened, focusing on her. "Then she must hold you in high esteem, my lady."

Lord Merriman turned his attention back to Con. "It helped, having you, His Grace, and my friend Reddington dance with her. I am grateful for the gesture."

"Go enjoy yourself with my cousin, Merriman," Con said cheerfully. "I believe the dance is about to begin. I may even go and pluck a wallflower from those seated and enjoy a dance myself."

The earl offered Tia his arm, and she placed her fingers lightly upon his sleeve. Touching him brought an unexpected jolt, and his gaze met hers, questions in his eyes. She smiled politely and said, "Lead the way, my lord."

They danced that set, and she saw that for such a large, tall man, he was graceful. Lord Merriman moved assuredly, and she couldn't help but think him a bit arrogant. She pushed the thought away, trying to enjoy the dance for itself, and not think on the disagreeable man she partnered with.

When it ended, Tia was out of breath and knew her face must be flushed.

"Might you care for a cup of punch, my lady?" he asked.

Though she did not want to spend additional time in his company, she was parched. Her thirst won out. "Thank you, my lord. I believe I am in need of a cup."

He escorted her to a table where a punch bowl stood and retrieved a cup for both of them.

"With so many gathered, it has grown hot inside this ballroom. Might you wish to step out onto the terrace to cool down a bit before the next set begins?"

Once again, she did not want to be with him, but the thought of a cool breeze appealed to her, and she must have an escort to go outside the ballroom. Tia nodded, and he led them through a set of French doors which opened onto the terrace.

They strolled side-by-side the length of the terrace, and she was thankful other couples were also outside, taking in the night air.

When they reached the far end, he came to a halt and said, "I owe you an apology, my lady."

His words startled her. An apology was the last thing she would have expected from him, and her face must have given her thoughts away.

"We have gotten off to a poor start," Lord Merriman continued. "I wish to remedy that . . . for the sake of Dilly. She thinks highly . . . of you."

"I believe people show their true colors when in private, my lord. I witnessed you being very abrupt with your sister when I first met you. Lady Dilly had spoken of you so lovingly, and yet the man I saw was anything but."

"Would you believe it is the . . . only time I have spoken sharply to her?"

She searched his face and nodded. "Yes, I believe I do," she said quietly. "Why were you like that with her?"

"I cannot go into the specifics, my lady. All I can say is that I desperately needed time alone that afternoon."

She frowned. "I will not intrude upon your privacy, my lord. That still does not excuse how rude you were to me when you came to dinner at my brother's townhouse."

He shook his head, looking shamed. "I will regret that terrible remark I made to you . . . for the rest of my life.

Tia heard the anguish in his voice and believed him to be sincere.

"For the sake of Lady Dilly, shall we call a truce between us? I think of her as a dear friend and do not wish to have the fact that you despise me come between her and me."

He looked startled. "I do not despise you."

They gazed at one another a long moment, neither seeming to know how to continue their conversation. Tia took a sip of her punch, while he drained his cup.

"Shall we return to the ballroom, my lady? I am certain you are engaged for the next set."

"I am," she confirmed, once more placing her hand on his offered sleeve. A delicious vibration ran through her as she did so.

Lord Merriman took her empty cup and said, "Thank you for dancing with me, Lady Tia. I will not ask you to do so again. I know there are plenty of other gentlemen who wish to claim your time. I am merely glad the air between us has been cleared and that I had the opportunity to make my apologies to you."

He bowed and left her. As he walked away, Tia almost called out for him to return and then stopped herself, thinking how silly she would have sounded. At least he had done the decent thing and apologized to her.

As her next partner claimed her, however, she almost wished that Lord Merriman had asked to dance with her again.

CHAPTER ELEVEN

TIA AWAITED LIA'S arrival in her mother's sitting room. The twins had arranged at supper last night for Lia to come an hour before morning calls began so that they might discuss the opening night's ball.

Lia now rushed into the room, and Tia embraced her, grateful that her sister had been willing to come and talk about last night's events.

But would she open their discussion to anything regarding Lord Merriman?

Already, she knew the answer was no. Though she had always confided in Lia regarding every matter, both small and large, suddenly she wanted to keep something to herself. She knew her sister had done the same regarding her feelings toward Rupert.

The trouble was that Tia now had conflicting feelings toward Lord Merriman. On one hand, she could not forget the rude man who had treated her insensitively. Then again, the earl had apologized to her last night for his behavior. The apology had seemed genuine. She also was confused by that odd feeling which occurred when she had touched him. Her feelings were completely muddled now. She would need to think on things and work everything out before she broached the subject with her twin.

"Let us sit," Lia suggested. "I want to hear everything from your perspective."

They took a seat together on the settee, holding hands as they often did.

"I also wish to hear what you thought of your first ball," she said. "Everything is not about me, simply because you are now wed. I thought you looked lovely last night in your ballgown. Did you experience queasiness?"

"No. That is reserved for early mornings only." Lia chuckled. "This morning, I did not even rise until almost eleven."

"I did the same. Town hours during the Season are certainly different from those in the country."

"I have done what has been suggested and kept bread by my bed. I tear off tiny pieces and nibble on them. It does seem to work. Though my belly still roils as I awake, it does calm with the bread. Rupert is pleased. He was becoming worried about me retching all the time."

"Rupert is going to be just like Julian and Val, acting like a mother hen where you are concerned," she teased.

They spent several minutes talking about some of the ballgowns they had liked, as well as discussing the midnight buffet.

"I tried not to let my eyes pop out when I saw the display of food," Tia said. "Of course, I was starving by the time we sat to eat. Thank Rupert for allowing the baron and me to join you for supper."

"It was enjoyable," her sister agreed. "And I did like the baron. He was most jovial."

"Alas, Mama did not like him one whit. You should have heard her go on and on in the carriage as we made our way home last night."

Lia frowned. "What did Mama not like about him? He seemed a most amiable sort."

"The fact that he was a baron."

Both girls burst out laughing, then Tia did an impression of her mother, berating Tia for dancing with a lowly baron and then deigning to spend supper with him.

Lia wiped tears away from laughing so hard. "You do Mama justice. I still do not understand why she is so focused on you wedding a man of high rank."

"She was pleased when Ariadne wed a marquess. You, on the other hand, only wed a viscount. I suppose it is up to me to bolster the Worthington family's reputation and set my cap for a duke. Perhaps Reddington will do."

"He was quite nice," Lia said. She studied Tia a moment. "I cannot tell if you are teasing me now, or if you are truly interested in His Grace."

"Reddington seemed nice enough. The trouble is that I barely got to speak to anyone last night after being introduced to so many. I know Mama had warned us that a ball was not the ideal situation to get to know someone. It is much too difficult to talk to a gentleman during a dance. I did visit with a few of them after we had danced and before the next set began, but the topics were very safe ones."

"The weather?" Lia inquired. "Of everyone I met last night, that seemed to be the subject by default." She shook her head. "I must say that I am grateful to have wed Rupert and not be going through what you are, my sweet sister. So, tell me about a few of the gentlemen who did stand out to you."

Tia mentioned the baron, along with Reddington and a viscount. She did not say a word about Lord Merriman.

"We should go to the drawing room now and look at your bouquets. I will admit that I stopped by there before coming to see you. Numerous flower arrangements filled the room, and more were being brought in as I left."

Why did Tia's first thought go to whether or not Lord Merriman had sent flowers to her?

She shrugged it off and stood, knowing the earl most definitely had not sent a bouquet. Linking arms with her twin, they ventured to the drawing room, where Mama and Eden were already present. She was glad she would have both of them nearby.

"Look at all the wonderful flowers which have come for you!" her sister-in-law exclaimed. "I am in awe that the drawing room looks like a garden."

Eden had never made her come-out into Polite Society. Though her father had been a viscount, she had been forced from her home when her cousin inherited the title, earning her living as a governess. This Season was also Eden's first glimpse into Polite Society.

Mama crisply said, "Look at the cards accompanying each arrangement, Thermantia. I have already done so, making note of each and the title the sender holds. Remember, the larger the bouquet, the more a gentleman is interested in you."

She and Lia went from one arrangement to the next, reading the cards. In truth, Tia was a bit overwhelmed at the number of gentlemen who had sent flowers to her.

When they had made a complete round of the room, she said, "Mama, I do not recall meeting some of the gentlemen who sent me flowers."

"There may have been a few who did not receive an introduction to you, Thermantia. Still, they are showing their interest in you by sending an arrangement, hoping to gain your notice. Over the course of the next few weeks, you will meet all of them."

She fretted that too many men's interests was twofold—that she was a duke's sister and that she possessed a fat dowry. Tia voiced that fear now.

Mama looked at her sternly. "It is natural for you to draw interest because you are Millbrooke's sister. That fact alone makes you one of the most sought-after girls of the Season. You could be a hunchback and bald, and you would still have men vying for your hand. And yes, there will be those who seek to court you not only for your social standing in Polite Society but the fact that your dowry is more than adequate."

Her mother's words filled Tia with dismay. "Then how am I to even know if someone likes me for *me*?"

Her mother replied, "That is why you have Millbrooke and me. Dyer, too. We will help guide you in your choice of a husband. I know much about the families these gentlemen come from, while your brother and cousin will know more about a man's reputation and intentions."

Mama's tone softened slightly, and she took Tia's hand in hers. "You will soon receive several offers of marriage, Thermantia. I do not believe any man will offer for you today, but they will during the weeks to come."

"How could they offer for me today?" she asked, bewildered. "I barely said two sentences to most of the bachelors I met at last night's ball."

"I have tried to explain to you that, for the most part, marriage is a business arrangement. It is to gain social standing within the *ton*. Unite powerful families. You will not know the gentlemen who offer for you very well. You may dance with them a handful of times. Perhaps stroll through the gardens with them at a garden party. It is not as if you are to become friends with them."

"But that is exactly what I do wish to do, Mama. I want to get to know the man I will spend the rest of my life with *before* we wed. What is the point of the Season if not to deepen a friendship and hopefully see it blossom?"

Mama sniffed. "You young people have such odd ideas regarding marriage these days. The old ways are tried and true. At least you will have a bit of say in whom you wish to wed. In my day, many marriages were arranged without giving the bride any voice in the matter. You did whatever your parents told you to do."

"I will not allow that to happen," Val said, joining them. "Tia is not going to be forced to wed anyone she has not gotten to know well." His gaze turned upon her. "You will receive a good number of offers to wed. I expect them to start coming in by the end of this week or next. Some of the men will speak to you first regarding their intentions. Others will approach me and not mention a word to you. I will make you aware of the gentlemen who speak to me, but I will not make any arrangements with them. You are to be a part of this, every step of the way, Tia."

Val turned his attention back to Mama. "I did not wish to interrupt you in the carriage last night, but you were wrong to berate Tia for supping with a baron. I want my sister to be as happy as I am with Eden. As happy as our other sisters are with their spouses. If Tia wishes to wed a baron, she will have my approval—and yours, Mama."

Mama opened her mouth to speak and thought better of it. Nodding, she merely said, "I understand, Millbrooke." Looking to Tia, she added, "I do wish for you to be happy. You will not be forced into a marriage by either of us. Unless you are foolish enough to be compromised, and then you will have no say in the matter."

"Mama, I am not going to go off with some gentleman and be caught kissing him," she protested. "I have better sense than that. I do need you to be patient with me, however. The Season is so new to me. I simply want to enjoy the events we are invited to and get to know a broad group of people. If I find I enjoy the company of a certain gentleman and he enjoys mine, as well? Then I will entertain an offer of marriage from him. But if the Season ends, and I have not found anyone who pleases me, I will simply go home to Millvale and try again next year."

Val said, "You do need to be discriminating, little sister. After all, marriage is for life. You must choose wisely. If you find the right man, I will encourage you to wed him. If you wish to wait, I will support that idea."

"You have already had your come-out delayed by your father's sudden passing," Mama pointed out. "That makes you older than the other girls making their come-outs. At nine and ten, Thermantia, you must not take too long, else you will be on the shelf."

Con entered the room, greeting everyone, and then he took Tia's arm for a turn about the room.

"What say you, Cousin? How was last night's ball for you? Did you fall madly in love with anyone?"

"May I say something in confidence to you?"

"You know that you can, Tia. I view you as more than my cousin. You are as my own sister. Tell me," he urged.

"The dancing was divine," she began. "It was the rest that was a bit . . . off-putting. I thought there would be more conversation. Other than the baron I supped with—who was very nice indeed—I did not learn much about any gentlemen whom I partnered with."

"That is why you will need Val and me to help guide you," he told her. "Much of the conversation during the Season is superficial. If you feel a spark of attraction, however, we will thoroughly investigate the gentleman and see if he is suitable for you."

"I am hoping if any call this afternoon that I will get to know them better."

Con shook his head. "That really will not happen, Tia. Has Aunt Alice not spoken to you about how these morning calls work?"

"She has made me aware that gentlemen who send flower arrangements are particularly interested in me, and that many of them will follow up on their interest by calling on me this afternoon."

"Those gentlemen will stay about a quarter-hour each," he informed her. "Many will come calling. I can see that by the number of flowers which fill this room. You will go from one to another, greeting them. Thanking them for coming to visit you today. Then they will be gone, and others will take their place."

"This is not how I pictured things to be," she revealed. "How *do* you get to know anyone? You have been coming to the Season for a few years now, Con. Perhaps you can explain it to me."

He chuckled. "You see I am here in Val's drawing room and not in any young lady's. I take the Season with a grain of salt. My allowance is barely enough to get by on. Until I come into my title, I have no plans to pursue any young lady. No flowers sent nor calls made."

"Thank you for being honest and looking out for me. I value your opinion. If I do find my interest piqued by a gentleman, I will certainly give his name to you and Val."

Parsons opened the door and announced three names, her first callers, and an endless stream of visitors came and went all afternoon. It was as Con had told her The afternoon passed in a blur, and Tia almost thought it pointless. She even made her way to Lia at one point and whispered to her twin how unsatisfied she felt.

"I do not envy you," Lia said. "Not after seeing how this afternoon has progressed. This is as overwhelming as seeing all the people at last night's ball. I feel doubly blessed to have met Rupert away from town and been able to get to know him." She grinned. "Are you certain you do not wish to come home with me after the Season and find a local Cumberland man to wed?"

"That idea is appealing to me more and more," she replied, seeing Mama motioning to her to come and greet the new arrivals.

At the very end of the time designated for morning calls, Parsons announced a final visitor.

"Lord Forsythe," the butler said, and her first dance partner entered the drawing room.

Tia had liked the earl and was pleased that he had come to see her. She did not recall him having sent a bouquet, however. If he had, his name would have stood out.

He bowed to her, and she offered her hand to him.

"You mentioned me being forthright last night, Lady Tia. If you do not mind, I wish to be so again."

"That would be refreshing, my lord," she said, laughing, already glad he had stopped by to see her.

"I wanted to let you know—in person—why I did not send flowers to you." He paused. "I had fully intended to do so because I enjoyed meeting you last night and most certainly enjoyed our dance together. In fact, I hope we might partner again in the future."

"I would enjoy dancing with you again," curious as to why he had turned up and yet not sent the traditional bouquet.

He swallowed. "I owe it to you to tell you that I do not wish to court you this Season, my lady."

Understanding filled her. "You found someone last night, didn't you? Why, Lord Forsythe, I am delighted to hear that. Thank you for being gentleman enough to tell me this." She smiled at him. "It makes me like you all the more."

"I hope you will not be upset when you learn who the young lady is who has captured my heart. It is Lady Delilah Drake." He looked at her, waiting for a response.

Beaming at him, Tia said, "I could not be more pleased, my lord. She is a good friend of mine."

"She mentioned that to me last night when we supped together. I did not want to be the cause of trouble between the two of you, but I am quite taken with her. My father told me long ago that it was the same for him when he met my mother. That he knew instantly they were meant for one another. While I will have to ask other ladies to dance at future balls, because I cannot take up all of Lady Delilah's dances, I fully intend to offer for her. I wished for you to be aware of this."

"You are a gentleman in every sense of the word," Tia praised. "My friend is blessed to have drawn your attention. I think you will suit beautifully. I hope that you, too, will become my friend, as well as Lady Delilah's intended."

Relief flooded his face. "Thank you for your approval, Lady Tia. I will not be calling upon you again, but I do reserve the right to ask for a dance every now and then." He smiled warmly at her.

She thought Lady Dilly to be a very fortunate girl and only hoped her friend might have feelings for Lord Forsythe.

Tia could not wait to see her friend at tonight's ball.

CHAPTER TWELVE

T HEY WERE HEADED to another ball. Hugo had not known there would be balls two nights in a row. He worried about being thrust into a crowded room again with so many others. It always took him time to recover from being around large groups. Though he had planned to recuperate this afternoon, since he had slept until almost eleven that morning, his mother had other plans for him. She had insisted he be present in the drawing room while Dilly received her suitors. For once, he agreed, wanting to see the type of men who turned out to visit with his sister.

The room had been filled with various gentlemen coming and going, along with multiple bouquets of flowers. Apparently, when a gentleman was interested in a lady, he sent flowers to indicate that interest, as well as dropping by during morning calls. Hugo had kept to himself much of the afternoon, keeping a watchful eye on Dilly, as Mama seamlessly guided her daughter about the room as he sat in the corner and observed the proceedings.

Only one man had even noticed Hugo's presence and had made an effort to come and introduce himself as the Earl of Forsythe. The earl had spent as much time talking with Hugo as he eventually did Dilly. Hugo watched their interaction closely and decided Forsythe would be a good candidate for his sister's hand.

"My earrings look wonderful with this ballgown, Mama,"

Dilly said. "Thank you again for giving them to me."

Mama laughed. "Darling, diamonds go with simply everything. When you have a husband, tell him so. It does not mean you do not wish for him to buy you sapphires or opals, but diamonds make every gown special."

"What did you think of the suitors who showed up this afternoon, Dilly?" he asked, eager to learn if she favored any, and hoping to hear Forsythe's name come from her lips.

Hugo assumed his sister and mother had talked about this at length during tea. He had made an excuse that he had to see his solicitor and had left the townhouse, walking the deserted streets of Mayfair. Teatime seemed the only time traffic died down in the fashionable part of town. As he had made his way home, however, he began to see carriages again, all of them heading in the direction of Hyde Park. He recalled Mama telling Dilly something about carriage rides in the park. At least he now knew to avoid the place after teatime and only use it as a refuge when others were not in the park in such droves.

"I found more than a few to my liking," Dilly said, answering his question. "But one gentleman truly stood out to me. I saw you speaking with him, Hugo."

Pleased, he said, "Ah. You mean Forsythe."

"Yes, Lord Forsythe. He is the one I shared supper with last night. I wish we could have spoken more, but we were at a table which seated eight. The conversation included all sitting at the table."

"That helps you get to know others," Mama said. "If Lord Forsythe is thinking of you as his potential countess, he will ask you to dance again this evening, Delilah."

"I hope he does," Dilly said, eagerness in her voice. "He is quite charming. I also find him to be most handsome."

Hugo had thought Forsythe's looks average. He was of medium height, with brown hair and brown eyes, but apparently, he had caught Dilly's eye. That meant Hugo needed to mention the earl's name to the Duke of Millbrooke. He or Viscount Dyer might know more about Lord Forsythe. Matthew, too, might also know something of the earl.

He had watched Matthew dancing with both Dilly and Lady Tia last night. His friend had mentioned it might be time to consider marriage. Despite his liking Lord Forsythe, it would be wonderful if Matthew would consider Dilly as his duchess. Then again, Matthew had not called upon her this afternoon.

What if he had visited Lady Tia instead?

A surge of jealousy rippled through him, startling him. Why would he care if Matthew had called upon Lady Tia? Yes, his friend had danced with her the previous evening, as he had Dilly. Yet Matthew had not visited the Drake townhouse to see Dilly this afternoon.

Hugo would find out tonight if Matthew had called upon any young lady today. If he learned that his friend had visited Lady Tia, he would make certain he did not judge Matthew in any way. After all, Lady Tia was his sister's friend. She was nothing to Hugo.

Yet he itched to see her again.

Again, he questioned why he seemed so addled when it came to Lady Tia. It must be because he found her quite attractive. Of the women he had seen or met last night, she was by far the most beautiful. He shook his head, wishing he could knock some sense into himself. Lady Tia despised him. Moreover, she was the daughter of a duke. She would have her pick from a cluster of eligible bachelors and never think to consider him.

Wait. *Consider* him? It was not as if Hugo were in the market for a bride. It was the exact opposite. The only time he had bothered dancing last night was with Lady Tia, and that was only because he felt he owed it to Millbrooke to do so since the duke had volunteered to dance with Dilly. The rest of the time, Hugo had watched from the sidelines, making certain each of Dilly's dance partners returned her to him after each set finished.

What if Lady Tia had learned she was the only woman he had danced with? Would she draw some sort of erroneous conclusion? Think that he might wish to woo her?

No, she seemed to be fairly level-headed. She would understand he had danced with her specifically to issue his apology to her. It eased his worry when she had told him she believed the apology to be sincere. It had been. Hugo had meant every word of it. He realized Lady Tia was a lively sort of girl, and Dilly had always been gregarious and unreserved herself. It was nice his sister had found a kindred spirit, especially after discovering that other girls making their come-outs had no interest in being friends with her.

"Merriman, keep an eye out for this Lord Forsythe. I am not familiar with his family. I shall do a bit of sleuthing myself."

"Mama! Do not be obvious," Dilly warned.

Their mother arched one brow. "I will be the soul of discretion, Delilah."

"I plan to mention the earl's name to Millbrooke and Dyer. Reddington, as well. By the end of tonight—or tomorrow at the latest—I should know more about him."

Dilly's nose crinkled. "It all seems so . . . detached. You and others looking into the earl."

"We must remain objective about Forsythe for the moment," Hugo told his sister. "You, too, must not wear your heart on your sleeve, Dilly. You do not wish to encourage this gentleman, only to have to discourage him if we find out he is not suitable for you."

"But I truly like him," she complained.

"I will admit I do, too," he said. "Still, I want to learn a bit more about his character. His background. If he is in need of a bride's dowry or if his family's finances are in order. Be kind to him. Dance with him if you wish. Just do not become too overly fond of him until we know more about him."

She crossed her arms. "Oh, all right," she said, sounding all of five years of age.

Hugo bit back a smile. His gaze met his mother's, and she nodded approvingly. It made him feel as if he were taking the appropriate care of his family.

Suddenly, the idea of family tugged at his heart. Though he adored Dilly, she would most likely be leaving his household soon. Mama was pleasant but a bit distant. A wave of loneliness swept over him. He had been alone for most of his entire life. His years in school had been a nightmare. His university years had turned out pleasant, though, with Anthony and Matthew by his side. But eventually, the two of them would wed and have families of their own.

Hugo realized that he, too, wanted a wife. Someone who would be a close companion whom he could turn to in good times and bad. And children. While his own father had been a poor example as to what a parent should be, he believed that he could be a decent father. Better than decent. He wanted to play on the lawn of Merrifield with his children. Teach them to sit a horse. Read to them. And if by chance one of them stammered, he would know exactly how to address the situation and intervene during the child's early years.

This might not be the Season to take a bride, but he would start giving the idea more thought. The qualities he would seek for Dilly's husband might very well be the same ones he wished in his own wife. Excitement filled him. As the Earl of Merriman, he was not the timid boy he had been. He was a powerful peer, with wealth at his disposal. Surely, he could attract a woman's notice.

Lady Tia Worthington came to mind, and he pushed the thought of her aside. She was not for him. He was merely infatuated with the unattainable. Hugo thought he might look amongst the wallflowers. Not every wallflower was plain of face. Some were bluestockings who did not appeal to many gentlemen of the *ton*. Others had small or no dowries, which also cost them the attention of most eligible bachelors. Some of them might merely be shy or withdrawn.

He had a plan now. See Dilly settled and then look to his own future. A majority of the wallflowers would not be going anywhere, whether it be this Season or next. He might as well dance with a few. He could even sup with one, along with Dilly and her supper partner. Just as he had practiced for years to be able to speak clearly and without much hesitation, it would take practice to attain a bride. The sooner he began his hunt, the better he believed it would go.

They arrived at the townhouse which was the site of tonight's ball. The pattern of the previous evening was repeated, with them joining a receiving line and waiting their turn to be greeted by their host and hostess. He entered the ballroom with his sister and mother, more confident tonight, greeting a few here and there of those he recognized, and then moving on.

He spied Millbrooke's party, which was smaller this evening than it had been on the previous occasion. The duke's aunt and uncle, Lord and Lady Marley, were not present. Neither were Lord and Lady Cressley.

"Let us speak to His Grace," Hugo said, guiding them toward the duke.

They exchanged greetings, and then he pulled Millbrooke and Dyer aside.

"I have a name for you," he shared. "Lord Forsythe. Of all the gentlemen Dilly met last night, he has shown the most interest in her."

"How does she feel about him?" the duke asked.

"She is taken with him. Almost a little too much after only one meeting. I wish to find out as much as I can about the earl."

"We can help with that task," Millbrooke guaranteed him. "We already know Forsythe from our schoolboy days."

"Forsythe was amongst the boys our age," Dyer continued. "He was good at sports. Usually made the captain of a team. I respected him for choosing fairly. He did not always select the most athletic players first. Sometimes, he would choose boys who were merely eager to please. Forsythe got the most out of them because, as captain, he had taken a chance on them."

Having always been selected last, Hugo admired Forsythe's

approach to games.

"He was average in his studies if I recall correctly," Millbrooke added. "Decent at languages and maths. I think geography challenged him a bit. But overall, he was a good egg. Now, you must realize that Dyer and I went to Oxford. I believe Forsythe attended Cambridge, so we cannot speak as to what happened to him after we last saw him. Still, he displayed good character then. I do not think him the type to change all that much."

"I agree," Hugo said. "What you have shared has greatly relieved me. Still, I plan to get to know him better."

"Why don't you invite him to join you at White's tomorrow morning, say eleven o'clock?" the viscount suggested. "Millbrooke and I will be there. You can join us. That way, we can converse as a group, and he will not feel you peppering him with questions."

"I would be most appreciative of that, my lord." Then he asked, "What of Lady Tia? Did she mention any gentleman she was particularly fond of? I am happy to learn what I can of him if you provide me with a name."

The duke chuckled. "Tia is very particular. While she enjoyed the dancing tremendously, it does not seem as if anyone stood out to her last night. Frankly, I can understand why. My drawing room was swamped with suitors this afternoon. I had trouble keeping up with who was who, so I know she had difficulty in doing so, as well."

He couldn't say why hearing this pleased him so, but it did.

"I will be on alert, Your Grace. Just pass along any name if and when your sister does provide you with one."

"I will."

Hugo turned, ready to get Dilly's and Mama's attention and have them move on. Then he met Lady Tia's steadfast gaze. Without thinking, he stepped toward her.

"Might you have an empty slot on your dance programme, my lady?"

"Only one, my lord," she said softly. "The supper dance."

Damnation. If he signed her card, he would be expected not only to dance with her but also to escort her into the supper buffet at midnight. He didn't know if he were ready to spend that much time with her. Then it came to him—he could do so and ask Dilly and her partner to join them. It would make the two girls happy, supping with one another, and Hugo could also learn more about Dilly's supper partner.

"I would like to claim it if I may."

She passed the programme to him, and he scrawled his name across the only vacant spot. It surprised him that no one had taken that dance, which many gentlemen felt to be the plum spot.

"Then I will see you later. Come along, Dilly. Mama. We must circulate and help Dilly meet those she did not have an opportunity to be introduced to last night."

They had only taken a few paces when Lord Forsythe appeared in front of them. He smiled at Dilly. Dilly smiled at him. Even Hugo could feel the pull of the couple toward one another. And after what Millbrooke and Dyer had said of the earl, he believed Forsythe would be an excellent choice of husband for his sister.

"Good evening, Lady Merriman. Lady Delilah. My lord." Forsythe's eyes rested on Dilly now. "Might I have the honor of dancing with you this evening, my lady?"

"I would like that very much," his sister replied.

Forsythe looked over the card. "I see the supper dance has not been spoken for. Do you mind if I engage you for it?"

Dilly's smile deepened. "I would be happy to spend supper with you, my lord."

The earl signed the programme, and Hugo said, "I will be spending supper with Lady Tia Worthington. Since Lady Tia and my sister are close friends, perhaps we could meet and spend suppertime together."

"I would like that very much," Lord Forsythe said.

"Then we shall see you at supper."

The earl looked uncertain a moment, as if he were trying to gather his courage, and then he blurted out, "Might I have another dance with you this evening, Lady Delilah?" He looked to Hugo and his mother. "That is, with your approval."

"It is granted," he said graciously, knowing it would please Dilly. It would also let the gossips of the *ton* know that Lord Forsythe had a *tendre* for his sister.

Taking Dilly's dance card, the earl signed it again, a pleased look on his face as he returned it to Dilly.

Bowing, he said, "I will see you later this evening, my lady."

Once he left, Dilly beamed up at him. "Oh, thank you, Hugo."

"I spoke to His Grace and Lord Dyer. They went to school with Lord Forsythe and deemed him quite a good man. Of course, I will still need to investigate him a bit further, but I think it is safe to say that if you wish to encourage his suit, you may do so."

They moved about the ballroom, several gentlemen signing Dilly's programme. If things did not work out with Lord Forsythe, Dilly would have other options to explore. Mama excused herself once Dilly's programme had filled, joining friends. After Dilly's first partner claimed her, Hugo moved to a section of the ballroom reserved for those girls who had not been claimed for the first dance. He went to one who was attractive, but she wore an ill-fitting gown, the color completely wrong for her.

"I am sorry we have not been introduced, my lady. I am Lord Merriman. Might I engage you for this dance?"

She looked startled by his request and nodded mutely.

"Her name is Miss Stanhope," one of her friends called out as he led her to the dance floor.

They joined another group in the country dance, and Hugo saw that what Miss Stanhope lacked in rhythm, she made up for in eagerness.

He danced with three other wallflowers, knowing they buzzed about him each time he led another of their group to the dance floor. While he wasn't able to converse much with any of them, due to the spirited dancing and frequent changing of partners during the dance, his confidence rose tremendously.

Eventually, he returned to where Lord Dyer stood, watching the Duke and Duchess of Millbrooke dance.

"They are well matched," Hugo remarked.

"Eden completes him," the viscount said. "My cousin was without purpose until his duchess came into his life."

"Do you intend to wed, my lord?" he asked, having not seen Lord Dyer dancing yet.

"Someday," Dyer said, a bit wistfully. "But nowhere in the near future."

Finally, the supper dance arrived, and Hugo went to where Lady Tia stood, talking with Dilly and another lady close to their age.

"I believe this is our dance, my lady," he said.

When he offered his arm, she looked a bit reluctant to take it. He couldn't blame her. When her fingers had brushed his sleeve last night, he had felt an odd feeling rush through him. It was a mixture of feeling ill and elated at the same time.

Gently, she rested her fingertips on his sleeve, and Hugo led Lady Tia to the center of the room.

CHAPTER THIRTEEN

TIA HAD BEEN distracted all evening.

Because Lord Merriman was dancing tonight.

She chastised herself for taking notice, but she couldn't help herself. He was a handsome man whose appearance was hard to overlook on the dance floor. Twice, he had been dancing in close proximity to her, almost causing her to lose count of her steps. She thought herself completely daft to have taken such a sudden interest in him. Despite his heartfelt apology, she did not consider him to be a gentleman. At least one she might be interested in.

Then why did her pulse begin to throb and her belly seemingly turn upside down when he had asked her to dance this evening?

And it would not simply be one dance with her. She would also share supper with him. Would he wish to join Val or Con at a table? Or even his friend, the Duke of Reddington? Tia had not seen Reddington all night. What if Lord Merriman seated them at a table for two? What on earth would they talk about?

Pushing aside her worries, she allowed him to guide her to the center of the room. The musicians raised their instruments again, and the dancing commenced once more. She wished the earl might stumble just so he would not seem so perfect, but he danced with his usual grace. It was not like her to wish ill upon others. She supposed it was her dislike of him which was bringing out the worst in her.

Yet was it truly dislike? She did not hate him. Tia merely found him unpleasant. Why was it that others were charmed by him and not her?

She gave up thinking and simply enjoyed the dance. Another ball would not be held for three days, and so she made the most of her time upon the dance floor. She even caught sight of a marquess who had called upon her this afternoon, his admiring gaze helping her confidence to soar.

When the dance ended, Lord Merriman took her hand and slipped it into the crook of his arm. Her grip tightened, feeling the hard muscle beneath her fingertips. His scent, too, was intoxicating, something she could not identify, mixed with bergamot. Tia fought to keep herself from leaning in closer and inhaling deeply.

"Compose yourself," she muttered under her breath, causing the earl to glance down at her, frowning slightly.

"We are to sup with my sister and a Lord Forsythe," he informed her.

Relaxing because she now knew they would have others with them, especially her new friend, Tia smiled up at him. "That is wonderful news, my lord."

"You do not have to look so happy, my lady. I am sorry you are forced to continue in my company for the midnight buffet."

If she hadn't known better, she would think his feelings hurt. "I am simply happy to spend time with my friend, my lord. And Lord Forsythe was my first partner at last night's ball. I think quite a bit of him. He is what I consider a true gentleman."

As they headed toward the supper room, he asked, "Did Forsythe call upon you this afternoon? Send you flowers?"

She sniffed. "Not that is any of your concern, but while he did call upon me, I received no bouquet from him."

Seeing his reaction, she continued. "I thought it odd myself, but Lord Forsythe explained to me that he only came to see me because he wished to tell me in person why he would *not* be calling upon me in the future."

She let the earl wrestle with that for a moment, secretly enjoying his discomfort.

"You see," she continued, "Lord Forsythe is most interested in Lady Dilly, my lord. He will not be calling upon me—or any other young lady. Only your sister. That is how much he already is devoted to her. I found that most refreshing, as well as thoughtful of him to let me know. Lord Forsythe did say he would ask me to dance upon occasion, simply because it would not do to ask Lady Dilly for every dance."

"I see," the earl mused.

Entering the room designated for the midnight buffet, they came across Lady Dilly and Lord Forsythe already seated at a table.

"We saved these seats for you," her friend said, happiness radiating from her.

After Lord Merriman seated her, Tia said, "Perhaps you gentlemen might go through the buffet line and bring something back to us."

Lord Forsythe rose. "I am happy to do so. Any requests, Lady Delilah? I will see if they are being served this evening."

"I will be happy with anything, my lord."

The two left, and she could not help but notice that Lord Merriman had not asked if she had any particular likes or dislikes. It did not surprise her, though. At least she had a brief respite from his company and was happy to spend it with her friend.

Lady Dilly said, "You orchestrated that so smoothly. Now, we have some time alone."

"Are you already madly in love with Lord Forsythe?" she asked, getting straight to the point.

Lady Dilly flushed scarlet. "Is it that obvious?"

Tia told of the earl's visit to Val's drawing room this afternoon, seeing how surprised her friend was by what Tia revealed.

"I did not know his feelings were so strong toward me."

"Do you like him?" she pressed. "Enjoy his company?"

"Immensely. When he called on me this afternoon, it was as if no other gentleman was present. All my attention was focused on him," Lady Dilly admitted.

"Well, he told me he would have to dance with others besides you, simply to keep the gossips from chattering too much, but you are the one who holds his heart."

Lady Dilly shook her head in disbelief. "Is it possible that I have found my husband on the first night of the Season?"

Tia reached for her friend's hand and squeezed it. "I think it is possible that you both have fallen in love. I hear it strikes quickly, at least according to those in my family."

They gossiped a bit about others they had met last night and tonight, and Tia shared how no particular gentleman had caught her fancy.

"I am not worried. My brother supports me, no matter what decision I arrive at. If I do not find a husband to my liking this Season, there is always next year."

Their supper partners joined them again, and Tia found her plate filled to the brim.

Apologetically, Lord Merriman said, "I did not know what you might like, so I tried to get something of almost everything on the buffet."

"If I ate everything here, you would have to find a wheelbarrow and roll me from the ballroom," she declared, causing everyone to laugh.

They spent a happy half-hour together, talking and eating. Tia learned more about Lord Forsythe than she did Lord Merriman, however. It seemed he was reluctant to talk about himself, and she found herself longing to know more of him. Maybe if she knew him better, she would grow to like him more. It would be difficult to be close with Lady Dilly without having to be around Lord Merriman.

Boldly, she suggested, "Might we leave the supper room and stroll the terrace, my lord? I could stand a bit of fresh air."

"Excellent idea, Lady Tia," Lord Forsythe said. "Would you care to do the same, Lady Delilah?"

Her friend's happiness seemed to overflow. "I would indeed,

my lord."

The two couples left their table, and they found numerous couples strolling the terrace when they ventured outside. Some had even gone down the stone steps and moved along the lawn.

"We should move from the terrace," she told Lord Merriman. "So many have come outside, it would be hard to navigate around them."

She had slipped her hand back into the crook of his arm, enjoying its warmth and the strength of his arm.

"Do you box?" she asked as they moved down the steps.

"No. Not at all. Why do you ask?"

Glad the lanterns lighting the way allowed their faces to remain in shadow, she said, "I thought all men boxed and rode to the hounds. I was simply trying to make conversation, my lord. While you often ask questions of others, you speak very little of yourself. I feel as if I know next to nothing about you, yet you seem to know quite a bit about me."

They reached the lawn, and he steered her toward the entry to the gardens. Though the entrance was lit, as they took a few steps along the path, she could tell the rest was dark. Even though Tia knew she should have asked to turn back, against her better judgment, she tightened her grip on Lord Merriman's arm as they proceeded.

When they had taken another two dozen steps, they were surrounded by darkness. He stopped, turning to face her. His hands took hold of her waist, and she could feel his heat through her ballgown and layers of undergarments. She swallowed, her heart racing like a galloping horse's. It was impossible to make out his features, only the heat of their bodies, close, but not touching.

"You wish to know about me?" he asked, his voice husky. "Why?"

Unsure of herself, Tia said, "Because you are my friend's brother. And you are fast becoming a friend of my own brother and cousin. I wish to know—"

He cut off her words, his mouth now on hers, moving, caus-ing delicious tingles along her hairline. Up and down her spine. His lips were firm, yet soft, and they grew more insistent. She wanted to ask why he kissed her when he didn't even like her, but the sensations were too enjoyable, and she was afraid her words might actually cause him to stop.

Instead, she stepped into him, her breasts pressing against the rock of his chest. Her hands moved to his nape, her fingers pushing into his hair. Oh, how silky it was!

A growl came from him, and his hands left her waist, His arm went around her, pinning her to him. His free hand grasped her nape, holding her in place. Her heart quickened, beating rapidly now as his tongue glided along her bottom lip, back and forth, hypnotizing her.

Then it ran along the seam of her mouth, urging her to open to him. Having never kissed a man before, Tia had no idea what was coming next.

But she was eager to learn.

When she opened to him, his tongue slipped inside her mouth, stroking her own, causing the place between her legs to come to life. It throbbed in a way she had never experienced, and she leaned more into him now, as if she couldn't get close enough. The kiss heated up, and she felt the urgency of it as it consumed them both. He deepened the kiss, causing her knees to go weak and something wild to race through her. Her arms wrapped around him, clinging tightly to him, wanting him to give her more.

Tia had no idea how long they kissed, only that it was the most heavenly thing she had known. Gradually, his intensity faded, and he returned to kissing her lips, breaking the kiss only to kiss her again. His lips left hers, trailing along her throat, causing her knees to buckle. Thankfully, he had hold of her and kept her from collapsing.

Then she sensed him withdrawing, not just physically—but emotionally. He brushed a final kiss against her swollen lips and then rested his brow against hers, both of them breathing rapidly.

"Why did you kiss me?" she asked.

"You wanted to know about me," he said softly, his breathing warm. "I thought a kiss might tell you all you needed to know."

She lifted her brow from his, wishing she could see what his eyes held. "It merely told me that you are skilled in the art of kissing, my lord. Obviously, you have kissed women before. You are very good at it."

"What? I have received a compliment from Lady Tia Worthington?" He chuckled softly.

"Please. Tell me," she insisted. "Why did you kiss me?"

"Because I thought I might die if I did not do so," he said, brushing his lips against her brow and then releasing her. He stepped away, that delicious warmth instantly fading.

"We must return to the ballroom, my lady," he said, his tone gruff, and she knew the wall he had erected around himself was once more going up, closing him off from the world.

And her.

"Why do you do that?"

"Do what?"

"Put distance between yourself and others. You must have a reason for doing so."

After a long pause, he said, "Call it . . . an unhappy childhood."

He took her arm, sliding a hand along it until he reached her hand. He took it and threaded it through his own arm, guiding her slowly along the darkened path.

"How can you even see?" she whispered, knowing they were close to the entrance because she could see the torch.

"My eyes grew . . . like a cat's." He paused in both speech and steps. "Because I had to . . . be ready . . . for when they came."

His words made no sense to her, but she had no opportunity to ask him what he meant. They had reached the entrance, and he stepped from the garden, guiding her close to another couple who happened to be kissing in the shadows and did not pay them any heed as they skirted by them.

As Lord Merriman led her to the steps and up them, he bent, his lips brushing against her ear, causing a chill to flicker through her.

"My curiosity is satisfied, Lady Tia. I suggest you keep what happened between us to yourself. Dilly would not understand. And if you tell a member of your family, Millbrooke in particular, he would be at my doorstep, beating down my door, demanding that I wed you at once by special license."

He paused. They were close enough to the doors leading into the ballroom now for the light to show his face. "And I doubt you wish to be chained in a marriage for the rest of your life with the likes of me."

Tia had no response, knowing what he said was true. If she even hinted to Val that Lord Merriman had kissed her, her brother would demand a marriage take place immediately. She did not like Lord Merriman. He did not like her.

Although she certainly had liked his kiss.

"Very well," she told him. "I will remain silent." Her gaze met his. "I do think it wise not to spend any unnecessary time in one another's company, my lord."

"No more dances," he assured her, leading her inside, returning her to where Val and Eden stood.

Giving Tia a charming smile, the earl said, "It was a pleasure supping with you, Lady Tia. I know my sister and Lord Forsythe also enjoyed your company." He glanced to Val. "I will bring Forsythe with me to White's tomorrow morning, Your Grace. We look forward to seeing you and Lord Dyer there."

With that, Lord Merriman left, causing Tia to feel very alone.

"Lord Merriman seems like such a good man," Eden remarked. "I am glad you have become friends with his sister and are friendly with him."

Her chin rising a notch, Tia said, "He is not looking for a wife this Season. Because of that, he and I have decided we will not be dancing with one another in the future. That way, it frees me up to spend time with other gentlemen."

She spied her next dance partner headed her way. Though her throat was thickening with unshed tears, Tia put on a bright smile and greeted the viscount. She recalled his title but not his name, and he did not provide it to her as he led her out onto the dance floor.

"Focus," she hissed under her breath as the music began, not wanting Lord Merriman to see her make a mistake while dancing as she pondered their kiss.

Tia *would* think on his kiss.

Later.

CHAPTER FOURTEEN

SIX WEEKS HAD passed since Hugo had kissed Lady Tia.
And he could still taste her . . .

They had only spoken a handful of times when they ran across one another, a stiff, formal greeting. He had stopped dancing entirely at balls. For the most part, he retreated to the card room. He knew that Lord Forsythe would be offering for Dilly at some point, and that the other gentlemen she danced with were merely filling time between her encounters with the earl.

He took midnight buffets with Lord Dyer, and they frequently sat with Dyer's cousin. Millbrooke usually had a large table of relatives, which included his brothers-in-law, the Marquess of Aldridge and Viscount Cressley. Hugo had become comfortable in the company of these men.

He and Dilly were on their way to Lady Swarthmore's tonight. It was to be a card party, and Mama had said those bored her, so she was staying in for the evening. Hugo hoped Lady Tia would not be in attendance because it would be harder to avoid her at such an intimate gathering.

Sitting across from Dilly in the carriage, he studied his sister, thinking she had grown even prettier as the Season had moved along. Part of it was the confidence she had in herself, thanks to her budding romance with Lord Forsythe. The more Hugo had gotten to know the young earl, the more he liked the man. When the time came, he could easily give his blessing to the couple. He only wondered when the offer might occur. Perhaps Forsythe was allowing Dilly to enjoy a full Season, and then he would request her hand in marriage.

They reached Lady Swarthmore's townhouse and were directed upstairs to her large drawing room. Mama had pulled him aside before they left and warned him that their hostess could be a vicious gossip and to make certain he looked after his sister this evening.

Right away, they were joined by Lord Forsythe. Dilly blushed prettily as her suitor greeted them, and he led her off to show her something.

Hugo saw one of his former bullies from his schooldays enter the drawing room. None of them had yet to associate him with the boy they had tormented all those years ago. For that, he was grateful. Forcing himself to be more social, he moved about the drawing room, speaking to others who were arriving.

Then he came upon Lord Dyer and Lady Tia.

"Good evening," he said, and they greeted him likewise. "Millbrooke is not in attendance this evening?" Usually, the duke and his duchess escorted Lady Tia to social affairs.

Lord Dyer chuckled. "He begged off from tonight's event. Cards used to be something he enjoyed immensely, but my cousin was eager to spend a quiet evening with his duchess and their babe."

"The same could be said for my sister and brother-in-law," Lady Tia added. "My twin was eager to have a quiet night with her husband."

He had learned Lady Cressley was increasing, and she and her husband only attended a few events each week in support of Lady Tia.

Continuing, she said, "Thank goodness my cousin was happy to escort me to tonight's card party, especially since Mama does not fancy playing much."

"My mother said the same. I am here tonight with my sister."

Curiosity eating him up, he asked, "Will the two of you partner together this evening at cards?"

The viscount laughed easily. "No, I have my eye on someone I wish to get to know a bit better. If you will excuse me, I will begin that endeavor now."

Lady Tia watched her cousin stroll away and then confided, "It is a widow he seeks out now."

Hugo found himself tongue-tied with it being just the two of them. All he wished to do was yank her into his arms and kiss her again.

"Might I join you?" a voice asked.

Lord Balch stood before them. He had been one of the chief boys who had led others against Hugo. The viscount was a good four inches shorter than Hugo was now, and he looked down upon the man with as much arrogance as he could muster.

It didn't matter—because Balch's full attention was centered upon Lady Tia.

"Rumor has it that you excel at cards, my lady. Might I ask if you have a partner for this evening's play?"

"I do not, my lord," she responded.

"Then we simply must play together," Balch insisted. "I am good enough at cards myself to guarantee that you and I will meet with victory this evening."

The viscount finally glanced at Hugo, not really seeing him. "If you will excuse us, my lord, Lady Tia and I are off to talk strategy."

His heart sank as Lady Tia placed her fingers upon Balch's sleeve, and they moved away to a far corner of the room.

Putting a smile upon his face and clasping his hands behind his back, Hugo continued making his way about the room, coming upon a small group which included Miss Stanhope. She weas the first wallflower he had danced with, and he had since learned that she was a bluestocking, which is why most gentle-men avoided her company.

"Good evening, Miss Stanhope. It is lovely seeing you present this evening."

"I feel the same way, my lord," she replied.

"Might you have a partner for this evening's play?"

"I do not at this point. Are you in need of one?"

He smiled. "I most certainly am, and I hear you have the intelligence which I seek in a partner."

"Then come let us talk gameplay, my lord," she suggested, looking a bit relieved to have found a partner.

She outlined her methods for taking tricks at whist, and Hugo couldn't help but be impressed with her strategies. He knew he had chosen wisely, and while he hoped they would not be up against Lady Tia and Lord Balch, if they did encounter them, he believed they would beat the viscount soundly.

After another quarter-hour, Lady Swarthmore had her guests gather around, explaining how match play would unfold this evening. She named the prizes to be awarded the winners, which he was uninterested in. All he wanted to do was play up to his partner's level in the competition.

Hugo was glad they had spoken before the first hand was dealt, because the couple they were paired to play against seemed to have no clue how to take a trick. They easily won, and they beat two more opponents after that. Then Lady Swarthmore interrupted play to let her guests know food and drink were now available in the library. Their next opponents agreed to take a short respite before they began playing, so he escorted Miss Stanhope to the library for some refreshments.

They spoke to a few other couples as they sipped their ratafia and nibbled on a most remarkable cheese, most congratulating them on their series of wins. Then they returned to the drawing room, ready for the next round of play.

Hugo and Miss Stanhope were victorious in two more matches, then came the moment he had dreaded.

They had been propelled into the finals with Lady Tia and Lord Balch.

Both couples took their places at the table, Lady Swarthmore's butler handing a new deck of cards to Hugo. He allowed

Balch to inspect the deck and then shuffled several times. Once the cards had been dealt, all playful banter ceased. When they had competed against other couples, a running conversation had taken place during the game. This time, however, things grew serious. It was obvious that their opponents were both skilled card players from their gameplay, but he and Miss Stanhope were no pushovers and took their fair share of tricks.

Victory came down to the final hand of the night, as Miss Stanhope dealt the cards around the table. His gaze met hers, and she nodded at him, determination in her eyes.

Lady Tia had been silent throughout the match. Each time she and Lord Balch had won, though, her partner had commented on how wonderful their play was and how poorly their opponents played. At one point, Hugo had to stop himself from smashing his fist into the smug viscount's nose, wishing to silence him.

While a majority of the guests had adjourned to the library to talk and eat, tired of card play, several couples had remained behind, watching this final game. He felt tension gather in his shoulders as he retrieved each card dealt to him and organized his hand. Thank goodness he did not have to speak when playing now because all his focus was on the cards themselves and not his speech.

Play was steady, and he was trying to recall which cards had been played in this round, especially spades. If Miss Stanhope did not have the Jack of spades, he thought they would be certain to lose. After taking a trick, Lady Tia led with the nine of spades, and his gaze met that of Miss Stanhope. She shook her head almost imperceptibly, and he realized victory would escape them this evening. His partner played the ten of spades, apparently the last of the suit she held in her hand. A few seconds later, Lord Balch took the trick with the Jack, also claiming the game and match.

Immediately, Balch began lording over Hugo and Miss Stanhope, extolling his play and that of his partner. While it was one thing to be excited to win, Lord Balch's words shamed them for their loss.

Lady Tia had been drumming her fingers upon the table and sharply said, "Stop."

Lord Balch looked at her quizzically. "My lady?"

"It is the mark of a true gentleman to be a gracious winner," she said, gazing at him steadily. "You are crowing about like some rooster, trying to impress a row of hens. We did not beat these two soundly, as you make it seem. It came down to this final trick, and it easily could have gone the other way. I will never partner with you again, Lord Balch. You are an ungracious winner, and I cannot imagine what a sore loser you would be."

With that, she rose from her seat and went to her cousin, who stood nearby. Immediately, Lord Dyer took her arm, and they moved to Lady Swarthmore, making a speedy goodbye.

As for Lord Balch, he stood gaping at Lady Tia. Then he seemed to recover a bit of his swagger and glanced to those standing about.

"I carried the chit the entire night. I will claim both prizes," he proclaimed.

Hugo was not about to let the viscount get away with what he had said. He placed his hand upon the man's forearm, squeezing tightly.

"What the bloody hell?" Balch asked, startled.

He looked the viscount in the eyes. "You will not disparage Lady Tia again. She proved to be an excellent partner to you. She fed you the cards you needed throughout our match, allowing you to take the glory in each game the two of you won. She is my sister's closest friend, and I will not have you sully her name or reputation."

He stared at Balch, daring the viscount to verbally spar with him.

Balch swallowed. "Lady Tia was an excellent partner to me," he said grudgingly. "I will see that she gets her prize."

"I believe she will have nothing more to do with you, Balch," Hugo told the man. "*I* will see that she gets her prize."

He could not deliver it directly to Lady Tia, but he could certainly give it to Dilly to pass along. He already knew Lady Tia was coming for tea tomorrow afternoon at their house, and she could receive her prize then.

Lady Swarthmore stepped in, looking a bit flustered. "I am so delighted play went as well as it did this evening," she told the guests still in the drawing room. "Please, go and have some more of my cook's delicious cakes and tarts."

Those gathered moved toward the door, including Lord Balch. Hugo was glad to see the man go. He had not changed one whit from the boy he had been.

Glancing to Miss Stanhope, he said, "I could not have asked for a better partner this evening, my lady."

With a sparkle in her eyes, she said, "Well, I enjoyed almost all of our evening together, my lord. Except the end, of course. I would like to have beaten that clod."

He chuckled. "I feel the same, Miss Stanhope."

Lady Swarthmore came toward them, thanking them for attending and giving Hugo a small box which contained the earrings which were tonight's prize for the winning lady. Then he escorted his card partner to the library once more. He saw her safely to her father and then went to sit with Dilly and Lord Forsythe.

"I hope you fared well at cards, Merriman," the earl said. "Lady Dilly and I only won one match this evening."

He had not seen Dilly or Forsythe present during the final match, so they had not heard how he had leaped to Lady Tia's defense.

"It is time we left," he told his sister.

Dilly gazed up at him. "I have asked Lord Forsythe to take tea with us tomorrow afternoon after my dress fitting. I would like you to be there, as well, Hugo."

Although he had planned to make himself scarce since he knew Lady Tia would be in attendance, he decided he would pass along her prize to her then.

"I look forward to seeing you tomorrow, Lord Forsythe," he told Dilly's suitor.

Hugo escorted Dilly to their waiting carriage, trying to tamp down the eagerness he felt, knowing he would see Lady Tia tomorrow.

CHAPTER FIFTEEN

TIA EAGERLY LOOKED forward to the last of today's callers leaving since she was to have tea with Lady Dilly. They had only grown closer over the weeks since the Season began. While no one would ever replace Lia as her most trusted confidante, Tia willingly shared much with Lady Dilly, who was mad for Lord Forsythe. Tia was looking forward to the day the earl would offer for her friend so that she could help with the wedding preparations.

"I really must go and lie down," Eden said, yawning. "If I am to stay awake for this evening's musicale, I will need a nap. Enjoy your tea with Lady Dilly, Tia."

Val followed his wife from the drawing room, and Tia couldn't help but wonder if Eden would have a chance to nap or not. She had caught her brother and his wife kissing upon numerous occasions from the time they wed. She smiled, happy that her only brother was so satisfied in his marriage, and also grateful that Eden had become a good friend to her.

"I am off to tea with Lady Swarthmore," Mama said. "She will want to share with me all that happened at her card party last evening."

"Why did you not go, Mama?" Tia asked.

"And miss a fabulous tea and the cakes her cook bakes? Lady Swarthmore can tell me all about her guests while we have our tea, and I did not have to waste hours of my time last night. I have never been fond of cards."

She thought it was because her father had been so fond of them that her mother had a dislike for any kind of card game.

"Enjoy your time with Lady Swarthmore," she said. "I must go see which of the footmen can escort me to tea."

"Oh, I can take you to Lord Merriman's townhouse on my way to Lady Swarthmore's," Mama said. "Have one of their maids see you safely home afterward."

While Tia had been perfectly willing to walk, the day was unseasonably warm, so she agreed to share a ride with her mother. Their coachman deposited her at the Merriman townhouse and did not drive off until he saw the butler admitting her.

Inside, however, she learned that Lady Dilly and Lady Merriman had yet to return from a dress fitting.

"I can wait in the drawing room for them. Or even the parlor. Whichever is more convenient, Coggins."

The butler informed her the drawing room was currently unoccupied, and she told him, "I will make my way there. No need to trouble yourself."

She mounted the stairs and headed for the drawing room. Until an unusual melody caused her to veer from her destination. Tia went and stood in the doorway of what she gathered was the music room. Lord Merriman was at the keys, his fingers flying across the ivories, lost to the world around him. She found herself entering the room and going to stand near him, watching his long, lean fingers dance along the keys. Though she had heard him perform previously, she was entranced now.

When he finished less than a minute later, she gasped. "That was incredible!"

He looked over his shoulder, looking startled to see her. "Wh-what are you . . . doing here?"

Wanting things not to be awkward between them, she said, "Apparently listening to you play better than anyone I have heard. Who is the composer?"

"Domenico Scarlatti. A contemporary of Handel. His works bridge the Baroque and Classical Eras."

"And the piece?"

"*Keyboard Sonata in D Minor*. One of . . . his most famous . . . works."

Tia noticed he had a habit of speaking very deliberately, even pausing often.

"Well, you played it wonderfully, my lord. I could sit and listen to you all day. You bring such joy to your playing, and that joy is spread to those who listen to you."

A pained expression crossed his face, and she gathered he was thinking of the hurtful comment he had made to her the night he and his family came to dinner.

"Do not worry, Lord Merriman. I am over the unfortunate remark you made to me. I fear I will never play even a tenth as well as you do. As I mentioned before, I have to concentrate on the finger patterns in a pianoforte piece. You, on the other hand, seem to absorb those patterns whole and interpret them in new ways."

Rising, he said, "I am blessed. To have a true ear for music. It has gotten me through many... trials and tribulations."

"Have you always played?"

"I only started when I was ten and eight, which was five years ago. Matthew—Reddington—challenged me to learn, and so I took up the instrument."

She shook her head in wonder. "I have played since I was six or seven, and I will never reach your level of accomplishment."

He smiled wryly. "I have practiced quite a bit . . . since I took up the pianoforte. Quite a bit since we came to town for the Season. Playing brings me comfort."

"You are not very comfortable at social affairs. At least that is what I have observed," she ventured. "At first, I believed you to be arrogant. Standoffish. A man who thought he was better than others around him."

The earl shook his head. "That is far from the truth, Lady Tia.

I am reserved. If I am quiet, it is because ... I believe I have nothing to contribute to a conversation."

She studied him a moment. "You do not speak often. I notice you ask questions of others and allow them to talk about themselves at length. Is that so you do not have to share things about yourself with anyone? Or is there another reason you do not wish to draw attention to yourself?"

He gazed down at her a long moment. "You see more than most others do. I ... am not very ... interesting. I would rather hear about others. You are correct ... in believing I ask questions to place attention away from me."

"I am sorry I misjudged you."

Lord Merriman nodded. "I also misjudged you. I thought you ... would be a poor influence on Dilly."

"Me, a poor influence? Why on earth would you believe that, my lord?"

He smiled. "It does not matter now. I realize how close you two are. You are the sister she never had."

"I felt perfectly comfortable with her the first time we met at Madame Laurent's dress shop. Lady Dilly was a breath of fresh air. While I had wanted to enjoy all the social events of the Season, I was most looking forward to making new friends. I have done so with her."

"What of finding a ... husband?" he challenged. "Isn't that what is most important?"

"Not to me," she admitted. "My three siblings all made love matches. They expect me to do the same, but in all honesty? Most of the eligible bachelors I have been introduced to simply bore me to tears. They say the same things, over and over, without any meaningful dialogue."

She moved away from him, roaming the room now, coming to stand before the windows which looked out on the square below.

"My biggest fear is that they only come to call on me or sign my dance programme because I am the sister to a duke, and they want to unite their family with ours for that reason alone. Or they see my hefty dowry as more attractive to them than I am and give me pretty compliments which they do not mean."

Suddenly, she sensed him behind her, body heat radiating from him. His arm snaked around her waist, pinning her to him, even as his lips brushed against her nape. A sigh escaped from her, and he kept kissing her nape. His mouth moved to the side of her neck. She tilted it to one side in order to give him better access. His kisses brought a shiver to her spine, and the place between her legs began to throb painfully.

"There are those who might wish for . . . an alliance with your brother," he said, his lips gliding. Nibbling. Then biting, causing her to gasp. He soothed the place with his tongue, and she gripped his forearm to keep from folding.

"It is hard for a women to read a man's intentions," she managed to get out, wondering exactly what his were toward her, and yet not caring as long as he kept kissing her. She had known men and women kissed on the lips, but she was learning kisses elsewhere could also be pleasurable.

Tia inhaled his bergamot scent, knowing she would forever associate it with this man. Wondering why she was attracted to him when she knew so little about him.

His lips left her neck, and his arm fell away. Boldly, she spun, wrapping her arms about him.

"You might be through with me—but I am not through with you."

His gray eyes darkened, and his mouth descended to hers.

The kiss was greedy from the start, demanding that she give everything to him. She recalled the lessons he had taught her during their prior kiss, and now she was the one to tease his mouth open, slipping her tongue inside, tasting him. Tia began to tremble, and his arms came about her, steadying her. She realized she trembled in need. In want.

In desire . . .

They both fought for command of the kiss, a thoroughly

enjoyable battle she would be happy to engage in at any time. Her nipples began aching as they rubbed against his chest, suddenly sensitive, eager for his touch. Somehow, he seemed to read her mind. He slipped a hand inside her bodice, his fingers hot as they caressed her breast. His thumb found her nipple, and he dragged the pad of it slowly back and forth, causing it to peak. Her heart seemed to want to burst from her chest, and she felt something hard between them.

Curious, she slid her hand along his hip and moved it between them, realizing it was his manhood which had swelled. Her fingertips grazed it. Even with his trousers between his cock and her fingers, she could feel its heat as he groaned into her mouth.

He broke the kiss, looking down at her, questions in his eyes. She had questions herself.

For both him—and her.

"Why did you kiss me again?" she asked, not ready to look inside herself for an answer she was uncertain about.

He shook his head sadly. "I have felt an attraction to you almost from the beginning. I know . . . it is wrong. I swear . . . I fight it whenever I am near you. I have no business . . . kissing you."

He gripped her shoulders, pushing his away from her, holding her at arm's length. "You can do far better than me, Lady Tia. My advice? Stay . . . away."

She gazed up at him, a long way since he was so very tall. "What if I do not wish to stay away?"

He frowned. "You must."

"I can do whatever I want."

His lips thinned. "You do not . . . need me. Open your eyes. You . . . will find someone worthy of you."

His hands released her, and he strode across the room. Stopping at the door, he said, "I advise you go . . . to tea now."

Stubbornness filled her. "Why are you trying to get rid of me? Oh, I know if we are caught alone, I am ruined. If Lady Dilly came upon us, though, she would not blab, forcing us to wed." Tia went to him. "Why can we not explore what is between us? See where it leads?"

"Nowhere," he said emphatically. "It leads . . . to nowhere. Go," he ordered.

"You are the most confusing man I know," she told him. "And just to let you know, I have kissed two other men since you." She paused, thinking of the stolen kisses and how they had disappointed her, having known Lord Merriman's kiss. "Their kiss barely affected me."

His brows arched.

"But when I kiss you? I feel we are just beginning upon some grand adventure." Her hands came to her waist, fists resting upon it. "I want to explore more with you, Lord Merriman. I do not expect you to offer for me. I simply want to see where this might lead us."

"We cannot," he told her. "Go and find yourself . . . a nice lord. And have a nice life."

Her eyes narrowed. "You want me. I can tell." She almost told him that she wanted him in return, but she bit back the words, not wishing for him to trample upon her pride if he refused her.

He snorted. "Go, my lady."

She sniffed. "You are the most confusing man, Lord Merriman. Far be it from me to be the lady who tries to figure you out."

Tia left the music room and headed down the corridor to the drawing room. She opened the door and saw Lady Dilly, Lady Merriman, and Lord Forsythe just starting to take a seat and was glad they had been delayed.

"Oh, there you are, Lady Tia," her friend said. "I feared you would be left alone because we were late leaving the modiste's this afternoon. I was hoping my brother would be here, however, to entertain you."

Not bothering to explain her own tardiness, she joined the

trio. "How did your fitting go? Is this the pink gown you have described to me?"

Lady Dilly began talking about the gown, with her mother chiming in. As the teacart was rolled in, Lord Merriman followed behind it. Tia's breath caught, surprised that he had made an appearance.

"I hope I am not too tardy," he said, looking so perfectly composed that she wished to throttle him.

"You are right on time, Merriman," his mother said. "We are getting a bit of a late start for tea. Madame Laurent was extremely busy this afternoon."

As Lady Merriman poured out for them, they discussed the musicale they all would attend this evening.

"I hear the singer is German," Lord Forsythe shared. "Supposedly, she is the most sought after soprano in all of Europe."

"I look forward to hearing her," Tia said. "While I am not the most accomplished pianist, I do enjoy listening to music." She turned to Lord Merriman. "I recall you played the pianoforte for us at my brother's. You are very talented, my lord. Perhaps I will have an opportunity to hear you play again sometime."

"Perhaps," he said coolly.

As tea came to an end, Lord Forsythe turned to Lord Merriman. "If you can spare a few minutes, my lord, there is something I wish to discuss with you."

"Certainly. Come to my study now."

The two men left. The minute the door closed behind them, Tia threw her arms about Lady Dilly.

"Oh, this is it!" she cried.

"Do you truly think he is ready to offer for me?" Lady Dilly asked.

"I cannot believe it has taken him this long," Lady Merriman said. "I expected an offer from Forsythe a few weeks ago."

"He wanted me to be certain, Mama," Lady Dilly explained to her mother. "Last night at the card party, he hinted to me that he might doing so today." She smiled brightly at Tia. "Oh, pinch me. Else I will think I am dreaming."

"I will do no such thing. I am not going to leave a bruise upon you," she told her friend. "Just think—you will be announcing your betrothal soon!"

Tia looked to the countess. "Might it be something you would have announced at tonight's musicale, my lady?"

"If it is true and Forsythe offers for my daughter, tonight's event would be the perfect time to make the news known. It will be a smaller gathering, most likely only fifty or so present. News travels quickly within the *ton*. By tomorrow night's ball, most of Polite Society will know of the engagement."

"*If* there is one, Mama," Lady Dilly said. "Lord Forsythe might be asking Hugo something mundane, such as to accompany him to White's tomorrow."

But Tia knew that was not the case, especially when the two men returned to the drawing room. Lord Merriman looked pleased, while Lord Forsythe seemed about to burst.

They joined them again, and Lord Merriman nodded, causing Lord Forsythe to declare, "I have offered for you, Dilly. And your brother has accepted my suit."

She noticed the earl called her friend Dilly, not Delilah, and that he had also dropped the use of her title.

Lady Dilly leaped to her feet, and Lord Forsythe took her hands in his, kissing her fingers.

"I knew you were the one for me from that first night," Lord Forsythe proclaimed. "You blinded me with not just your beauty, Lady Dilly, but with your sweet nature."

"I felt the same, my lord," her friend said, happiness written across her face. "Oh, I cannot believe we are to be wed!" She turned to Tia. "And you must help me plan my wedding."

As they embraced, Tia said, "I would be happy to do whatever you request, Lady Dilly."

Flush with her happiness, Lady Dilly said, "Then please call me Dilly. I feel as if you are a sister to me."

"Then I am to be Tia to you," she told her friend.

They debated for a few minutes whether a summer or autumn wedding would be best.

"You do not have to decide anything just yet," Lady Merriman said. "Enjoy your betrothal. In a few days, when things have calmed down, we can speak again of the ceremony. Where and when to hold it. And we must visit Madame Laurent again so that she might begin creating your wedding gown."

Dilly turned to her. "You will come to the wedding, Tia, won't you? Wherever it is?"

"I would not miss it for anything," she replied, her gaze meeting that of Lord Merriman's.

He reached into his pocket, withdrawing a small box. "I forgot. This is for you, my lady. From Lady Swarthmore."

"Whyever would Lady Swarthmore give you a present?" Lady Merriman questioned.

"Lady Tia won at cards last night," Lord Merriman said. "Unfortunately, she had to leave before the prizes were awarded."

"Open it," encouraged Dilly. "I recall Lady Swarthmore saying that the lady's prize last night was to be earrings."

Tia opened the box, seeing the sapphire earrings inside.

And knew exactly which gown she would pair them with tonight.

CHAPTER SIXTEEN

T IA SAT BEFORE the mirror and fastened her new sapphire
earrings onto her earlobes. She had held back two gowns
this Season, hoping to save each for a special occasion. One was a
blush ballgown, the barest of pinks, which flattered her complex-
ion. The other was what she wore tonight, an iced-blue gown
with just a hint of color in it. Not only did it make the earrings
stand out, but it caused her eyes to sparkle. It also was a perfect
shade against her strawberry blond hair.

She was glad that not a single gentleman had mentioned the
color of her hair since the Season had begun. All four Worthington siblings had varying shades of red, with hers being the softest
of reds, cut with blond. She rather liked her hair's color.

And she hoped Lord Merriman would appreciate everything
about her appearance this evening, especially the gown. It was cut
lower than what she usually wore, revealing more of her breasts.
From having overheard a conversation between Val and Con
once, she knew men appreciated the sight of a woman's breasts.

The earl was such an enigma to her. One minute, he blew
hot, filling her with heat and making her seem boneless as he
kissed her. Then he turned cold and haughty, barely acknowledg-
ing her existence. She knew he was attracted to her—just as she
was to him—but Tia did not understand why he would kiss her
and not wish to pursue her. He had never sent a single bouquet to
her, nor had he even visited once during morning calls. If

anything, he avoided her as if she carried the plague.

Then again, his duty was to his sister, and he must spend every afternoon chaperoning Dilly in their drawing room. Yet how many suitors could be calling upon her friend these days? Dilly had told her of the numerous flower arrangements she had received at the beginning of the Season, but as Dilly spent more and more time with Lord Forsythe, surely that number had begun to dwindle. With Dilly and Forsythe now becoming betrothed, Tia doubted any suitors would be calling upon her friend once the news of the couple's engagement was announced at tonight's musicale.

It should free up Lord Merriman. Lady Merriman would be enough to chaperone the couple, and from what Tia gathered, engaged couples were sometimes even left alone, in order to get to know one another better before they became husband and wife.

Should she be so bold as to invite the earl to Val's drawing room some afternoon?

Sadly, Tia shook her head. She might try to tempt Lord Merriman tonight with her appearance, but she was not going to chase after him as she had seen many other young ladies do in pursuit of other eligible bachelors this Season. As far as making friends with others, she found most of the girls making their come-outs to be interested in only one thing—finding a husband. That single-minded purpose kept them from gaining friendships with other girls. It had been almost shameless how these young ladies, along with their mothers, had pursued the available gentlemen of the Season. No wonder Con liked to hide in the card room during balls.

She thought about her cousin Tray coming to town next Season. By now, Tray would have finished up his university studies. With Verina making her debut into Polite Society next Season, it would make sense for Tray to come to town for the first time. She doubted her cousin would be interested in securing a bride just yet. He had gained his title when he was but ten years of age, and Tray had become the man of the family at that time. It had been a heavy burden placed upon the shoulders of one so young, and she hoped he would come to the Season and relax, enjoying all it had to offer. Verina was eager for children, and Tia had no doubt that her younger cousin would make a fine match next Season.

Venturing downstairs, she found Val and Eden in the foyer.

"Where is Mama?" she asked.

"Mama said she is tired and told us to go without her this evening," her brother informed her.

Missing an event was not like Mama. "She is not ill, is she?"

"Not at all," he assured her. "I think Mama is ready to have a quiet evening to herself."

They went to the carriage and a short time later arrived at Lord and Lady Tallon's townhouse. This was the first musicale Tia had attended, and she was looking forward to it. She also could not wait to watch Dilly and Lord Forsythe share their good news with those in attendance. Lady Merriman was right. After tonight's announcement, most everyone would learn of the betrothal by tomorrow night's ball. She wondered when the engagement announcement might appear in the newspapers.

As they entered the townhouse, she saw there was no receiving line, which was a relief. In the carriage, Val had told her sometimes a musicale took place in a ballroom, but oftentimes, the smaller number of guests invited could be accommodated in a drawing room or library. The Tallons' butler took them upstairs to the drawing room now, and she saw the furniture had been moved back against the walls, and chairs had been brought in, placed in rows in a U-shape. She spoke with several others and then saw Dilly arrive. Her friend simply glowed with happiness, and Tia knew it was a love match. She had come to know Lord Forsythe better since the beginning of the Season, and Tia thought the pair simply perfect together.

The couple made their way toward Val, Eden, and her now, with Lord Merriman and his mother following.

"You look splendid," she cried, embracing Dilly.

"I was about to say the same about you, Tia," Dilly exclaimed. "This gown is gorgeous on you. And those earrings simply make it. You will be wearing these earrings for many years to come."

She smiled and saucily replied, "I suppose my cardplaying skills paid off."

They both laughed, and she glanced to her left, seeing Lord Merriman looking at her as if she were a morsel he wished to gobble up.

Good.

"Good evening, my lady."

"Good evening, Lord Merriman," she said coolly, not seeming to encourage him. The gown is what would reel him in. She only wished she could dance with him this evening, but dancing did not go on at a musicale. Then Tia chided herself. The earl was not a fish to reel in. If he were only taken with her physical beauty, she would find him dull and uninteresting. She almost regretted wearing the gown now, thinking she had been wrong trying to appeal to him.

"I hear tonight's gathering is small," he said to her as the others began speaking with Val and Eden.

"Yes, I could tell by the number of chairs set out for the performance."

His gaze burned into her as she asked, "Do you really wish to talk about the number of guests present tonight, my lord? Or do you have something else to say to me?"

Before he could reply, the Duke of Reddington appeared at his elbow. "Why, Lady Tia, you are the most beautiful woman present this evening. I must compliment you on your gown. The color is exquisite."

"Thank you, Your Grace. I have not seen much of you lately," she told him, batting her lashes at him. Perhaps it wouldn't hurt to have Lord Merriman the tiniest bit jealous, even though Tia had no interest in the Duke of Reddington.

"I heard at White's today how you won at cards last night," the duke said. "Are those the earrings which were the prize Lady Swarthmore offered?"

"They are indeed, Your Grace. Thank you for noticing them. I have no other jewels, and so I will wear these proudly, having earned them."

The two of them spoke back and forth, Lord Merriman simply listening to the conversation. Yet the entire time she spoke with Reddington, Tia was very aware of the earl's presence.

Their host got their attention, asking everyone to take a seat. Her group filed into a row, and she wound up with the duke on one side of her and Lord Merriman on the other, at the end of the row. Blithely, she ignored him, continuing her conversation with the duke.

Then Lord and Lady Tallon appeared at the front, and the guests fell silent, turning their attention to their host and hostess.

Clearing his throat, Lord Tallon said, "We are greatly honored tonight to have Fräulein Engel singing for us. She has dazzled audiences across Europe, and tonight will be no different."

Lord Tallon held out his hand, and the opera singer approached. A string quartet began tuning their instruments as the fräulein took her place in front of those gathered.

In perfect English, with only a slight accent, she said, "Thank you for having me this evening. I look forward to performing for you." Then she looked to the musicians and nodded.

For the next hour, Tia was transported. The music took her to another time and place, and she was lost in Fräulein Engel's angelic voice.

The applause was thunderous when the opera singer nodded brusquely and moved from being the center of attention. Lord Tallon took her place.

"We will take a brief respite before the fräulein sings for us again. Lady Tallon has planned some light refreshments. You can find them in the library. Our servants will direct you there."

"It was transformative, wasn't it?" Lord Merriman said quietly.

It had certainly been so. Tia had not been aware of him next to her during the singer's performance.

"I finally understand how you must feel when you play," she told him. "You have always seemed to become lost in the piece you play. I found myself mesmerized as the fräulein sang."

"Have you attended the opera this Season?"

"No, I have not. I did go with Val and Eden to the theater one night. I realize now that I was as caught up in the actors' performance as I was in Fräulein Engel's singing tonight. It is wonderful to discover how art can move a person."

"The fräulein will be singing in a new production early next week. Perhaps you might care to attend one of the performances with me."

A thrill shot through Tia. Smiling, she said, "I would enjoy doing so, my lord."

"I will arrange for a box then. Dilly and Lord Forsythe might wish to accompany us. We could even stop afterward for a late supper."

"That would be a most wonderful evening," she said, trying to contain her excitement.

She did not worry about a chaperone at that point. She wasn't certain if by being betrothed, Dilly might act as a chaperone for her. Or perhaps Lord Merriman would bring his mother along for that purpose. All Tia knew was that her spirits were soaring. For the first time this Season, she was truly happy.

"Are we going for refreshments?" Eden asked.

Glancing up, she saw only she and Lord Merriman were seated on their row, blocking the others from passing. Quickly, she stood as he did the same, stepping aside and allowing her to exit the row.

He offered his arm to her. "May I escort you to the library, my lady?"

"Thank you," she said, placing her fingers atop his sleeve,

experiencing that frisson of electricity that she now believed was desire as she brushed against him.

Most of the other guests had already arrived in the library, and she was displeased when she caught sight of Lord Balch. She had gone to visit Lia today, and as they had strolled in the park, Tia had shared with her twin of how the viscount had behaved so poorly after their win at cards. Lia had been appalled that a gentleman would act in such an ugly manner, much less in front of a drawing room full of others.

She noticed Lord Balch stood with Lord Calley. This was a man Tia had danced with once early in the Season, and his flirtatious manner had made her uncomfortable. Val had confirmed it, telling her to avoid Lord Calley in the future. If she had known that Lord Calley was a bosom friend of Lord Balch, she would never have agreed to partner with Lord Balch at cards.

Lord Merriman steered them away so they would not encounter the pair, who eyed them with interest. Then Lady Tallon rang a tiny bell, claiming their attention.

"We have some most wonderful news to share with our guests this evening."

Tia knew this must be the announcement regarding Dilly's betrothal.

"I have been informed by Lady Merriman that her daughter, Lady Delilah Drake, is now engaged to the Earl of Forsythe."

Polite applause broke out, and Tia watched her friend blush at being the center of attention.

"Come," Lord Tallon said, waving the couple over to join him and his wife.

Footmen now arrived with trays of champagne, and Tia took a flute, ready to celebrate her friends. Once all the guests had champagne in hand, Lord Tallon raised his flute.

"A toast to Lady Delilah and Lord Forsythe. May they find lasting happiness together."

As she sipped the bubbly liquid, which tickled her nose, happiness filled Tia. Her friend had chosen well. Lord Forsythe would make for a fine husband.

"This certainly is good news," Reddington said, joining them. "I have enjoyed getting to know Forsythe since you have brought him to White's with you several times, Merriman. I believe he will make Lady Delilah very happy. Congratulations, old friend, in helping find your sister a husband."

"I liked Forsythe from the beginning," Lord Merriman said. "He was taken with Dilly from their first meeting. I do not believe any other gentleman would suit Dilly as well as Forsythe does."

Suddenly, Lord Balch and Lord Calley joined their small circle of three.

"Your Grace," the two men said deferentially, in unison.

An odd feeling swept over Tia, and she wished to turn away from these supposed gentlemen. She glanced to Lord Merriman to ask him if they might get some punch, but his gaze was fastened upon the pair.

"So, your sister is engaged to be wed, *Merriman*," Lord Calley remarked.

She did not like the tone Lord Calley used.

"The two of you favor one another quite a bit," Lord Balch added. "Calley and I had not put it together before this evening." His gaze bore into Lord Merriman.

"Put what together?" she asked, dread now filling her.

Balch smiled, a chilling smile, which caused Tia to shiver.

"Calley and I realized upon hearing the name Drake—and seeing that Lady Deliliah is your sister—that we knew you from before, Merriman. As Hugo Drake."

Lord Calley's eyes gleamed. "Do you recall our schooldays, Drake? My, we had such fun, didn't we?"

She sensed Lord Merriman tensing next to her and did not know what to do or say. Her eyes flicked to the duke, and she saw concern on his face.

"Wh-wh-what's the m-matter, Drake?" Lord Balch said, affecting a stammer. "Has the c-c-cat got your t-t-tongue?"

Suddenly, everything became crystal clear to Tia. How Lord Merriman always seemed to take his time before he spoke. How he sometimes paused in the middle of a sentence, as if having to gather his thoughts. How his speech was very deliberate, much more so than anyone else she had ever spoken with.

He had stammered as a boy—and these two had made fun of him for doing so.

Anger now came off Lord Merriman in waves. "G-g-get away from m-me," he said, turning scarlet. "I d-d-d-do not wish t-to speak t-t-to you."

She winced, pity filling her as he reverted to stammering.

"Poor Drake," lamented Lord Calley. "You might have grown into an imposing figure, but that sad little boy who could barely utter a word is still hiding just below your surface." He looked to Tia. "I would avoid this man's company, my lady. After all, if you wed, your children might be as cursed as he is."

"B-B-Bastard," Lord Merriman got out.

Tia saw anger, mixed with panic—and fear—now filling the earl's face. She placed a hand on his arm, but he shook it off.

"You are p-p-p-pathetic," he spat out. "The t-t-two of y-you r-r-r . . . almost d-destroyed m-m-me."

Lord Balch beamed. He looked around, waving a hand, and she saw the entire library of guests were now looking on in horror. "I see you have already done that to yourself, my lord."

With a cry of anguish, Lord Merriman fled the room. She watched as Dilly and Lord Forsythe, their faces drained of color, raced after him. Lady Merriman, her head held high, went to Lord and Lady Tallon.

"Thank you for your kind invitation," she said, her face giving nothing away.

The room filled with silence as the countess left the library. Then everyone was abuzz with gossip. Tia turned on the pair of laughing men, her voice raised, causing all those present to take note.

"You should be ashamed of yourselves. As boys, you intimidated a child because he had a speech defect. It is obvious you harassed him to a point where you almost broke him. And you humiliate him tonight, even as adults? Your brutish behavior is mean-spirited."

Lord Calley laughed harshly. "You are aligning yourself with a very flawed man, Lady Tia. You deserve to raise brats with Merriman that blubber on, barely able to communicate."

Heat filled her face. "I am not betrothed to Lord Merriman," she declared. "His sister is my closest friend, and I would not see you sully his reputation. Teasing amongst boys is one thing, my lord. Bullying is quite something else. I would think as a grown man, you would be past such terrible behavior."

"Your own behavior is lacking, my lady," Lord Calley shot back. "Why, I doubt there will be a gentleman within the *ton* now who would want someone as outspoken as yourself as his wife."

"Enough!" cried Val, rushing across the room. "You will not besmirch my sister's reputation, simply for defending a—"

"Do you wish to duel, Your Grace?" Lord Calley demanded.

"No, Val," Tia said, moving to her brother and taking his forearm, willing him not to reply. "Dueling is about honor. These two cads have none. They only blacken their own reputations when they defame Lord Merriman or me. The members of Polite Society will see they are the ones with tarnished reputations. I beg you not to meet either of them on the field."

She knew her brother was an excellent shot. If he killed either of these men, he would have to flee to the Continent and never be able to return to England.

His face, dark with rage, caused her to add, "You are the head of our family. Do not give this pair the satisfaction of drawing you into a duel. You would have to live abroad the rest of your life because you would easily kill these spineless men. Think of Eden—and William."

"But they have insulted you, Tia," her brother insisted.

"I care not for their insults," she declared. "I trust Polite Society will see these two for what they are. Despicable, immature, dishonorable fools." Slipping her arm through Val's, she added, "They are not worthy of our time, Brother. Let us leave."

As she and Val turned, Lord Calley shouted, "Coward!"

Tia spun about, hurrying to him. She paused, looking at him steadily. "*You* are the gutless poltroon, my lord. Not Millbrooke."

Then she slapped him. Hard. The pain raced from her stinging palm, reverberating up her arm, but she kept her face a blank, not wanting to give him the smallest bit of satisfaction.

Returning to Val, she linked her arm through his. They headed toward Eden, whose face was as white as a ghost's. She trembled visibly, but she smiled at her husband, slipping her arm through his free one. The three of them headed straight for their hosts, who stood slack-jawed.

"Thank you for a lovely evening," Eden said calmly, looking every bit the duchess she was. "I am sorry we have to leave before hearing Fräulein Engel sing again."

In unison, they stepped from the room. By the time they reached the foyer, Tia was shaking all over. Their carriage was quickly summoned, and Val handed them up.

Once inside the vehicle, Eden burst into tears, and Val pulled his wife into his lap, shushing her, giving her light, reassuring kisses. She buried her face in his chest, and he looked to Tia.

"The repercussions from tonight's events will affect you," he said quietly. "More than it will us. If you would like, we can return to Millvale in the morning."

Anger sizzled through her. "Leave town? And let those bloody bastards think they have won?" She shook her head. "I will not turn tail and let them run us out of town, Val. If anything, I plan to go to every social event and hold my head high. I did nothing wrong. *They* are the ones in the wrong."

Her brother sighed. "The gossip will be malicious. What happened tonight will be embellished and greatly exaggerated by those present tonight until the event will in no way resemble what actually occurred. While Merriman's reputation will be affected, *you* will suffer the most, Tia."

"Why do you think so?"

"Because you came to Merriman's defense. Bravely, yes, but your name will be linked with his. It will be impossible for you to make a match this Season because of it."

She huffed. "You know I was not attending the Season this year to land a husband."

"I know," he said gently. "But your name will be associated with Lord Merriman's all the same. Any gentleman previously interested in you will now shy away."

"Then let him," she declared. "I plan to remain in town. I do not care what the gossips say."

He looked at her sadly. "I hope you know what you are doing. We will have to alert Mama to what occurred in order to prepare her. Lia and Rupert. Ariadne and Julian. They need to know because they, too, will face gossip merely because of their association with you."

"What about Lord Calley and Lord Balch? Shouldn't they be the focus of the gossip?"

"They will face some," Val assured her. "But you standing up for Lord Merriman, even in his absence, will be a bigger part of the story. I only hope you can weather the storm ahead."

CHAPTER SEVENTEEN

HUGO BLINDLY LEFT the room, the many faces staring at him a blur. He raced down the stairs and when he reached the foyer, he pushed past the footman, flinging open the door himself and hurrying out into the night. All he wanted was the safety of his carriage.

He found his coachman, who looked startled to see him, and threw open the door, leaping into the carriage and slamming the door behind him. Panting, he dropped his head into his hands.

Everything was ruined. His secret was out. His two chief persecutors had finally taken enough notice of him to recognize Lord Merriman as the pathetic boy they had abused. By confronting him in front of other members of Polite Society—and especially in Lady Tia Worthington's presence—he had been so rattled that his stutter had reappeared. All the years of working daily, trying to overcome his deficiency, had been shattered in a few moments.

He tore at his hair, a growl coming from him, as he felt the life he had carefully built slip through his fingers. Though the gathering at Lord and Lady Tallon's had been small, every person present in that library would share his or her account of what they had witnessed. The gossip would spread like wildfire, and he would no longer be welcomed at social affairs. Or worse, he would attend one and find that others mocked him, either behind his back—or to his face.

He worried about the consequences of tonight's debacle and how much Dilly might be affected. Would Lord Forsythe withdraw his offer of marriage, seeing that his brother-in-law was the laughingstock of Polite Society? Or would Forsythe do the honorable thing and keep fast to his commitment to Dilly?

The door opened. He raised his head and saw Dilly enter the vehicle, her eyes filled with tears. She sat across from him, taking his hands.

"Oh, I am so sorry, Hugo."

"No, I am the o-one who should apologize. F-for ruining your night."

Mama took a seat beside him, placing a hand on his leg. "It will be all right, Merriman."

"No. It most certainly will not, Mama," he said bitterly, watching his sister's fiancé join them inside the vehicle. He thought it a good sign when Forsythe linked his fingers with Dilly's.

Then the earl looked at Hugo. "My feelings toward Lady Dilly are steadfast. My commitment to her—and this family— unwavering. You have my support, Lord Merriman."

"You have a good heart, Forsythe," he said wearily, trying his best to watch his speech, even in front of those dearest to him. "I do not expect you . . . to stand by my side in this matter. I appreciate your . . . loyalty to my sister, however. Hopefully, the two of you can wed q-quietly. For me, I shall return to the country."

"No," Mama said, her tone resolute. "Those men will not chase you from town." She reached for his hand and squeezed it. "I knew sending you away to school would be awful, Hugo, but your father insisted. You were but a small boy then, powerless against the bullies who bedeviled you. Your suffering was great— but you are a grown man now. You are an earl. A wealthy earl. Why, you are friends with two dukes."

"Do you truly think Reddington or M-Millbrooke can support me through such troubles, Mama?" he asked.

"I believe your friends are your friends and will remain so," she said, confidence in her voice. "If you allow those two dishonorable scalawags to affect the way you think of yourself, then you are dicked in the nob."

He grimaced. "I am not mad, Mama. Merely trying . . . to be practical. No one will be comfortable in my presence. No one— even a loyal friend—should be forced to take a stance with me. I cannot attend any social events. Because the gossip will fill the room."

Hugo squeezed her fingers. "I have already made much of your life miserable as it is."

"Do not say such a thing," she huffed. "Your father is the one who ruined both our lives. Thankfully, we are rid of him."

"Well, now that Forsythe here will not abandon Dilly, it m-matters not if I go to social affairs."

"Give it some time, Lord Merriman," Forsythe said. "Yes, the gossips will be in full force the next few days, but they will move on to another topic. There will be another couple who elopes to Gretna Green, or some lady will be compromised by a rake. After a week, you will be of little interest to them."

He met Forsythe's gaze. "Do you truly think so?"

The man shrugged. "Isn't that how gossip works? The gossip mill will churn on, feeding upon new victims to smear."

Though Hugo understood in theory what Forsythe said, he doubted it would be true in this instance. He imagined entering a ballroom or White's. Immediately, talk would die as others scrutinized him.

Even worse, he had finally decided because Dilly was spoken for that he might test the waters and see if Lady Tia had any interest in him. Now, however, she would avoid him at all costs.

Sighing, he promised, "I will not leave town. To do so would be victory for those two bloody cocksuckers. I still feel you should wed. In a quiet affair."

Dilly sniffed. "I will not let those two men dictate what my wedding will be like. Mama and I have an appointment with

Madame Laurent tomorrow afternoon so that she might create a wedding gown for me. I will not be rushed. Lord Forsythe and I will have the ceremony we wish to have. *When* we wish to have it. And *where* we choose to speak our vows."

"I admire your gumption, Dilly," he told her. "And your loyalty, my lord," he said to Forsythe. Looking to his mother, he said, "I am sorry about how . . . I responded . . . to this evening. I should not have fled the scene." He hesitated. "If you do not wish for me to be at your wedding, Dilly, I would understand."

She burst into tears. "You must come, Hugo, else I will not wed."

"I will be there," he assured her, still hoping she would have nothing to do with him so that she and the family she created would not be tainted by association.

The coachman drove to Lord Forsythe's first, and he told them goodnight, promising to visit with them at tea tomorrow afternoon.

"I will also go to White's in the morning and see what damage has been done. And I must extract a promise from you, my lord."

Knowing how loyal the earl had been to his sister, he nodded. "Anything."

"I know you will not want to attend tomorrow night's ball."

"Heavens, n-no!"

"But as I said, the gossip will end. You say you will remain in town. Skip the next few events, but after a week's time, I believe you should return to socializing. Let Polite Society see you are not cowed by those two blackguards."

Though it pained him to think of facing others, Hugo nodded, and the earl departed. The carriage started up again, and they remained silent the rest of the way home. He told himself he must double the time he practiced each day. Read aloud more. Sing more. Anything to rebuild his shattered confidence.

When they reached home, he bid his mother and sister goodnight.

"You are not retiring?" Mama asked.

"I think I will go play my pianoforte," he told her, knowing the instrument would bring him comfort.

Retreating to the music room, he sat before his instrument, cracking his knuckles before beginning to play. He launched into a complicated invention by Bach, knowing the tricky fingering would command all his attention. He needed to have something to keep his mind from going back to those horrifying moments when he had been humiliated. The fact it had occurred in front of Lady Tia upset him all the more.

Hugo played for a long time, but he could not find solace in music tonight. He wondered if he ever would again. He cursed Balch and Calley aloud, thinking they were still taking things from him, and shouted, "I will not let you rob me of anything else!"

"Good. I was hoping you would come around."

Wheeling, he saw Matthew sitting nearby, his ankle casually crossed over his knee as he slouched in the chair.

Standing, Hugo confronted him. "Why are you h-here?"

"I thought you might like to know what happened after you left the musicale."

Panic filled him. He rushed to his friend, lifting his hands, examining the knuckles.

"No, I did not beat either Calley or Balch to a bloody pulp." Matthew grinned. "I would have liked to. Lady Tia did slap Calley, however."

"She *what*?"

"You heard me."

He sank into a chair before his knees buckled and sent him crashing to the floor. "No. She did not."

"She did," his friend insisted. "Calley was completely taken off-guard. It is too bad Lady Tia did not punch him in the nose and bloody him. As it was, the outline of her palm was stark against Calley's cheek. He and Balch slithered off."

Leaning forward, Hugo rested his forearms on his thigh. "Tell me. Tell me everything."

He listened as Matthew recounted the events in the library after Hugo had left. How his mother had conducted herself as a true lady, thanking their hosts with composure and departing. Then how Lady Tia dressed down Balch and Calley in front of the crowd.

"She was magnificent in her defense of you, Hugo. Of course, Calley did his best to malign her in front of everyone, so much so that her brother sprang to her defense."

"I would expect no less from His Grace. Millbrooke is a true gentleman in every sense of the word, unlike those two scoundrels who plagued me tonight."

"Things grew heated," Matthew continued. "Then Calley taunted His Grace, asking him if he wished to duel."

"*Duel?* Oh, please, tell me no. That the duke . . . had sense enough . . . not to fall into such a trap."

Matthew shrugged. "I believe His Grace would have been quick to agree to such a thing, but Lady Tia intervened." He thought a moment. "She said that dueling was about honor and that Calley and Balch had none. She refused to let Millbrooke agree to a duel, even though they had greatly insulted her."

He felt even worse than he had in the heat of the moment, when he could not get out a few words without stammering. While it had been admirable of Lady Tia to defend him, she had been foolish to do so, and he told that to Matthew now.

"Lady Tia seems to believe in the goodness of mankind. That Polite Society will shun Balch and Calley for their actions," his friend revealed.

"I doubt it," he said flatly. "She has ruined herself. For me. And there is nothing that I can do . . . to repair her reputation."

"You could offer for her."

"Wh-what?"

"You heard me, Hugo. I said offer for her. Any woman willing to defend a man so heatedly—and even strike one of his detractors—must hold feelings for you." Matthew paused. "And I suspect you have feelings for Lady Tia, as well."

Raking his hands through his hair in frustration, he said, "Even if I did, I doubt she wants to have anything to do with me, Matthew. Or even if she did, Millbrooke would . . . stand in the way. He will not see his sister wed to the likes . . . of me."

"So, you do have feelings for her?" Matthew pressed.

"I do," he finally admitted to his friend.

And himself.

"Then you must act upon them."

"I let my family convince me not to leave for Merrifield. They thought if I did so that I would never forgive myself. For backing down in such a manner. I agree with them. I do not want to be chased off. But it is one thing to take a stand in Polite Society. It is quite another to . . . risk everything . . . and offer marriage to a woman whom I am not even certain likes me."

He rose. "No. For now, I will remain in town. Lick my wounds a bit before I appear at another *ton* event. It would be mad to offer for Lady Tia now. If ever."

Matthew came to his feet. "I have advised you what to do. I cannot put words into your mouth."

"Much less . . . say them for me," he teased.

Matthew laughed. "There is that. Let me know when you are ready to seek the company of Polite Society again, Hugo. I will go with you to White's. Accompany you—and your sister and Forsythe—to any event."

"The one good thing which came from this evening . . . was finding the depth of the earl's feelings for Dilly. If he will not abandon her over something such as what we witnessed tonight, then I know he will remain every faithful to her."

He went to the decanter and poured brandy into two snifters. Handing one to Matthew, he said, "To better days ahead."

They clinked glasses and downed the brandy. It burned the entire way down to his belly.

"Go home and get some sleep, Matthew. Thank you again for coming to me and relating all that went on in my absence."

"We are friends for life, Hugo. Nothing you could do would ever chase me away."

He wondered if he had lost Millbrooke or Dyer's friendship over tonight's episode.

And if he would ever have the courage to see if Lady Tia might wish to pursue a relationship with him.

CHAPTER EIGHTEEN

TIA AWOKE THE next morning and found Lia sitting beside the bed. Seeing her sister caused Tia to burst into tears.

"It will be all right," Lia said, stroking Tia's hair.

"Did Val send for you? Eden?" she asked.

Lia smiled serenely. "No. I woke up last night and knew something was wrong. I got out of bed and paced the bedchamber, waking Rupert. He convinced me to return to bed, but I did not sleep a wink after that. At first light, I rose and dressed, and we came straight here. Val was at breakfast. He told us what happened last night at the musicale."

Tears blurred her eyes. "Oh, Lia, it was so awful. Lord Balch and Lord Calley are terrible men. They apparently terrorized Lord Merriman when they were at school together years ago. He stammered as a boy, and I can only imagine how cruel they were to him."

"Lord Merriman is such a thoughtful, kind man," her twin said. "He must have worked incredibly hard to lose his stammer."

"I have noticed how deliberately he speaks. He must need to concentrate anytime he speaks. No wonder he often lets others dominate the conversation."

"Val said Lord Merriman left the musicale very upset."

Tia nodded. "He was. I wanted . . . to go after him. I wish I had."

"Instead of slapping Lord Calley?" Lia asked, grinning at her.

"Oh, so Val really did tell all." She sighed. "I could not help myself. Lord Calley was trying to goad Val into a duel, which was utter insanity. Val is a wonderful shot."

"I assume Lord Calley believed Val would have deloped," Lia said, referring to the practice of wasting a first shot in a duel by firing into the ground or in the air. "Then Lord Calley could have done the same, without losing his honor."

Tia snorted. "I would not have trusted Lord Calley to behave honorably under any circumstances. If Val deloped, Lord Calley may well have fired upon Val—and we would have lost our brother. Eden would have no husband, and William would have grown up without his father." She shivered. "Even though Val was trying to keep my reputation from being tainted, I have implored him to walk away from the idea of a duel."

Lia looked puzzled. "If Val was going to honor your wishes and walk away, why did you strike Lord Calley?"

She sighed. "Because he called Val a coward for listening to me. I couldn't help myself, Lia. I was so angry in that moment. Lord Calley and Lord Balch made a mess of a perfectly delightful evening, one I was enjoying very much."

"With Lord Merriman."

"Yes," she said, tears now spilling down her cheeks. "I have been quite ambivalent in regard to my feelings toward Lord Merriman, but I believed our relationship was turning a corner last night. I had high hopes, only to see them dashed by those two fools. They humiliated Lord Merriman. Ruined the betrothal announcement of Dilly and Lord Forsythe. Called my integrity— and Val's—into question."

"I do not think Lord Merriman will hold the actions of them against you, Tia," Lia said softly. "Especially if he has developed feelings for you."

"He was shamed in front of everyone, Lia. Not just me. He began stammering when he spoke. It was agony watching him trying to say what he wished to. I did not hide my shock, and he would have noticed it. I am a reminder of his greatest failure in front of the *ton*. There is no going back to how things were." She hiccupped. "And no moving forward for us either."

Tia burst into tears, sobs racking her body. Lia climbed into the bed, holding her fast, crying along with her. Her tears soaked Lia's gown, and she apologized. She placed a palm against her sister's belly, which was more noticeable these days.

"I have upset you. That cannot be good for your babe."

"I was already upset," Lia said. I knew you were in distress. I only wish I had come to you last night."

"Talk about anything else but last night," she begged. "Nothing about the Season. Let us speak about the babe or Crestbrook."

They lay together, talking of everything which concerned her sister these days. How Lia wondered what childbirth would be like. If Rupert would find her body attractive as it swelled.

"Rupert adores you. He will continue to adore you," Tia assured her twin. "And while childbirth is sure to be painful, look at William. He is the light of Val's and Eden's eyes. The same is true of Penelope. Ariadne and Julian adore their daughter. Nor do I see either Val or Julian coming up short in paying attention to their wives. Rupert will be the same."

"I hope so." Lia paused. "If you do not wed after the Season ends, will you come to Cumberland with us? Stay for the babe's birth?"

Tia laughed. "If any man had the idea to make me his bride, I am certain that thought will have died after last night's happenings. I promise to come to you. I need to see when Dilly and Forsythe will wed. I must attend their wedding."

Lia's brow furrowed. "Do you believe Forsythe will still wed Lady Dilly after what happened last night?"

"Of course. Forsythe is not a fickle man. He is very protective of Dilly. They had not set a date for their marriage. With what happened last night, they may even wish to wed quietly, without any fuss." She stroked her twin's cheek. "But once they are wed, I will be happy to come to Crestbrook. In fact, I will stay with you until you return for the Season next spring if you would like for me to do so. As long as Rupert does not mind."

"Oh, that would wonderful, Tia. Rupert is so fond of you. He knows I am happier when you are near."

"I think I will call on Dilly this morning and see about her wedding plans," she announced. "Would you like to come with me? You can be my chaperone."

"I would be delighted to do so," Lia declared.

Instead of ringing for a maid to help her dress, Lia attended Tia, making her feel as if it were the old days again. They went downstairs and found Val and Rupert still in the breakfast room. Eden had joined them. Tia was glad that Mama usually remained in her rooms until noon. At some point, Mama would have to be told of last night's events, and she dreaded that conversation.

"How are you?" Eden asked, her worry for Tia obvious.

"I am well." She held up her hand. "My palm is still tingling some, though," she teased.

"Remind me to always be on your side if a fight breaks out," Val said, laughing.

"I would like to go and see Dilly now," she told them. "Lia has volunteered to go with me."

"Do you think it wise to go to Lord Merriman's house?" Eden questioned. "We know the gossip will be ferocious for a few days."

"I need to see Dilly," she insisted. "She would want me there."

"I agree with Eden," Val said. "While I know Dilly is your friend, it *is* Lord Merriman's residence. It might not be the wisest move to be seen entering it, Tia. We already know your name will be coupled with Lord Merriman's, whether you wish it to be or not."

"What if Lady Dilly took a ride in our carriage with you?" Rupert suggested. "I could go to the door and see if she might be available. Lia and Tia could wait in the coach. If no one sees Tia, then no one is the wiser."

"I like that idea," Eden said. "Do you need me to accompany you?"

"No," Tia said. "But if you would help Val explain things to Mama, that would be very helpful."

Eden laughed. "Oh, you are quite the character, Tia."

"Val has a better chance of . . . stating things in a unique way," she said. "If I tell Mama about the incident, she will most likely banish me to the country for the rest of the Season. Mama has always favored Val. His narrative of the situation would be much more acceptable than mine ever could be."

Lia spoke up. "Tia is right. Val can do no wrong in Mama's eyes. He will break the news to her in a way Mama will find acceptable."

"Just do not tell her that Calley challenged you to a duel," Tia added. "Or maybe you should. The thought of losing you in a duel will drive the thought of my actions totally from her mind."

"Leave it to me," her brother assured her. "I will lay the groundwork and then tell Mama only what she needs to know. I doubt anyone—even her friends—will address the matter with her."

"Shall we go to the carriage then?" asked Rupert.

He escorted them outside, and Tia gave the coachman the address. They arrived a few minutes later.

"Wait here. I may be gone several minutes," Rupert told them. "I will also give you time to speak privately. I can have our coachman leave me at White's."

"You are kind to do this for me, Rupert," Tia said.

Her brother-in-law patted her hand and exited the carriage. He returned ten minutes later.

"I spoke with Lady Merriman and explained that I was wed to your twin, Tia. She finally granted permission for her daughter to ride with you, understanding how it might not be the wisest thing for Tia to visit Lady Dilly at home. They have an appointment at the modiste's at one o'clock this afternoon, so you must have Lady Dilly back no later than half-past twelve."

Relief flooded her. "The appointment is for Dilly's wedding gown. If she is keeping that, all must be well between her and Lord Forsythe."

Moments later, the carriage door opened, and Dilly climbed in. She fell into Tia's arms, and they hugged tightly, both of them crying.

"Thank you for coming to see me," Dilly said. "Lord Cressley explained why you did not come in, and Mama agreed that was best."

By now, the carriage was heading through the streets of London, and Rupert said that he would leave them shortly. No one spoke until they arrived at White's. Rupert kissed Lia, and then told Tia and Dilly goodbye.

Once the footman closed the carriage door, Tia asked, "How is Lord Merriman?"

"I have not seen him today," Dilly admitted. "But I do know that Reddington stopped by last night. Alfie—Hugo's valet—told me so. They have been good friends for several years now. I am certain Reddington's visit helped my brother."

"I assume because you are to see the modiste that your wedding is still on," Tia said.

Dilly brightened. "Oh, yes, it is. Forsythe was a rock last night, a steadying hand for all of us. He will not desert me at such a time. He continues to offer his friendship and support to Hugo."

"Do you know when you might wed?" Lia asked.

"We are not certain of our plans yet. All I know is that those two clods will not force me to wed quickly, nor will Hugo leave town for the country."

That was good news. Tia had worried that Lord Merriman might quit town abruptly after what had happened.

"Will you be at tonight's ball?" she asked.

"Forsythe and I will attend. Mama will serve as my chaperone." She hesitated. "I know Hugo does not plan to come to any events for a week or so, but he will return after that. Forsythe convinced him that Hugo is not the one in the wrong. *He* was the injured party." She bit her lip. "I only hope the *ton* recognizes that and responds accordingly."

"It is good Lord Merriman will return to events," Lia said. "That is encouraging news." Her gaze met Tia's.

"Yes, Lia is right. While it will help Lord Merriman to have a brief respite from Polite Society, it will be important for him to return—if only to face down the gossips, much less Lord Calley and Lord Balch."

"Do you think those two will even show their faces after last night?" Dilly asked worriedly.

She knew her friend had no idea of what had gone on after her departure, and Tia was not going to explain the confrontation between Val, Lord Calley, and herself. Instead, she patted Dilly's hand.

"I think everything will turn out for the best."

Tia only hoped she would have a chance to speak to Lord Merriman soon. She feared he would brush her aside in order to spare her from any association with him.

And she was determined not to let that occur.

CHAPTER NINETEEN

AFTER THEY DROPPED Dilly at home in time for her to make her appointment with Madame Laurent, Tia and Lia returned to White's to retrieve Rupert. He entered the carriage, looking grim, which caused her heart to sink.

"What is it?" cried Lia.

But Tia already knew. Her brother-in-law did not have to voice his concerns because they were evident by looking at his face.

Lacing his fingers through his wife's, Rupert said, "We should talk about this with Val. I saw Julian just now, and he went home to retrieve Ariadne. They will meet us at Val's. Con will be there, as well."

It was even worse than Tia thought if the entire family in town would be gathering to discuss the situation. Lia sensed the tension and tried to speak of other things, but she finally gave up, and they rode in silence.

Once home, Parsons admitted them and told them everyone awaited them in the drawing room. As she climbed the stairs, Tia felt as if she were mounting the gallows to her execution. Suddenly, the gravity of the situation struck her. She had gone into the Season lighthearted, not worrying about whether or not she found her husband this year. Something told her that she might never find one after the events of last night, and she would die an old maid, set upon the shelf before she even reached a score.

When they entered the drawing room, she noticed Uncle Arthur and Aunt Charlotte were also present. Ever since her own father's death, Aunt Charlotte had stepped up, making herself the unofficial spokesman of the three related families. Her eyes cut to Mama, who sat looking lost, as if she had failed her children.

"Come join us," Aunt Charlotte ordered, and the three of them took seats in the group.

Her aunt's eyes flicked over Tia now. "This is nothing short of an unmitigated disaster," she crisply announced.

Mama made a noise of distress. "Oh, Charlotte, do you truly think so? Millbrooke is a duke. Everyone knows that dukes are a law unto themselves."

"Millbrooke will not go unscathed in this instance," Aunt Charlotte determined. "Then again, he is already wed, with an heir. It is Thermantia who stands to lose everything."

"I think things will blow over, Aunt Charlotte," her brother said. "Tia did nothing wrong." But Val did not look convinced by his own words.

"She stood up for a man. One severely lacking."

Her aunt's statement riled her. "You believe Lord Merriman is lacking simply because he stammered a bit? It was the first time we have heard him do so. He was provoked terribly by Lord Calley and Lord Balch. It was obvious they had bullied him as a child. Most likely, his stammer was a reflex."

"True," Aunt Charlotte conceded. "It would seem Merriman had outgrown it, but since he fell back into it so easily, it is apparent he merely has tried to control it all these years. You know as well as I do, Thermantia, that the *ton* harshly judges others, especially if they prove to be slightly different."

"I still do not see the problem," Mama protected. "Lord Merriman seems to be quite amiable. He is an earl and wealthy."

"Do you want your daughter stuck with someone such as he?" Aunt Charlotte demanded. "Do you wish for your grandchildren to stammer like idiots?"

Con spoke up. "You go too far, Mama."

Aunt Charlotte gave her son a withering look. "I do not go far enough."

Again, her aunt's words caused Tia's anger to bubble up, and she said, "There is no understanding between Lord Merriman and me." Then she burst into tears.

Lia wrapped an arm about her twin's shoulders. "Can you not be more supportive, Aunt?" Lia asked. "Obviously, Tia is very upset. She is hurting."

"She should wash her hands of Merriman. His sister, as well. Lady Delilah and Lord Forsythe will also be marked by this scandal," Aunt Charlotte predicted.

"How long do you believe the gossip will go on?" Eden asked. "Yes, two lords acted in a most ungentlemanly way toward Lord Merriman last night. And yes, the earl was most upset, stuttering a bit as he rebuked them."

Aunt Charlotte's brows rose. Her tone condescending, she told Eden, "It is not merely that. Thermantia dragged Millbrooke into the mess. Why, he was challenged to a *duel!*"

"A duel?" Mama echoed weakly, her dismay obvious. Looking to Val, she said, "You spoke of no duel, Millbrooke."

Val took charge of the situation. "That is because no duel was planned, nor will one be fought, Mama. One of those bloody fools was disparaging my sister, and I came to Tia's defense. This man threw out the notion of a duel, which neither Tia nor I considered for a moment. Duels are fought over honor, by men *with* honor. I think this scandal will die a quick death. Mama said it best. I am a duke, and while others might wish to gossip about this unfortunate incident, it will slide off me in the long run. Tia, too."

Aunt Charlotte's eyes held doubt. "Just because you say it will does not make it so, Millbrooke. I believe Thermantia's Season is over. You should return to Millvale and give the gossip time to die down."

Tia wiped angrily at the tears on her cheeks. "I refuse to let those two chase me from town," she declared. "They were in the wrong. Neither Val nor I were. If the *ton* needs to gossip about someone, it should be those two who are ostracized, their reputations in tatters."

"And yet the two of you will be the chief subject at tonight's ball if you attend it," her aunt predicted. "Merriman and his sister, as well."

"I just came from being with Lady Dilly," she revealed. "Lord Forsythe is standing beside her. They will still wed. He did not cry off."

Aunt Charlotte sniffed. "If they do wed, it should be done quickly and quietly, and then they should retreat from town. They are on the edge of this scandal. It would be best for the chit if she did wed and then chose to have nothing to do with her brother."

Lia said, "I think there is one thing we must address—and that is Tia's feelings toward Lord Merriman."

Suddenly, all eyes in the room were upon her, and Val gently asked, "Do you have feelings for Merriman? Do you love him?"

"No. Yes. I don't know," she said, frustration filling her. "I do have some kind of feelings toward him. I am not certain exactly what those feelings are. I believe he, too, has feelings where I am concerned. I thought we were on the verge of exploring them last night."

"No good will come of your association with this earl," Aunt Charlotte told her.

Uncle Arthur cleared his throat. "But if you do have tender feelings for him, my dear, I know you do not wish to thrust them aside. I have seen Lucy and Dru in love, and our daughters would both agree and tell you to see things to the end. If you do not, you will always regret it."

Ariadne finally spoke. "I agree, as well, Uncle Arthur. It is obvious Tia is confused by her feelings toward Lord Merriman, so she must resolve them before she can move forward." Her sister looked kindly at her. "If it is love, scandal will not kill it. Gossip may try to poison your relationship with Lord Merriman, but if you are meant to be together, you will find a way to do so."

"Thermantia should not even be seen with this earl," Aunt Charlotte complained. "If he is a true gentleman, he will not wish to ruin her future. He will have nothing to do with her."

"Then that would make Merriman and Tia miserable," Julian declared. "I agree with Val. When the next scandal arises—and we all know it will—the gossips will turn toward it in full force. While they are like a dog with a bone, if they are tossed fresh meat, the bone suddenly becomes obsolete."

New tears formed in Tia's eyes. "So, you are saying that I must wait for someone else to be facing scandal and heartbreak before I am able to resolve my own situation?"

Lia patted her on the back. "Lady Dilly did say that her brother would be absent from events for the next week or so. You would not be able to see him anyway, Tia."

"I say you continue attending the events to which we have accepted invitations," Val proclaimed. "You have the support of everyone in this room. Polite Society will see that we have rallied around you. I do not think they would lightly take to arousing the wrath of a duke."

Her gaze met her brother's. "You think I should go ahead and attend tonight's ball then?"

"I do," he confirmed.

She decided to wear the blush ballgown which she had been saving for a special occasion. Tia needed to look her absolute best tonight and would don the ballgown as her armor going into battle.

Hours later, she sat in her brother's ducal carriage. They rode in silence.

Mama took Tia's hand. "All will be well, Child," she said, trying to comfort Tia.

They joined the receiving line upon arrival. Everyone's gaze turned upon her as they did so.

"Chin up," Eden said quietly. "You have done nothing wrong.

Do not be cowed by their stares."

They reached their hosts for the evening, and Val introduced her to them. Instead of the usual warm greeting, the earl and his countess nodded brusquely, silently urging them to move on.

When they entered the ballroom, she saw everyone who had been gathered in the drawing room this afternoon standing together. Relief swept through her, knowing she had her family by her side. They joined the group, and Lia and Ariadne complimented her gown.

"You look like a Greek goddess," Ariadne praised. Her sister smiled. "I have never been prouder of you. You spoke out against an injustice you witnessed. Lord Merriman will learn of this. It will draw his favor."

Tia looked anxiously to everyone who entered the ballroom now. Each party deliberately moved the opposite way of where she and her family stood. No gentlemen came, asking to sign her programme. Her mouth grew dry. She wished to flee, and yet she knew it was important to remain in here tonight, calm and composed.

A gentleman finally approached, and she heard the audible sighs of relief come from those gathered around her.

As he drew closer, however, Val shook his head. He only did so when it was a known rake, and Tia knew he expected her to turn down a dance with this man.

Smiling, the newcomer said, "I assume your dance card is not filled as it usually is, Lady Tia. Let me do you the favor of dancing with me."

"I think not, my lord," she said politely.

His eyes cut to Val and then returned to her. The man shrugged. "Do not say I didn't warn you, my lady. You will be sitting amongst the wallflowers this evening—and every evening to come."

His words were like a knife to her heart.

She was then approached by a gentleman who looked to be in his mid-forties. Again, Val shook his head, and she politely declined.

He looked her in the eye. "If you wish to wed, my lady, you will not have the selection which has been available to you previously. I believe I will be the best you can do. If you change your mind, come and find me."

She was appalled by his words.

Another gentleman approached her, introducing himself. He was very socially awkward, and she asked, "Why have you not wished to dance with me before, Mr. Bannister?"

"You always have so many admirers about you, my lady." He swallowed. "I was challenged to ask you to a dance. I hope you will accept."

"And who might have issued this challenge to you?" she demanded.

He flushed scarlet. "Lord Balch and Lord Calley, my lady."

She drew in a quick breath, looking about the ballroom. She found Lord Balch standing beside Lord Calley. They each had a glass in their hands and raised it to her in a mock toast.

Her gaze returned to Mr. Bannister. "I do not accept dances issued on a dare," she said crisply. "I will not be dancing with you this evening, Mr. Bannister, nor any other evening."

It was almost time for the dancing to begin, and Tia had not collected one signature on her program. Val assured her that each of them in their family would dance with her.

"No," she refused. "I will take my place with the other ladies who are not otherwise engaged."

She saw the Duke of Reddington headed their way, and Tia hoped he would have news of Lord Merriman for her.

"Good evening," he greeted. "Lady Tia, might I claim a dance with you this evening?"

"You may, Your Grace," she responded, handing over her dance card to him.

"I would like to sign for the supper dance if that is agreeable with you."

She knew that would give them a chance to talk and nodded.

After the duke left, it seemed all eyes in the ballroom had been on them. Because of that, a few other gentlemen quickly came and signed her programme, none of whom she knew. Val did not shoo any of them off, so at least she would not stand on the sidelines all evening. Fortunately, one of them chose the opening set, and so it allowed her to be out on the dance floor when the dancing commenced.

She did, however, head to the area and sit when she was not engaged for a set. During one of those unclaimed times, she sat beside Miss Stanhope, whom she recognized from having played cards with earlier in the Season at Lady Swarthmore's.

"Miss Stanhope, it is so nice to see you this evening."

"I know I am not supposed to address such matters, Lady Tia, but I heard how you defended Lord Merriman last night at the musicale. While I know it has affected how Polite Society now views you, it is never the wrong time to do the right thing, no matter what the consequences."

"I will take your words to heart, Miss Stanhope, and I appreciate you sharing that with me."

Finally, Reddington came to her for the supper dance. She liked Lord Merriman's friend and told him after their dance that she appreciated that he had sought her out this evening.

As they moved toward the buffet room, she said, "Obviously, you saw my programme was blank before you signed it. At least by doing so, it caused a few others to brave the *ton*'s wrath and do the same."

"Do you mind if we take a table for two, Lady Tia?"

"I would prefer to do so, Your Grace."

He led her to a table and told a nearby footman not to allow anyone to sit at it. Then he guided her to the buffet line.

"I do not wish to have you sitting alone all that time."

"Again, I appreciate your consideration."

The duke helped fill her plate, but Tia was not very hungry. They returned to the table for two, the duke seating her.

"How is he?" she asked.

"As you might suspect, Merriman's spirits are low. I actually went to see him last night. I found him at his pianoforte, but even that did not seem to offer him much solace."

"I was with Dilly earlier today," she shared. "Dilly said that Lord Merriman would skip several events."

"He believes his absence for a week or more would be beneficial, both to his sister—and you. I must say that I admire you for turning out tonight, Lady Tia. It has not been easy for you."

"It most certainly has not," she agreed. Then she decided to ask him the question which burned in her heart. "Did Lord Merriman mention me last night?"

For the first time, the duke looked uncomfortable in her presence. "I believe anything my friend wishes to say to you should come from him. Not me."

She bit her lip. "I am afraid after what happened last night, he will push me away." She hesitated before adding, "That is the last thing I hope he will do."

Reddington offered her a small smile. "I think if you are open to a future with Merriman, he would feel the same."

Hope sprang within her. "Would you at least let him know I am thinking about him, Your Grace? That is, if you see him."

"I plan to visit him every day," the duke assured her. "I will let him know that you asked after him and would be receptive to a conversation with him."

She nodded. "That will be enough. I will ask nothing further of you."

"After I pass along your message, I will remove myself from the situation. I cannot resolve it for you." He grinned. "Much as I would like to."

As supper ended, Reddington asked, "Shall I escort you back to the ballroom?"

Knowing she had drawn no signatures for after the buffet, she said, "No. To Millbrooke's table instead. I believe we are going to make it an early night."

"Very well."

He rose and pulled out her chair, helping her to stand. Reddington walked her to Val. All the while, she could feel eyes upon her.

"Thank you, Your Grace," Mama said. "You are a true gentleman."

Reddington bowed and left.

Slipping into a chair, Tia told Eden, "I am engaged for no other dances tonight. Shall we make it an early evening and be in our beds before dawn for once?'

Eden sighed. "I would like nothing better. Val?"

"I think we did what we set out to accomplish," her brother said. "We came. We spoke to others. We danced. Let us retire."

They made their way to their hosts, thanking them for the evening. While the countess eyed them with disdain, the earl said, "It took courage for you to come this evening. Especially for you, Lady Tia."

She thanked him, and they departed the supper room, going straight to their carriage. Val had asked his coachman to park two streets down, facing away from the ball's site, in order to make for an easier departure.

Once they arrived home, she rang for a maid and undressed to ready herself for bed. Tia climbed beneath the bedclothes after placing the night rail over her head. She relaxed for the first time since the horrible encounter with Lord Balch and Lord Calley.

As she fell asleep, she decided to wait a week. If Lord Merriman had not yet made an appearance in Polite Society by that point, then she would go to him.

CHAPTER TWENTY

HUGO AWOKE, SURPRISED he had gotten any sleep at all. He rose and threw on some clothes without ringing for Alfie. Unwashed and unshaved, he ventured downstairs and out the door, heading straight to Hyde Park. The streets of Mayfair were quiet at this time of morning. Members of the *ton* would be sleeping now, having only returned to their beds from last night's ball only an hour or so ago.

He reached the park and entered it, knowing he would have it to himself for the next few hours. While a few gentlemen might ride in Rotten Row in an hour or two, the rest of the park would be deserted. No nannies or governesses bringing children here to entertain them for an hour or two. No carriages driving through, stopping to speak with others doing the same.

As he walked, he began singing aloud, his rich bass filling the air, mingling with the sounds of birds chirping. It was exhilarating to sing in the open air, no one around to judge him. Then he moved to reciting poetry, concentrating as his tongue formed the words to complicated lines. The practice did him good, helping to bolster his confidence, which had been shattered by Balch and Calley at the musicale.

Finishing up his recitation of a favorite Samuel Taylor Coleridge poem, he suddenly realized someone walked beside him and came to a halt, grateful to see Matthew there with him. His friend merely nodded, and they continued walking side-by-side for another good hour, no words necessary between them.

A melody kept playing over and over in his head. While Hugo had dabbled with writing a few piano compositions on his own over the last few years, none had come to him so fully formed as this one did. He let the melody play on, working out various chords to use with it, knowing his muse was none other than Lady Tia Worthington.

Matthew finally broke the silence. "Shall we sit a bit?"

He nodded, and they made their way to the closest bench. As he sat, weariness seemed to seep into his very bones.

"I suppose you are checking on me, as a physician might an ailing patient."

"What are friends for if not to be there when one is in need?"

They sat in companionable silence for several minutes, and then Matthew spoke again.

"It is worse than I would have suspected," he began.

Hugo had known he would be chewed up and spit out by the gossips of the *ton*, but he had not thought they would disparage him to his dearest friend.

"You must not defend me, Matthew. I do not want you to lose any of your standing in Polite Society because of your association with me. If you are to cut ties, I completely understand. I know you had mentioned searching for a bride this Season, and I—"

"I may have spoken of that. As usual, I have found no young lady who interests me enough to pursue the idea. And as far as abandoning you when you are in need? I thought you knew me better than that, old friend. What I am referring to is not you, Hugo. It is Lady Tia."

He winced, knowing he had dragged the beauty into his own misery. He had been shocked—and then thrilled—to learn that she cared enough about him to defend him after he had left the musicale. But just as he had worried that Matthew would be tainted because of their friendship, it seemed the same had occurred with Lady Tia.

"How bad is it?"

"I arrived at last night's ball only minutes before it began. I observed not a single gentleman in her vicinity. Lady Tia had all her family gathered about her in a strong show of support, but they were like an island to themselves."

It pained Hugo to hear this. "Go on."

"I asked if I might dance with her, and she handed me her blank programme."

Matthew's words stung him. Usually, Lady Tia's dance card filled long before a ball began.

"She is that much a pariah?"

His friend nodded solemnly. "After I signed her card, a few others from the fringes of Polite Society approached her, but it was obvious that she was not meeting with the success she has experienced since the start of the Season."

"Perhaps it will get better," he said, instinctively knowing that it wouldn't. He had dragged the woman he loved into the mire with him.

The woman he loved . . .

He had never admitted to himself that he did love her—and now it was too late to act upon it.

"You should encourage her to go home to the country," he said quietly. "Or speak with Millbrooke about it. By the time next Season comes around, I would hope that the gossip surrounding her might have died down."

"That is the last thing she will do," his friend told him. "I asked to claim her for the supper dance so that we might speak. Of you."

He swallowed. "What did she say?"

"Obviously, she asked how you fared. I did not lie to her, Hugo. I told you you were despondent." Matthew paused. "Still, she wondered if you might have spoken of her."

Panic soared through him. "You did not tell her . . . that I have feelings for her? I spoke to you in confidence about that."

"I would never voice a man's feelings for a woman. That is

for you to do, Hugo."

He raked his fingers through his hair, frustration filling him. "How can I tell her of my feelings, Matthew? I only have just admitted to myself that I love her. I cannot tell her this because I have ruined her life. She needs to stay as far away from me as possible in order to repair her reputation. I know I allowed Dilly to talk me into remaining in town—and even attending a few more events this Season—but I am no good for Lady Tia."

"She holds feelings for you, as well, Hugo," Matthew informed him.

He gasped. "What?"

"Once again, it is for the two of you to sort things out between you. I believe, however, that she does hold you dear, my friend."

"Even after I made an absolute fool of myself? You heard me, Matthew. My stammer returned in full force."

Matthew smiled at him. "And even hearing that, she as much as admitted to me that she cares a great deal for you. Do not be foolish, Hugo. Do not let the opinions of Polite Society guide you." His friend's gaze met his. "Listen to your heart. Let it show you the way to Lady Tia—and happiness."

He shook his head. "Millbrooke would never entertain an offer from me at this point. He would want better for his beloved sister."

"Millbrooke wants his sister to be happy. As he is, with his duchess. That man could walk away from Polite Society and never look back, simply because he wed the woman he loves and needs nothing else but her and his family." Matthew studied him. "Do you truly love Lady Tia? Are you willing to ignore others judging you in order to spend a lifetime with someone who feels about you the way you do about her?"

Tears swam in Hugo's eyes. "How could she want me? I stammered so badly, Matthew. Barely getting out words. I fled my former tormentors instead of standing up to them."

"Listen to you speak. Even now, you are practicing daily. You have not stammered once during our conversation this morning. You did not tuck your tail and run home to Merrifield. You are braver than any man I know, Hugo. You simply must convince yourself of that."

Matthew stood. "You have a choice to make now, my friend. Keep silent—and lose Lady Tia—causing both of you to be miserable for the rest of your lives. Or you can declare your love for her and pursue happiness. The choice is yours."

Hugo watched Matthew walk away. His friend had not minced words with him.

Could he build a life with Lady Tia after such a terrible incident? Would she consider his suit?

Resolve filled him as he came to his feet. He would never know unless he spoke to her of his feelings. She still might reject him, not wishing to have to stand alone as two against all of Polite Society. At least he would know and be able to move on with his own life after he learned her thoughts.

He made his way back through the park, trying to work out things in his mind as he returned to his townhouse. What he would say to her. Where he would say it. He knew she was loved by her large family and would have them to walk with her, no matter what path she chose.

Passing Rotten Row, he saw a few riders, including a pair who raced their horses the entire length. He thought what fun it would be to ride beside his wife about Merrifield.

Hugo entered his residence and went to his study. He wanted to consult his list of what events were scheduled for today and where they would take place. A garden party was to be held at two o'clock this afternoon. Another ball would take place this evening. Mama had committed them to both events. He decided he would seek out Lady Tia at the garden party. It might be easier to approach her at a smaller event with fewer in attendance.

He rang for Alfie, telling his valet he needed a bath, shave, and hair trim.

"Unkempt as you are, you look like you have a spark in your

eye, my lord. I'm happy to clean you up and make you presentable to others. It is about time you climbed back upon the horse who unseated you."

Hugo had poured out his heart to Alfie, telling the valet how his stammer had returned when Lord Calley and Lord Balch had mocked him. His old friend had sympathized but told Hugo at some point, he would need to take a stand.

Not only did he need to share his feelings with Lady Tia, he must also lay the ghosts of the past to rest.

He returned to his bedchamber, awaiting the hot water. Once it came, he soaked in his bathing tub for a long time, trying to work out everything in his head. He had learned to do so, especially when it came to important things he had to say. The better prepared he was, the more likely he was to keep the stammering at bay.

Alfie dressed him in clothes appropriate for the garden party, and then he went to find his mother and sister to let them know he would escort them to this afternoon's event. Mrs. Coggins told him Mama was in her sitting room, and so he made his way to her.

She eyed him carefully as he crossed the room. "You look as if you are going somewhere, Merriman. Perhaps a garden party?" she asked hopefully.

"Yes, Mama. I intend to speak to Lady Tia while I am there."

His mother rose and came to him, placing her hands on his shoulders and brushing a kiss against his cheek.

"You must love her a great deal to face down the gossips so soon."

Her insight surprised him. "How did you know?"

"A mother knows things about her boy, no matter how old he is, Merriman. I wish I could have been a better mother to you. I wish I would have stood up more for you. With him."

He took her hands in his. "Mama, you did the best you could in an impossible situation. He is gone from our lives and rotting in Hell. Do not let him haunt you anymore."

She smiled gently. "Then perhaps I will make for a better grandmother than I did mother."

He kissed her brow. "Let me know when it is time to leave for the garden party."

Hugo went to his study. It was impossible to accomplish any work. He merely sat at his desk, playing out various scenarios in his mind. He even recited a poem or two aloud to bolster his confidence, as well as practice what he wished to say to the woman he loved.

He did not stammer a single time.

The door flew open, and Dilly rushed in. "Is it true, Hugo? Mama said you are coming to the garden party with us."

"I do not wish to be a coward," he told his sister. "I need to face my demons." He grinned. "And one special angel."

Her eyes widened. "Do you mean . . . Tia?"

He nodded.

Dilly rushed to him. Throwing her arms about him, she said, "Oh, I think you would be wonderful together, Hugo. If you wed, Tia would truly become my sister."

"It remains to be seen what she might say, Dilly. I know she has been ostracized because of her association with me."

She frowned. "Matthew spoke to you, didn't he? About last night's ball."

Nodding, he said, "He told me she was a pariah at the ball. It is all my fault."

"It is the fault of those two bloody dolts, Hugo," Dilly said, fire in her eyes. "Do not ever let men who are not gentlemen make you believe you are something which you are not. You are smart. Kind. Brave. And I could not be prouder of you."

"Then wish me the best, my little sister, for I feel as if I am marching today into the nine circles of Dante's Hell."

CHAPTER TWENTY-ONE

TIA DRESSED FOR the garden party. Lia had come over early to lend her support.

"Are you certain you even wish to go this afternoon?" her twin asked.

"I am not going to let those two sods think they have won," she said, bristling with anger. Then she forced herself to relax. "Besides, I have always adored flowers. Strolling through the gardens at a garden party will hopefully lift my spirits."

She had not received a single bouquet today. Usually, by this time, the drawing room was filled with the sweet aroma of wisteria, gardenias, and irises, bouquets from men she had spoken to and danced with. After last night's disaster, Tia wasn't certain she would ever receive a flower arrangement again. She would not let it bother her, however.

Because she only wanted flowers from one man.

Hopefully, Lord Merriman would return to Polite Society in the next few days. Dilly had assured Tia that her brother had not left for Norfolk. She had worried that he would return to his country estate, simply because it would be harder to chase him down if he had. Val would take her to Merrifield if she asked him to do so. She only hoped it would not come to that and that she might speak with Lord Merriman here in town.

Perhaps she should ask Dilly or Lady Merriman to invite her to tea. Then again, Tia had no idea if the earl was taking tea with his family these days. The Duke of Reddington had let her know that Lord Merriman was in poor spirits. He might be locked in the music room for all she knew, seeking comfort from his pianoforte.

"I have a plan," she told Lia. "I am going to speak to Lord Merriman when he attends an event. Dilly has shared with me that her brother is merely taking a brief respite from the social swirl. That he will soon return."

Lia looked upon her with sympathy. "Will you share with him your feelings?"

"I must. If I do not, he may be lost to me forever. My greatest fear is that he will feel as if he is some anchor about my neck, weighing me down, when that is far from the truth. If he would wed me and we stayed in the country the rest of our lives, I would be happy."

Her sister frowned. "Are you certain that is what you want? You are a very outgoing person, Tia. You like having people around you. And what of our plans to always attend the Season to be with family? To have our children grow close?"

"We could always come to town and visit with everyone in the family—and not attend events," she said stubbornly.

Lia took Tia's hands in hers. "I want what is best for you. I always have. I have never been jealous of you in any respect. But I cannot see you isolating yourself for any man, Tia." Lia paused. "If he truly loves you, he will—"

"But what if he doesn't?" she asked. "I do love him, Lia. I do. I think about him constantly. I would be miserable if he is not in my life. I would change everything about myself to be with him," she said earnestly.

Lia squeezed her hands. "If Lord Merriman does love you, he will not wish for you to change. Simply take things a day at a time. We shall go to this garden party this afternoon. The ball tonight. And then we will let tomorrow sort out itself when it arrives."

They embraced, and Tia knew how fortunate she was to have

Lia. No one understood her the way her twin did.

"I am ready," she said after fastening the sapphire earring onto her lobe, and they went downstairs, where she found Ariadne and Julian waiting with Val, Eden, and Rupert.

Going to her sister, she hugged her. "Thank you for accompanying us today."

"You know Julian and I stand firmly with you," Ariadne assured her. "This garden party may be all you need to attend today. You are welcome to come home with us after it. Spend some time in the nursery with Penelope. Even stay the night."

"Are you worried about me going to tonight's ball?" she asked.

"A little," Ariadne admitted. "I know last night was trying for you."

"I actually talked to a few very nice ladies last night when I was not engaged in a dance. Miss Stanhope, in particular, was a good conversationalist, and she also excels at cards. I think we could possibly be friends. I would not mind spending more time with her this evening."

"You do not have to decide now," Eden said. "Let us go to this garden party."

"Please," she said. "All of you are so worried about me. You do not need to be. I am going to be fine."

"Of course, you are," Mama said, joining them. "You are a Worthington. You are made of strong stuff."

They went outside, where three carriages stood. Her brother said, "We should leave one of the carriages here."

"Ride with us, Tia," Julian encouraged. "That will give me a chance to tell you what Penelope is up to."

Everyone laughed, and she joined Ariadne and Julian, along with Lia and Rupert, and rode with them, while Val, Eden, and Mama took the Millbrooke carriage. Julian kept them entertained with stories of his daughter, and she appreciated him all the more for it.

As Julian handed her down, he said, "I am here for you, Tia. If

I need to bash in someone's nose on your behalf, it would give me great pleasure. Working on the London docks, I learned to fight dirty, so I am your man."

"Perhaps I should have you show me how to fight dirty, Julian."

"My best advice? Kick a man in his balls. It works every time."

She burst out laughing, all the tension within her leaving. "If we see Lord Calley or Lord Balch here, I might just do so."

They entered the house, where a servant led them to a set of French doors. Exiting them, Tia saw about fifty others gathered on the terrace, spilling down the steps and lingering below. A few couples were entering the gardens. As she surveyed the crowd, she felt a hush fall as conversations ceased. Every eye turned to her. She swallowed.

Then Val slipped an arm through hers, and Eden did the same on her other side. Together, the three of them moved into the crowd. Others turned away, continuing their conversations once more, and Val led them to the punchbowl, where Lia and Rupert joined them.

"I have always found it helpful to hold something in my hands," Eden said.

"Are you certain you trust me with a cup of punch in my hand?" Tia asked. "I just saw Lord Calley and Lord Balch are here. I am sorely tempted to pour a cup over their heads."

"Avoid them," her brother advised. "The *ton* already has enough to talk about." He looked at her beseechingly. "Do not give them more to feather their nests with."

"I shall take the high road," she promised her brother.

"Let us go about and greet those here," Ariadne said. "Hold your head high. I will be with you. Julian, as well. No one will dare cross him."

Her brother-in-law did have a bit of a menacing air about him. She doubted either Lord Calley or Lord Balch would dare approach her, much less speak derisively to her if she were in his presence.

"Very well."

They set out, moving through the crowd. Ariadne had a commanding presence, and no one dared turn her away. Tia actually found people speaking to her and not just her sister and brother-in-law.

One lady, an elderly countess, said to her, "Those two scoundrels acted dreadfully, Lady Tia. Poor Lord Merriman. I would hate to be in his shoes. Simply steer away from the three of them. That is the best advice I can give you."

Tia had no clue as to how to reply, and Julian simply guided them away and to the next group. Then she felt an odd tingling and turned.

Lord Merriman had arrived—and was looking right at her.

Her heart leaped within her chest. She started to move toward him, but Julian held firm to her arm.

"Let him come to you," he said. "People have talked about how brazen you were, slapping Lord Calley. I am not saying let the *ton* rule your actions, Tia, but a little decorum would not hurt."

Julian then released her arm. He and Ariadne stepped away from her. For a moment, she worried, being left alone in the midst of so many others, but Lord Merriman's gaze met hers. He walked with purpose toward her, and she eagerly awaited him. Tia was aware that once again, all conversation had ceased, and everyone watched with great interest, sharpening the knives of their words to come.

He arrived in front of her and bowed. She offered him her hand, and he kissed her fingers, bringing a rush of desire racing through her. She wanted his mouth on hers again. His hand on her breast. His scent invading her senses.

"Lady Tia," he rumbled in his deep voice.

"Lord Merriman," she responded.

He continued holding her hand. She knew she should withdraw it, but it felt so right being in his.

"Wh-wh-what are y-you d-d-d-doing?" a voice to her left said, causing Lord Merriman to grimace. Yet he stiffened his spine and turned toward it.

"Are you . . . mocking me, Lord Calley?" he asked, releasing Tia's hand as he glared at the intruder who had joined them.

"N-no. N-n-not a b-b-b-bit," Lord Calley replied, his eyes gleaming.

Lord Balch joined him. "G-g-give it a r-rest, m-m-m-my lord. Can't y-you see Merriman is t-t-trying to w-win Lady T-T-T-Tia's favor?"

"Enough," Lord Merriman said sharply. "The two of you were good-for-nothing bounders as boys. You haven't changed . . . a bit. You hurled cruel insults and threatened m-me when I was young. I was weaker. Smaller. Too vulnerable . . . to fight back."

Lord Merriman stared down the pair now. "I am no longer afraid. Of you. Of your taunts. Yes, I stammer. Yes, I overcame it—but I work diligently. Every single day. To keep it away." He shook his head. "I let you rattle me at the musicale. I refuse to be cowed by you ever again."

He looked out over the guests, who gawked at them. "These two showed how . . . uncouth they are when they mocked me. Then . . . and now. Their boorish conduct was . . . disrespectful. Not fit for true gentlemen. They are rude. If anything, you should b-be talking about *their* boorish behavior. Not maligning me or belittling Lady Tia. She was the only one who called them out for acting . . . so atrociously."

He turned to her. "I think you are . . . the bravest woman in the world."

Her heart soared, hearing his words of praise.

Once again, he faced the two men who had mimicked his stammering. "You ridiculed me. Beat me. Humiliated me when I was a boy. You shamed me in front of the *ton* as a man. You have disgraced yourselves. And your families. I hope the gossips do what they do best now. V-vilify you. Scorn you. You are exposed now. Everyone present knows you possess no honor. No good character. Leave now—or I shall make you leave."

Lord Calley laughed, and Tia cringed.

"You think to make *me* leave? I am not the one others are talking about. *You* are the one who is not welcome, Merriman."

"Polite Society has no room for such unprincipled men," Val said, stepping next to Lord Merriman in a show of support, causing Tia to fill with pride.

"His Grace is right," Rupert said, coming to stand next to Val. "Who wants to socialize with such disgraceful cads? It goes against the very rules of Polite Society."

Julian joined them. "Give me a solid fellow such as Merriman any day. One who is respectful."

Con, whom she had not seen, became the next addition to the group. "Merriman has more honor in his smallest finger than either of you will ever own."

Tears formed in Tia's eyes, watching her family back Lord Merriman. Then Lord Forsythe came forward.

"I plan to wed Lord Merriman's sister—and I am happy I will count Merriman as my brother."

Lord Calley looked at the men standing there. "You five are *all* fools," he declared.

"No, we are men of honor," Lord Merriman said, his voice firm, ringing out. "And we look down upon anyone who does not hold honor dear."

Lord Calley snorted. "You are but a small part of Polite Society. No one cares what you say."

Then Tia saw the Duke of Reddington move forward. "But they do care, Calley. I am a duke. So is Millbrooke. Aldridge, Dyer, and Cressley are well thought of, as is Forsythe. And each of us calls Lord Merriman friend. To me, he is my closest friend. I would take one Merriman over a thousand of you. You do not have the ear of the *ton* as you think you do. Look about, man. See what is on their faces. You and Balch have completely disgraced yourselves. You will not be welcomed at any future events. No true gentlemen will ever call either of you friend again. You have worn out your welcome."

Calley and Balch looked helplessly at one another. Balch started to speak and then seemed to think better of it. He tugged on Calley's sleeve, and they made a quick retreat.

Lord Merriman said, "You have all put your own reputations on the line. To stand with me. I will never be able to repay you. But know this. I will always be there for you. No matter what happens. Call upon me. Anytime."

Val offered his hand. "Friends, now and forever."

Tia's eyes misted with tears as each of them shook hands with Lord Merriman. Then he turned to her, closing the distance between them.

"I had not thought to act so publicly, Lady Tia, but the time . . . is right."

He captured her hands in his, and she heard those present gasp.

"My stutter left me . . . vulnerable . . . as a child. Even now, I must think carefully as I speak. I have feared vulnerability . . . my entire life. Thinking it was a weakness." He smiled. But I do not mind being vulnerable with you. Open with you. Only you. You have my heart. My soul.

"My love."

"I love you, too," she revealed. "I will always love you."

His smile lit up his face. "Then I suppose the best thing to do is wed as soon as possible."

Blinking away her tears, she cried, "Yes!"

Then, in front of everyone, he took her into his arms. His mouth descended upon hers, his kiss full of all the love they shared—and promise. Of all the days to come. They would stand strong together, having the support of both their families, large and small.

Tia knew her love for him would only grow deeper and richer as the years progressed.

CHAPTER TWENTY-TWO

"THE NEWSPAPERS ARE calling it the wedding of the Season," Eden said, helping to fasten a strand of pearls around Tia's neck.

Tia fingered the pearls. "They are beautiful and the perfect touch to my wedding gown," she told her sister-in-law. "Thank you for allowing me to borrow them."

Lia bent, placing her hands on Tia's shoulders, pressing her cheek to that of her twin's. "You make for a most beautiful bride. Oh, I am thrilled you have found love with Hugo."

After Hugo's very public declaration of love and offer of marriage, the past four weeks had been a blur, as wedding preparations had begun in earnest and the banns were called. Dilly had suggested that Tia and Hugo wed at the same time she and Lord Forsythe did. Instead of a country wedding in Kent, as she had always thought would take place when she did marry, Tia had agreed to wed at St. George's, the parish church of Mayfair, and one of the most fashionable in London.

She and Hugo had gone to tour it, along with Mama, Dilly and her mother, and Lord Forsythe. From the vicar, they had learned that the church was the greatest achievement of designer John James, who had been a student of Christpher Wren. The building had stood for over eighty years, and it had become the place for couples from Polite Society to wed if they chose to hold their ceremonies in town. Close to a thousand couples had spoken their wedding vows at St. George's last year, and the vicar who spoke with them said that number was increasing every year.

After settling on a date, the two couples had sent out joint invitations, and this particular double wedding ceremony was on the lips of everyone in the *ton*. Mama had told Tia to expect the church filled to the brim. Frankly, she didn't care who was in attendance. All she wanted was to start her life with Hugo.

They'd had several long talks over the past few weeks. Her fiancé had been brutally honest with her, sharing how difficult his childhood had been with a father who had a heavy hand, especially when it came to a son who stuttered. Hugo didn't know if his stammering had been a result of the beatings he received or if the stutter had appeared first, resulting in subsequent discipline, which only made his stammer worse.

She had cried hearing of his time at school, but Hugo had insisted she know all before she committed to a life with him. They even spoke of what they would do if one of their own children stammered. He believed that with time, practice—and love—it could be conquered.

Hugo also spent many hours in the company of her family. He had already become friendly with Val, Con, and Rupert. Julian was quickly added to Hugo's circle, and the Duke of Reddington and Lord Forsythe also became part of their group. Tia was thrilled when Lucy finally came to the Season, bringing Judson and their newborn daughter. Elizabeth had been born at the very beginning of March, and Lucy and Judson had decided to linger at Huntsworth a while, especially because Lucy's sister Dru was increasing. Dru would give birth in mid-July or slightly later, so Lucy and Judson had only come to town for a few weeks, in order to show off Elizabeth and spend quality time with their extended family. Fortunately, the couple would attend today's wedding before returning home tomorrow. They were neighbors not only to Ariadne and Julian, but to Dru and Perry, as well. Lucy wanted to be present when Dru gave birth to her first child.

Tia envied the sisters being able to live so close to one another. She and Lia would be far apart, with Lia and Rupert in Cumberland and she and Hugo in Norfolk, practically on opposite sides of England. Still, as Ariadne said, that was what the Season was for—to gather at a central place and spend time with family during several pleasant months. By next spring, Lia would be a mother—and Tia herself might be increasing. The thought should have frightened her since she knew so little about raising children, but she and Hugo would shower any offspring they had with love, the most important gift of all.

Lia had sat Tia down for a most interesting conversation. In it, her twin explained some of the particulars of lovemaking, so Tia would not be caught unaware. Fortunately, they were comfortable with one another, allowing Lia to be quite frank. A few of the things her twin shared sounded impossible, but Lia assured her that everything would work like magic between her and Hugo.

"Just trust in your love for one another," Lia had said, the best advice Tia could have received.

She had only heard him stammer twice since their betrothal. Those times had occurred when he was overtired. He had explained that it took a great deal of concentration to speak, and that was why sometimes he paused as he did, breaking what he wished to say into parts. It didn't matter to her. She loved her handsome fiancé with all her heart. He was everything—even more—than she had ever dreamed of holding dear.

Mama appeared. "Millbrooke says it is time to leave."

Lia kissed Tia's cheek. "I will see you in Hanover Square."

She took a final look in the mirror. "I suppose I am as ready as I ever will be," she told Eden, Ariadne, and Mama.

Downstairs, her sisters followed Julian outside to Rupert's carriage, while she and Mama joined Val and Eden in his. The ride to St. George's did not take long. As they pulled up in front of the church, she admired its six Corinthian columns and lofty tower. While the architecture outside the church was spellbinding, the inside was quite plain, with tall, boxed pews and a high pulpit. Mama had hired a florist to provide a plethora of flowers to dress up the church.

Val handed each of them down, and she saw that Lady Merriman and Dilly were standing on the pavement. Smiling, she hurried to her friend.

"Are you ready to speak your vows?"

"I have been forever," Dilly declared. "I could have wed Forsythe that first night. I was that certain he was the one for me."

They entered the foyer of the church, and Eden led the two mothers inside. Val would be escorting Tia to the altar, and Reddington now came toward them. Since Dilly had no living father and her brother, who usually would have been the one to see her to her groom, was already at the altar, the duke had stepped in to guide Dilly down the aisle.

Reddington greeted them. "I have never been to a double wedding. I quite like the idea, especially for siblings."

"You will soon be the groom awaiting your bride," Val predicted. "I think it is time to take you on and introduce you to someone who could be your duchess."

The duke laughed. "Let us get through these weddings first, Millbrooke. Then perhaps at the wedding breakfast we can start this search."

Their moods lighthearted, the four took their places at the entrance. As the organist began to play, Dilly and Reddington stepped down the aisle first. She and Val were to allow them to reach the altar before they, too, would march along the aisle.

"You are happy, aren't you?" her brother asked. "You do love Hugo?"

"Deliriously happy," she assured him. "And yes, it is because I love Hugo that I am floating amongst the clouds, Val."

He smiled at her. "We four Worthingtons have all made love matches. Lucy and Dru, as well. I suppose we need to work on Con next, along with Reddington. I think when our cousin falls in love, he will fall hard."

Her brother then guided her down the aisle, past hundreds of guests. She felt their presence but did not look at a one of them. Her eyes met that of her husband-to-be, and joy filled Tia.

The ceremony took slightly longer than most, simply because there were four of them to repeat their vows after the vicar. She thought it incredibly special to be sharing this day with Dilly, a friend who would now become a sister to her.

Forsythe slid the wedding band onto Dilly's finger, repeating the words of the vicar. Then Hugo did the same with her. Her eyes never left his as he said, "With this ring I thee wed, with my body I thee worship, and with all my worldly goods I thee endow: In the Name of the Father, and of the Son, and of the Holy Ghost. Amen."

Tears stung her eyes, happy tears, knowing she would spend the rest of her life with the best man she had ever known. That they would live to the fullest as they raised their family and cared for their tenants. She could not wait to go to her new home—and start making it their home.

The final prayer was offered, and then they were pronounced husband and wife. Tia kissed her new husband, thinking how she had entered this Season not believing she would find love, much less marry. All her plans had gone out the window, and for that, she was grateful. She wanted to live every minute to the fullest, with Hugo by her side.

They marched back up the aisle, Dilly and Forsythe following them, to the cheers of all present. The fickle *ton* had, as usual, changed its mind, and now the four of them were the darlings of Polite Society. Tia knew it would not last.

But her and Hugo's love would last forever.

As the two couples exited the church, Tia saw dozens of people gathered outside, average citizens of London who had turned out to wish them well. She found it odd, in a way, that complete strangers would be there when the *ton* itself only a short time ago had ostracized both her and Hugo. Still, they had been accepted back into the fold. She knew now, more than ever before, that the most important thing to depend upon was family.

"This way," Hugo said, leading them to Val's carriage. Her brother had told the two couples to take it to the wedding breakfast, which was to be held at Ariadne and Julian's townhouse. Though Lia had broached the idea of hosting the breakfast, Rupert had not wanted his wife to take on so much in her delicate condition.

Ariadne, who was a superb hostess, had eagerly agreed to hold the wedding breakfast in their honor, saying that any time any of the cousins decided to wed in town, she would be happy to do so.

They settled themselves in the carriage, and she waved to a few of those gathered in the streets, and they waved back to her. Then Hugo reached over and drew the curtains, blocking out both spectators and sun.

He looked to Dilly and Lord Forsythe and said, "It you will excuse me from conversation, I plan to kiss my wife the entire way to Aldridge's place."

Dilly blushed a bright red, while her new husband chuckled and said, "I like the way you think, Merriman."

Both grooms turned to their brides, and Hugo enveloped Tia in his arms, making good on his promise. His kisses stirred her blood, and she was eager for their wedding night to occur. She still wasn't certain about the exact mechanics of everything, but she trusted Lia when her twin had told her that their passion would make up for her lack of knowledge.

Hugo did not break their kiss until the carriage came to a halt. When he did so, he smiled at her and whispered, "There will be more of that later—and much more beyond."

Both grooms handed down their brides, and they ventured inside to where the wedding breakfast would be held. Though hundreds had graced St. George's for the ceremony, Tia and Dilly had agreed they wished for the wedding breakfast to be a private affair. It would only involve their families and the Duke of

Reddington.

Ariadne had decided to hold the breakfast in their ballroom and had small tables brought to it. A string quartet picked up their instruments and begin to play as the two couples entered the ballroom. There was also a long table holding the buffet, which contained foods each of them favored.

"Lady Aldridge has thought of everything," Dilly said.

"My sister is very organized. So is my sister-in-law," Tia added, thinking of the fete Eden had planned at Millvale last year, an occasion which would occur each year. She and Val had journeyed back to Millvale recently for that celebration before returning to town for today's ceremony.

The families arrived, and Ariadne said it was to be a casual affair, having them all go through the buffet line. The food was delicious and as the meal ended, champagne was brought out on trays by footmen. Val waited until everyone present held a flute and then stood, raising his glass high. Everyone followed his lead.

"Today has been a most special day," her brother began, smiling at Tia. "The last of my siblings has wed, along with Lady Dilly."

She noted Val's use of Dilly's nickname. Her entire family used it now, and Lady Merriman had given up protesting its use, seeing how happy her daughter was.

"Lord Merriman and Lord Forsythe are two very fine men," Val continued. "I know each will hold his wife dear. Here is to two long, happy marriages—and many children to come."

Tia sipped on the champagne, thinking the bubbly liquid was a visual symbol of the joy she felt bubbling within her.

"I think it is time to dance with our wives!" Hugo proclaimed, and the two couples moved onto the dance floor.

Lucy, Judson, Ariadne, and Julian joined them, and the musicians played a lively country dance. She couldn't help but glow with pride, watching her husband move. He was so lighthearted today. He had made it through his vows without stammering once, which she knew had been very important to him. She would always be conscious of his speech, helping him to realize when he was overtired and needed a respite from conversation. Love for him bloomed within her, making her grateful that she had wed for love.

They danced for another hour, and then Hugo whispered in her ear that it was time to go. They went about, saying their goodbyes to all present.

When they reached Lucy and Judson, she said, "Thank you so much for coming to town and being a part of our day."

"We were so happy to be here," her cousin replied. "I wanted Judson to meet the Worthington cousins and, of course, we had to show off our darling Elizabeth."

"Send word once Dru has given birth. I hope she and Perry will be able to come to town for the Season next year so we might meet their babe."

"When will you leave town?" Judson asked.

"We will remain here another week," Hugo shared. "Just long enough for me to escort my wife to a few events. Then I am eager to take her home so she may see Merrifield for the first time."

Tia would have left for Merrifield tomorrow, but Hugo wanted to give his staff time to prepare for their arrival. He had sent word about their upcoming marriage, and the staff was to prepare her room, as well as move Lady Merriman's possessions to the dower house. She had told her mother-in-law that would not be necessary, but Lady Merriman said she preferred to give the couple privacy in their own home. She did promise to come and dine with them upon occasion. Tia had worried that her mother-in-law might be lonely living alone, but Hugo assured her that his mother enjoyed solitude.

They stopped to visit a moment with Con, and she told her cousin, "I have a favor to ask of you."

"I cannot refuse any favor you ask of me on your wedding day," her cousin teased. "What do you wish for me to do for you?"

"I met a lady amongst the wallflowers, and I wish for you to dance with her at least once, Con."

"Dancing is a specialty of mine. I will seek out this lady. What is her name?"

"Miss Stanhope, the daughter of Viscount Samuel. She is quite pretty, but her beauty is hidden by gold spectacles. She revealed herself as a bluestocking, which is why gentlemen steer away from her." Tia paused. "I liked her, Con. Very much. I was hoping if you danced with her, it might bring the attention of other gentlemen to her."

"I shall do so at tomorrow night's ball," he promised. "Perhaps I will engage her for the supper dance, and if you and Hugo are in attendance, we could sup together."

"We will be there," her husband said. "Definitely ask Miss Stanhope to dance. I myself have danced with her before. She is most interesting."

When they reached Lia and Rupert, Tia hugged her twin tightly. As she did so, she felt something odd and stepped back. Lia's face showed her own surprise, and her hands went to her belly.

"It was the babe. It moved!" her sister said, taking her husband's hand and placing his palm flat against her belly.

Rupert frowned, and then suddenly his face held joy. "I felt it, too!" He kissed his wife enthusiastically.

Lia's eyes now misted with tears. "I am glad I could share this moment with you," she told her sister. "Especially since we leave for Crestbrook tomorrow."

Tia knew Lia was ready to return to their country home and settle in, especially now since her twin was also wed.

They finished their goodbyes, and Dilly and Forsythe did, as well. Everyone accompanied them outside, to where their separate carriages awaited them. They thanked Ariadne and Julian for hosting the wedding breakfast. Tia touched Penelope's cheek, thinking how the little girl had danced amongst them and how Hugo had sweetly scooped up the child and danced with her in his arms. In that moment, Tia knew more than anything she was ready to have his babes.

The ride to Hugo's townhouse was short since it lay nearby. She knew this morning that her things had been transferred from Val's townhouse to her new husband's. She also had hired a new lady's maid who would attend to her here and accompany them back to Merrifield. The woman was a cousin of Alfie's. Tia liked the cheeky valet and was excited to finally have a maid of her own.

They entered Hugo's residence, and he said, "This is your home now, my dearest. Our home for when we come to town for the Season. Are you tired?"

"Not a bit," she declared.

"Since you aren't, would you accompany me to the music room?" he asked. "I have a surprise for you."

Tia tried not to show her disappointment, thinking they would have immediately gone upstairs to make love. Still, she knew how music soothed her husband. Perhaps he needed to play a bit before they consummated their marriage.

"You know I enjoy hearing you play," she said. "As long as you are the one at the pianoforte and not me, I am happy to accompany you there."

They entered the music room, and she believed they would spend many enjoyable hours here. She might even request that her talented husband play for her every night before they retired.

He led them to the instrument, and she reluctantly released his hand. Hugo sat and looked up at her.

"I have written something. What I play now, I play for you, my love."

CHAPTER TWENTY-THREE

HUGO BEGAN TO play, and she watched his fingers dance upon the ivory keys. The melody was tender. Poignant. It tugged upon her heartstrings, knowing that he had taken the time to create this song just for her.

When the last note sounded, he gazed up at her anxiously. She framed his face in her hands and bent, pressing a soft kiss upon his lips.

"No one has ever given me a greater gift, Hugo. It is a haunting melody. Is it difficult to compose a song?"

He rose, his large hands cradling her cheeks, his thumbs caressing them. "Not when I have such wonderful inspiration. This song, I hope, will be the first of many which I hope to write for you."

His lips touched hers briefly. "I never expected to wed this Season, Tia. I certainly never dreamed I would fall in love, but it is the most wonderful feeling in all the world." He hesitated a moment. "Are you ready to go upstairs and truly begin our life as man and wife?"

She gave him a wicked smile. "I thought you would never ask, Husband."

Laughing, he swept her into his arms, easily carrying her up the stairs to her new bedchamber. She reached down and turned the doorknob, pushing the door open for him.

Her new maid sat in the corner, waiting for her. She smiled at the couple and rose. Hugo set Tia onto her feet.

"I will come to you soon, my love," he promised, giving her a quick kiss on the lips.

Anticipation filled her as she was dressed in one of her new night rails. She had tried on a sample one at Madame Laurent's shop, Lia accompanying her. Tia thought it almost indecent, but her sister and the modiste had smiled knowingly, telling her the flimsy material was exactly what she needed. She glanced down, seeing the night rail left little to the imagination, hoping Hugo would approve of it.

And her.

"Shall I leave your hair up, my lady?"

It had taken a good hour to create the hairstyle she now wore, and she thought it would be good to keep her hair pinned. That way, it would not interfere with whatever they did in their bed. Lia had told her that she and Rupert actually shared a bed, sleeping together each night. Lia only used her bedchamber as a dressing room since Rupert preferred keeping her with him. Tia wondered what Hugo's preference would be. It seemed almost scandalous to sleep all night in a man's bed, even if that man might be her husband.

The maid excused herself, and Tia paced, nervous energy filling her. Then she heard a tap on the door and went to it.

No one was there.

Confused, she closed it, only to hear the same noise again. This time, she realized it was coming from another door. She moved toward it and when she opened the door, Hugo was on the other side.

"Our rooms adjoin?" she asked.

"Yes. There is a bathing chamber between them, with our bedchambers on each side of it. You also have a place to store your wardrobe." He caressed her cheek. "But you can investigate that later. Right now, I wish to explore you. All of you."

He stepped into her room, closing the door behind him. She wet her lips, knowing some of what was to come, but still not certain how it would play out.

Hugo took her hands and lifted her arms to the side, his eyes moving up and down her body, drinking her in.

"You are breathtaking," he said, awe in his voice. "But I would ask for one adjustment to be made." He paused. "Might . . . I take your hair down?"

"If you would like. I thought having it pinned up would keep it from being a distraction."

He brought her hands to his lips, pressing a fervent kiss against her knuckles. "Your hair is one of the things I cherish most about you. The color is so unique."

"Ariadne calls it strawberry blond."

"That is a good description. It is a lovely shade of red, with blond strands kissing the red."

She went and sat at her dressing table. Indicating a jar, she told him, "Place the pins in this."

With great care, he removed each pin, and eventually, her waves tumbled past her shoulders and down her back. Then Hugo took up her brush and ran it through her tresses. His touch was light, bringing tingles rushing up and down her spine.

Their gazes met in the mirror, and he said, "I love you, Tia. Just saying the words aloud . . . brings a thrill to me."

"I love you, too. I feel we have joined some exclusive club. Only a handful of Polite Society make a love match. My family has been blessed with several. All my siblings. Lucy and Judson. Dru and Perry."

"How many more cousins are yet to wed?" he asked.

"Con, whom you know. He is the only one of the Alingtons left to do so. All three Fultons still remain unwed. Tray is the eldest. Verina is the middle child. And Justina is the youngest."

He bent, his lips grazing her nape. "I look forward to making their acquaintance."

Shivers ran through her as his lips moved against her skin.

Then Hugo helped her rise, and he took her in his arms. They kissed, heated kisses, ones which declared their desire for one another. Her pulse began to race as his fingers ran through her locks.

Breaking the kiss, he asked, "What do you know of love play?"

"A little. All from Lia. She said passion would guide us and that whatever we enjoy is what we should do together. She mentioned sometimes things would grow unorthodox, but pleasing one another should be our ultimate goal."

"I agree. If I do something you enjoy, tell me. I will do the same," he promised.

He began kissing her again, his kiss demanding. Deep. Causing desire to ripple through her. He guided her to the bed and removed her night rail before helping her onto the bed. She watched him untie and shrug from his banyan. He wore nothing under it, and she admired his lean, hard body, the muscles sleek.

For an endless time, they explored one another's bodies, their hands gliding, their mouths following. She thought Hugo would kiss every inch of her, so thorough was he. Then as he kissed her deeply, his hand ran across her belly, going lower. Her core anticipated his touch and began pounding, as if to signal him where to go. One finger stroked the length of her seam, and Tia whimpered.

"You like that?"

"Yes," she whispered. "Do it again."

He did.

The third time he ran his finger along her, it stopped midpoint, then pushed inside her. She moaned as he began stroking her, the caresses deep, causing her to tremble. His motion was steady. Teasing her. Tempting her. Then he shocked her, lowering his mouth to her belly, gliding his tongue along it, then going lower. She knew where it headed but still could not fathom what he was about to do.

As Lia had explained, he parted her with his fingers and slipped his tongue inside her. She let out a groan, clutching the bedclothes as his mouth made love to her most secret place. Her hips began rising as a thick anticipation suddenly blanketed her.

"Something's coming," she said, panting.

He paused a moment, looking up at her, their gazes connecting. "Let it come."

Hugo returned to her, nipping and licking and thrusting until that unknown feeling exploded, washing over her. Her hips gyrated as waves of pleasure engulfed her. Whatever it was came hard and fast, completely controlling her.

When the feeling began to subside, he kissed his way back up to her mouth, once again drinking from her. As he did, he hovered over her, and she felt something hard now between her legs, realizing it was his manhood. As he kissed her deeply, he thrust into her. The action brought a little fear because this was definitely the unknown, but the larger part was the wonderful sensations that begin to drift through her.

He broke the kiss. "May I continue?"

She loved him for asking permission. "You may."

"Wrap your legs about my waist," he instructed. "It will allow me to go deeper, which should add to your pleasure."

She did as told, and his next thrust immediately set off beautiful sensations within her. As he moved in and out of her, Tia caught on to the movement of the dance. Her fingers pushed into his hair, and she kissed him passionately, giving everything she had of herself to this wonderful man. He gripped her buttocks, kneading them, his kisses still demanding as they moved as one.

Then that lovely feeling began building within her again. She held tightly to him as it struck her with great force. The same must be happening with him, because they both cried out in unison, each calling the other's name.

When it finally subsided, Hugo collapsed atop her, covering her face in kisses. She unlocked her ankles and lowered her legs, feeling incredibly elated. He pulled himself from her and lay on his side, turning her and pulling her toward him, her back pressed into his chest. Tenderly, he kissed her neck, his arms about her, and she knew he would protect her with his life.

"That was . . . incredible," she said, stroking his arm. His leg had now wrapped around hers, and Tia felt as if she were in a cocoon.

"I thought so, too," he said, his voice low and rough.

"Can we be any happier?" she asked.

"Can we love one another even more than we do in this moment?" he countered. "I believe so. I think every day with you as my wife will bring us closer together, and our love will grow beyond anything we might ever imagine."

"I cannot wait to bear your children, Hugo. Watching you dance with Penelope today made me see what a wonderful father you will be."

"I do yearn for children," he told her. "And I want to be a father they can love. One they can come to and share their emotions. Their troubles and sorrows. But also their happiness and triumphs."

"We will make mistakes," she said. "Neither of us is perfect. My parents, Papa, in particular, was very cold and unapproachable."

"You know my father was a monster. I want to be nothing like him. I will shower our children—and you—with love every day, Tia. Every single day."

"I am so happy to be your wife and know that we have so much in common. That we look forward to the family we will build together. We will lead by example, showing our children what it is to love. To care. To do good."

Her eyes grew heavy. "Oh, I am yawning. I can barely hold my eyes open."

"Then close them, love. And know when you awaken, I will be here. I will always be here for you. Now—and forevermore."

"Might we sleep together each night?" she asked.

He dropped a kiss upon the top of her head. "I would not have it any other way."

"Then I can fall asleep. Because whenever I awaken, you will always be there. Goodnight, Hugo, my love."

"Goodnight, my sweet Tia. The first of thousands of nights together."

She snuggled into him—and drifted off to sleep, dreaming of him and the years to come.

EPILOGUE

London—1828

TIA AWOKE FIRST, Hugo's body curling about hers. Contentment filled her. Even after all these years, she still adored her husband.

They had built a good life together, having two daughters and two sons. Their eldest, Jane, would wed today in St. George's, just as they had twenty years ago. Jane had insisted upon a double wedding ceremony, having grown up hearing the stories of her mother and Aunt Dilly marrying together. The other bride today would be Lia's oldest daughter. Her sister had given birth to twins Edward and Mary seven months before Tia herself brought Jane into the world. Lia also had borne two more girls and a boy.

All their children would be here, along with many of their family members. The cousins' pact had held all these years, and they brought their spouses and children to town with them each Season. While they were selective about the events they attended, they saw family every day for months. Tia looked forward to the Season each spring, wanting to visit with all her cousins, but especially because she was able to spend time with her twin. They remained in touch with one another through the year via letters, but nothing could replace the time they had together in person.

Missing from today's ceremony would be Mama and Aunt Agnes. They had lost them many years ago, as well as Uncle Arthur. Only Aunt Charlotte remained from the older generation, and she adored being the matriarch of their three families. Her aunt had been disappointed when none of the cousins continued the tradition of naming their children after Roman and Byzantine rulers and their wives, but Tia and Hugo had agreed they wanted to name their children ordinary, sensible names.

Hugo stirred, which caused desire to stir within her. Soon, they were making love, their kisses slow and delicious, their orgasms shattering.

"Do you recall our wedding day?" her husband asked, in the afterglow of lovemaking, Tia in his arms.

"Like it was yesterday," she replied. "Where has the time gone, my darling?"

He chuckled. "I am finding more gray in my hair these days than black."

She cradled his cheek. "And it makes you look ever so distinguished. My gray hairs, on the other hand, age me."

He kissed her softly. "You will always remain ageless in my eyes, love."

They cuddled several more minutes, and then Tia said, "I must go and dress. You, too. We cannot lay abed all morning. We must be at St. George's to see our daughter and niece wed."

As she climbed from the bed, he watched her with admiring eyes as she tossed on her dressing gown and belted it.

"Jane has chosen wisely," Hugo said. "Just as her mother did."

"Jane is a good girl. A very smart one. And she is very much in love."

"Again, just as her mother is," he said, pulling the cord to ring for Alfie.

Tia blew him a kiss and sailed through the connecting rooms, returning to her own. She rang for her own maid, who brought her tea and toast.

"Something to keep your belly from growling in the church," the servant teased.

Once she was dressed, she went to her daughter's room. Jane sat before her dressing table, a maid putting the finishing touches on her hair. She wore the sapphire earrings Tia had won many years ago playing cards. She had gifted them to Jane on the night of her come-out Season this past April.

And here her babe was now a grown woman, ready to wed and have babes of her own.

"Mama!" Jane cried.

"Hold still, my lady," the maid warned. "I'm almost done."

"Very well," Jane said, waiting until the final pin was in place. Then she rose and came to Tia, embracing her. "Oh, Mama. I cannot believe my wedding day is finally here."

"Frankly, neither can I," she quipped. "When did I grow old enough to have a daughter who could wed?" She caressed Jane's cheek. "One who might very well make me a grandmama by this time next year."

Jane's eyes grew wide. "I had not thought of that."

She dismissed the maid, and then said, "You have been so busy, but there are a few things I wish to tell you now. I want you to know something of the marriage bed."

"Really, Mama?" Jane protested.

"It is better to have some knowledge of it than going into things blind."

For the next several minutes, she had a frank discussion with her daughter, who blushed profusely as they spoke. Tia did not care. She wanted Jane happy, and part of that would mean she would want to be happy when it came to love play.

"It sounds a little complicated," Jane said when Tia finished. "And you and Papa . . . doing that. Why, it is scandalous!"

"There is nothing wrong with a little bit of wicked behavior in a marriage. Trust me. You will be thankful I prepared you."

A light tap sounded on the door, and Hugo leaned in. "Are you ready, my little love?"

Jane went to her father, wrapping her arms about his neck, pressing a kiss upon his cheek. "I am not so little anymore, Papa. I am a grown woman."

"You truly are," he said, seeming to look at her with fresh

eyes. "But the carriage and all those guests await at St. George's. We must be on our way."

"Where are my brothers and sister?" Jane asked as they made their way down to the foyer.

"Uncle Val came and collected them a good hour ago," Tia told her daughter.

"And Mary will meet us there, won't she?" Jane asked anxiously.

"Knowing Mary, she has already greeted every guest in attendance," Hugo teased.

They drove through Mayfair to St. George's, and Tia couldn't help but think of entering this church on her own wedding day, Dilly by her side. Matthew had escorted Dilly to the altar that day. Now, he was officially one of their family by marriage.

Mary stood out front with Edward and Rupert. Jane rushed from the carriage to her cousins, embracing them both.

"I can go inside, now that you are here," Edward said. "Mary was mad with worry, thinking you would be late."

He kissed his twin's cheek and then looked to her. "Ready to go inside, Aunt Tia?"

She looked at her sweet girl. Cupping Jane's cheeks, she said, "The next time we speak, you will be wed." She glanced at Mary, touching her cheek. "Both of you."

"Go inside, Mama," Jane ordered. "And try not to cry."

"Oh, I told Mama the same," Mary said, laughing.

Edward held out his arm, and Tia took it. "I hope your mother saves me a place next to her."

"She did. On the front row. There is room for you, Uncle Hugo, and Papa, as well."

Edward led her down the aisle, and Tia couldn't help but admire how beautiful the church looked, with all the wonderful flowers on display. It made her think of how Hugo brought her flowers each week. When they were in town, he would have them sent. When they were at Merrivale, he would go to the gardens or hothouse and clip them himself.

Joining Lia, they held hands, and her twin said, "It seems as if only yesterday when we were the brides, speaking our vows with our very handsome grooms."

"Time marches on. I am happy that both our girls have made love matches, Lia. Just think—another wedding breakfast held at Ariadne's. I love how our family traditions continue."

Soon, the organ came to life, and they watched Rupert escort Mary down the aisle. Hugo and Jane followed them. After both men had handed off their daughters to the two waiting grooms, they came to join their wives.

Hugo threaded his fingers through hers. "It is a happy day, my love," he whispered in her ear.

She beamed up at him. "And we have so many more happy ones yet to come."

About the Author

USA Today and Amazon Top 10 bestselling author Alexa Aston lives with her husband in a Dallas suburb, where she eats her fair share of dark chocolate and plots while she walks every morning. She enjoys travel and sports—and can't get enough of *Survivor* or *The Crown*.

Her Regency and Medieval historical romances bring to life loveable rogues and dashing knights. Her series include: *The Strongs of Shadowcrest, Suddenly a Duke, Second Sons of London, Dukes Done Wrong, Dukes of Distinction, Soldiers and Soulmates, The St. Clairs, The de Wolfes of Esterley Castle, The King's Cousins, Medieval Runaway Wives,* and *The Knights of Honor.*

www.ingramcontent.com/pod-product-compliance
Lightning Source LLC
Chambersburg PA
CBHW060402310726
48976CB00003B/916